TRANSFORMERS™

REVENGE OF THE FALLEN

ALAN DEAN FOSTER

Based on the Screenplay written by Ehren Kruger and Robert Orci and Alex Kurtzman

BALLANTINE BOOKS · NEW YORK

A Del Rey Mass Market Original

Copyright © 2009 by Hasbro Inc. All rights reserved.
Copyright © 2009 Paramount Pictures and DreamWorks LLC
Based on Hasbro's Transformers® Action Figures

Published in the United States by Del Rey, an imprint of The Random House Publishing Group, a division of Random House, Inc., New York.

TRANSFORMERS and the distinctive logo thereof are trademarks of Hasbro, Inc. Used with permission.

DEL REY is a registered trademark and the Del Rey colophon is a trademark of Random House, Inc.

ISBN 978-0-345-51593-3

Printed in the United States of America

www.delreybooks.com
www.transformersmovie.com
www.hasbro.com

OPM   9   8   7   6   5   4   3   2   1

For my nephew, Shelby Hettinger,
From Cybertron to Texas,
With every good wish, from Uncle Alan

PROLOGUE
17,000 B.C.

The tiger was faster than its pursuers. It was stronger, quicker, and far more deadly. Hunting alone, it could take down prey that was considerably larger than itself. But still it ran. Because it had learned that the slower, weaker, feebler creatures now close on its trail could kill its kind. They had done so often within the realm of the tiger's memory. If they could, they would do so again, eager to claim its pelt and teeth and claws. They represented by far the most lethal threat to the tiger's domain and dominance that it had ever encountered.

Until now.

The men pursuing the big cat breathed steadily and evenly. Each was an experienced hunter, each eager to be the one to deliver the final blow or ultimate spear thrust. They knew well the tiger's ways. Knew all its tricks, its favorite hiding places, which trail it was most likely to take in its increasingly futile attempt to escape their hand-hewn weapons of obsidian and bone. They would run it to ground or corner it against the shore of the sea, kill it, and claim its strength as their own. They were the masters of the land in which they lived. Nothing could stand against them—not tiger, lion, or even the great elephant. Nothing could . . .

Fifty tons of metal terminating in a broad, gleaming foot came crashing down between the hunting party and its quarry.

To their credit, none of the intrepid hunters fainted. They did not retreat, either, but that was because they were paralyzed by the vision that had appeared before them. Blissfully indifferent to the complications imposed by the first stirrings of complex thought that now afflicted the hunters, and therefore spared any need to ponder the reason behind the cessation of their pursuit, the relieved tiger plunged down into a small arroyo and made good its escape.

The hunters were not so lucky. It was immediately evident that they were in the presence of a god. Their tribal pantheon made room for many gods. There was the god of the hunt, who had plainly chosen to abandon them. There was the god of good weather, who allowed them to track and follow the prey animals that sustained their people. There were gods of clean water and spring berries and fish and female fecundity. But this god was new to them.

Eight times the height of a man, it towered above the tallest in their party. The god was roughly man-shaped, with two arms, two legs, and a head. But there any similarities ended. It was made not of flesh but of a bright, shiny substance, fragments of which the tribesmen occasionally encountered in broken rock or stream pebbles. Instead of being curved and soft like a person, the god was all flat lines and hard surfaces. And its eyes . . . its eyes . . .

The intent look with which it was now regarding them was not warm.

Though their concept and command of language

was rudimentary, to a man the hunters knew what they had to do. As one, and without a sign from their leader, they fell to their knees and pressed their foreheads to the earth in supplication. The enormous metal shape standing over them regarded this action with an indifference that bordered on contempt. Since the creatures showed no sign of moving, in the interest of accumulating an additional bit of information about the world on which it found itself, it bent over and picked one of them up.

Too shocked to faint, the unfortunate hunter, who found himself held tightly in metal fingers and lifted high, was now too frightened to slump into the unconsciousness he so desperately sought. Instead, he was brought close to a face that was an angular caricature of his own. Where human eyes should have been was a pair of enormous flat spaces that glowed like the sky at sunset after a heavy rain. Their color and aspect were anything but reassuring. The man squirmed slightly but could not free himself. On the ground below, his terrified companions tried to bury their faces in the mud and prayed they would be ignored.

The metal giant examined the specimen of local bipedal life with the same advanced probing instrument it had utilized to record the makeup of everything from trees to fish—and with the same lack of emotion or empathy. Big insect, small insect—this world was overflowing with them. It duly noted the specimen's heart rate, body temperature, weight, chemical composition, and other characteristics. The thing in its grasp was alive, a biological entity not dissimilar from the thousands of others whose makeup the giant had already noted and recorded. Placing this newest organism in the appropriate category of native bioforms, the giant unclenched his fingers, turned, and strode off in the direction of the rising sun. During the entire episode, it had not uttered a sound or indicated in any way that it recognized its captive and his frightened companions as any more intelligent than the field mice that fled from its gigantic feet—or, for that matter, the rocks that were crushed beneath its great weight.

Falling from a height of some forty feet, the freed hunter hit the ground hard. The impact stunned him, but with the aid of his fellows he was able to stand on his own two feet. Their small stature notwithstanding, men who hunted tigers and elephants and antelope were as tough as they were wiry. Much grunting and gesticulating ensued until the leader of the small band growled for them to be quiet.

In the silence that followed, a new sound became audible. The giant was unlike anything they had ever seen. This noise was unlike anything they had ever heard. By dint of gestures and protowords, several members of the group indicated that no matter what their leader ordered, they were returning to the communal cave as fast as their feet would carry them. The leader did not try to stop them.

The same curiosity that had elevated his kind to their present level of dominance drove the leader and several of his companions to investigate the source of the strange new noises. Though the indifferent god had left them, his enormous strides carrying him over a ridge and out of sight, the hunters picked their way carefully. Outstanding trackers, they had no difficulty following the sound to its source. What they saw when they finally peered over the rim of the bluff on which they were walking and into the canyon below stunned them almost as much as their encounter with the metal god.

The canyon was full of smaller gods. Though differing in size and shape from the giant who had interrupted the chase, their appearance was sufficiently similar to that terrifying entity for the relationship to be unmistakable.

Among the old men of the tribe who could no longer participate in the strenuous activity demanded by a hunt was one who had mastered the ability to make small baskets out of dried reeds the women collected from the shore of a shallow lake. He had taught this valuable skill to others, and now teenage children and women with deft fingers helped in the making of the useful baskets. Confronted by a sight outside their experience and for which they had no other frame of reference, the crouching hunters could only conclude that the small gods, under the supervision of the big one, were weaving the most elaborate basket they had ever seen. And they were making it not from dried reeds, but out of bits and slabs of shiny rock not unlike themselves. The basket was huge, glistening, and tapered to a high point. They could not begin to imagine what its purpose might be. It certainly was not meant to hold dried fish or freshly gathered fruits. The mere look of it frightened them, though they could not have said why this should be so.

Keeping under cover, they observed the activity for much of the remainder of the day. Since neither the big god nor his smaller minions came toward them, the hunters were convinced that they remained undiscovered in their hiding place atop the bluff. This was not the case. Every one of the machines was aware of their presence. The machines also noted the occasional appearance of birds in the sky, small mammals scurrying in the underbrush, and beetles and other bugs underfoot. Since none of these native organic creatures interfered with their work, they paid them no heed.

The bold hunters on the bluff would have been discomfited to learn that in the hierarchy of possible threats to the work being conducted below them, they ranked no higher than the worms and considerably lower than a pack of wandering wild dogs.

Despite rampant, not to say runaway, development in the course of the preceding decades, the sprawling megalopolis of Shanghai still boasted areas that could be relatively dark and quiet—especially after ten at night. Even in bustling modern China, not all enterprises operated around the clock. Not every commercial venture burned power by keeping its lights on when the last shift had left for the day. The outskirts of the business park that was home to assorted heavy industries was nearly silent. A minimum of lights pushed against the darkness at an assortment of locations where such illumination was deemed necessary for security reasons.

A sizable chunk of the ancient city had sacrificed its homes and alleys, its noodle shops and kiosks, to make way for the extensive industrial compound. A few of the old neighborhoods still clung to its fringes, saved from demolition when the developers' voracious appetite for land had finally been sated. Most of those who dwelled within the surviving houses counted themselves fortunate. Their homes had been spared, the living was cheap, and they had benefited from good jobs in the factories while being spared the need for an expensive commute. Their preserved hutong was safe, too. Spillover from the advanced security that protected the commercial development kept thieves and vandals away from their homes.

In the absence of the delivery trucks that rumbled to and from the industrial complex throughout the day, the surrounding streets were comparatively quiet. Exhausted workers slept, while behind closed doors and windows those who could not rest parked themselves in front of garrulous televisions or plied the Internet. Young lovers stole moments of intimacy where they could in a city where privacy was among the scarcer commodities. Elders contemplated how much their lives had changed in the preceding decades, much as elders have done since the time when their predecessors prowled for food in fields and jungles instead of massive grocery stores.

A nomadic distributor of such food was presently plying its lonely way among the district's deserted streets and avenues. The ice-cream truck was squat and battered, and had visibly been heavily used. Its bells tinkled an oddly familiar melody while the intensity with which its headlights illuminated the surrounding streets and structures suggested hidden power quite out of keeping with its scruffy external appearance. Equally iconoclastic was the English-language sticker that decorated part of the truck's rear bumper:

DECEPTICONS—SUCK MY POPSICLE

Out of the darkness a trio of powerful motorcycles came thundering. Their leather-clad female riders were beautiful, alluring, and as alike as identical triplets. Occasionally their outlines wavered like the advanced holograms they were. Though not real, they were all part and parcel of the single entity to which they belonged.

The lateness of the hour neither inhibited the two children who came running after the ice-cream truck nor diminished their desire for its produce. Waving yuan, the boy and girl tried desperately to intercept it. Short legs being no match for large tires, they were too late. Despite their imploring shouts they rapidly fell behind, slowed, and finally came to a discouraged and disappointed stop. Then the truck abruptly halted, turned, and with headlights dimmed came straight toward them.

Brother and sister, too startled to get out of the way, could only stare as the truck bore down on them. In the absence of an adult to snatch them up and carry them to safety, scream at them to run, or deliver any other instruction, they stood dumbly in the middle of the street and gaped at the oncoming vehicle. At the last possible instant the truck did the impossible: it split perfectly in half. As if mounted on individual gyroscopes, each section sped past the paralyzed children, one on each side. Whirling around to maintain eye contact, brother and sister became simultaneously aware of two subsidiary impossibilities. The more obvious one was that the two halves of the ice-cream truck had rejoined to once more become one. The other was that it had left in its wake a small mountain of Popsicles, Dreamsicles, drumsticks, and other frozen treats both imported and domestic. Instantly putting aside all thought of the magical vehicle that had nearly run them down, the delighted children piled into the stack of frozen treats with an enthusiasm that would have done their physical education instructors proud.

On another street, a speeding black semi was in the process of disgorging contents of a very different kind. No treats these, frozen or otherwise. The small Hummers it unloaded carried men clad in full hazmat gear. In addition to their protective clothing they bore a variety of cutting-edge search-and-seek instrumentation. They also packed weaponry designed to deal with whatever their searching might find. Their expressions matched their gear and reflected their determination.

Ice-cream–seeking children aside, the industrial complex was a hive of uncharacteristic nocturnal activity. Blackhawk choppers had joined the rapidly deploying hazmat teams and began to circle the district. They were backed up by Cobra gunships. Bigger copters of Russian design mounting heavier weapons formed still another line of aerial defense.

No shots were fired. No disinfecting elements were deployed. The increasing number of weapons-wielding arrivals worked in silence, searching for . . . targets. The men and women of several squads began to slip out of their bulky hazmat suits. The insignia on their uniforms identified them not as waste workers but as soldiers.

One such group preparing to exit a rapidly descending chopper, was led by a somber-faced major who was better prepared than anyone else in the area to deal with the unknown possibilities it currently presented. Better prepared, that is, except for the master sergeant crouched beside him. As always, Epps had his iPod with him, but for once it was tucked away in a secured pocket. There was a time and a place for swaying to the music, and this particular night in industrial Shanghai was neither. Like Major William Lennox, the sergeant was all business. Behind them, highly trained troops readied themselves to follow the pair's lead. Though they had been well briefed and given some idea what they might expect to encounter, all of them knew they would have to rely on the expertise of the two battle-hardened Americans.

Reaching up, Lennox gently repositioned his light-weight headset. "Break, all stations, this net: cordon and search. People's Republic has put out an appropriate cover story, so the area should be clear of civilians. 'Toxic spill'—had to evac the district for search and rescue. That's us, 'cept for the 'rescue' part. Don't need to restate how important this is—and how in all probability dangerous. Six sightings in eight months; gotta make sure this one does *not* get out in the public eye. 'Specially after Rome. So keep it tight and let's make this operation as clean as possible."

The chopper's skids made a grinding sound as they touched down on the thick concrete.

"All right, everybody—let's rock."

Led by Lennox and Epps, the troops poured out of the copter and quickly spread out, keeping in contact while seeking cover. No one spoke. There was nothing more to be said, and any communication would come from their commanding officer and his assisting noncom.

Flipping the visor of his advanced headgear down over his eyes, Epps hastily activated its integrated radiation tracker. The heads-up display showed him what he expected to find, in spades.

"Lotta interference on this one," he muttered to the man standing alongside him. "Gamma signature's at four bars."

"*Four?*" Lennox added something under his breath. "You gotta be kidding me. That's not what we came for."

Behind them, one of the team members offered his own assessment. "Either it's cloaking its signal, like in Rome, or we're getting echoes off all this heavy metal."

Lennox nodded, pondering. Reaching a decision, he whispered sharply into his headset's pickup. "Tell our four-by-four friend that he's clear."

A moment later another black truck appeared. A second squad of experienced soldiers scrambled out, the last one getting off just as the vehicle began to change shape. Bending, folding, rising into the night sky, it assumed the form of a familiar silhouette, scarred but unbowed. Taking a step forward, it crouched down wordlessly behind Epps and Lennox, looming over them. Neither man was intimidated by its proximity.

Quite the contrary.

Turning, Epps favored the new arrival with a welcoming nod. The metal giant responded with a slow nod of its own. Epps grinned knowingly.

"Let's kick some alien ass."

Lennox's tone was disapproving. "Epps, you're getting cocky."

The sergeant shrugged diffidently. "Sir, that's just me, dealing with my fears about some classified, violent, otherworldly predator. Each of us has our own way of preparing for these encounters. Me, I like to get a little confrontational." His tone turned serious. "Isn't like I don't know what's coming."

Lennox started to say something, then just nodded tersely. Looking up and past the noncom, he regarded the metal shape that now blocked out much of the night sky behind them.

"Ironhide, we've got echoes. Steel stacks, two o'clock."

The huge Autobot was peering past the much smaller humans, probing with sensors far more advanced than anything they possessed. "He's here," the giant murmured softly. "He's close."

"Then let's make sure he doesn't get far." Raising an arm, Lennox gestured at the squad assembled behind him. "Move out."

Spreading out around the straightening, silent Autobot, the soldiers brought to mind ancient Carthaginian warriors flanking one of Hannibal's war elephants. Each man was prepared to defend himself but also to operate in support of the far more powerful giant in their midst. Though the electronic eyes and sensors that were part of their gear were greatly inferior to Ironhide's own, the Autobot could not investigate every place at once. At such times an aggregation of humans proved invaluable, able to provide a plethora of supplementary search capacity. When even a second or two of additional warning about an incoming attack or possible ambush could prove decisive, an extra pair of simple organic eyes was always welcome on the perimeter.

This tactical methodology, involving humans operating directly alongside their Autobot allies, soon proved its worth. It was one of the human soldiers whose instrumentation first intercepted the revealing undulation. Halting, he lifted a warning hand.

"*Thermal ripple,* three o'clock."

Instantly, every man in the group stopped in his tracks and turned detection equipment and weapons in the indicated direction. So did Ironhide, who had learned the benefit of having a multitude of human scouts. Silently, he broadcast an alert of his own.

"Sideswipe, deploy . . ."

The corvette that shot down the ramp protruding from the rear of another semitruck seemed utterly out of place among the swiftly dispersing soldiers and their prosaic military vehicles—until it shifted shape into that of a particularly sleek Autobot armed not only with guns but also with a variety of Cybertronian swords. As Sideswipe rushed to take up position, Ironhide was already issuing his second order.

"Arcee, guard flanks."

The triplets riding identical motorcycles rezzed once, twice, and winked out. The disguise they presented had become superfluous as the Autobot altered, changing into her multiple yet integrated shape. Three single-wheeled killing machines now advanced where the cycles and their simulated riders had formerly idled. As befitted Arcee's personality and in contrast to her fellow Autobots, both the voice and the aspect of the tripartite Cybertronian emanated a decidedly nonmasculine cast—though her words were anything but feminine.

"*Locked and loaded,* Ironhide."

Deep within the complex, Ironhide advanced cautiously, flanked on both sides by alert and ready humans.

He's close, he thought to himself. *Truly close.* But where? If their target was cloaking, he was doing an exceptional job of concealing his presence. If not for his own unique detection gear and that which had been devised by the humans, no one would suspect that anything boasting an offworld origin was anywhere in the vicinity. Surely their target must know by now that he was being stalked. Yet the nearer pursuit drew, the tighter their quarry's cover seemed to become.

Where in the name of the Allspark was he hiding?

A sound followed, motorized and moving fast. Raising both arms, Ironhide turned in the direction of the rising noise. If it was to be a straightforward, head-on attack, then he needed to . . .

He sighed and lowered his weapons as the ice-cream truck came skidding around a corner.

He shook his head. "Twins, just . . . *try* and stay out of trouble. Watch the big boys—and learn." He looked around, searching the silent, dark human industrial complex. "This is no place for improvisation."

Obediently, the truck puttered to a stop. The tinkling musical tune it had been emitting switched off. As the two Autobots, one huge and experienced, the other smaller and new to the conflict, regarded each other, the human soldiers kept advancing. Detectors were signaling like mad as the squad closed in around a massive earthmover parked behind stacks of large-diameter concrete water pipes. The presence of knee-high weeds suggested that the area had not been disturbed in some time. Still . . .

The audible blip-blip of the tracker integrated into Lennox's headgear was firing away at his consciousness like the drum machines that seemed to underlie half the music Epps favored. *Something* was causing the device to go crazy. But there was nothing here. Nothing but the earthmover, which gave not the slightest indication it was anything but a standard construction machine.

Something wasn't right. The earthmover was clearly not a Decepticon. Sitting in front of them squat, unmoving, and devoid of a single revealing indicator, it simply could *not* be a Decepticon.

But, he realized abruptly, it *could* be something else. He took a sudden step backward.

"It's a *reflection*. A diversion!" Whirling, he found himself confronted by . . .

. . . a couple of local children. Their eyes were wide, their expressions curious, and their hands full of rapidly melting frozen treats. Turning to a couple of nearby soldiers, Lennox spoke through clenched teeth.

"Guys, I ordered this district locked *down*. Get these kids outta h . . ."

Too late.

Enormous cement pipes were heaved aside as the actual earthmover whose duplicated image had drawn the soldiers' attention changed shape and came at them from an entirely different direction. Men dove for cover. Not all made it as crashing pipes were joined by the irresistible mass of the Decepticon known as Demolisher. Firing as they retreated, the squad scattered while Lennox swept up the stunned children and hustled them to safety.

Rising and roaring in the midst of the open area, Demolisher struck out with his own weapons as the soldiers poured fire in his direction, spraying the enormous Decepticon with everything from sabot-tipped stinger missiles to portable SAMs. Rocking and rolling, it slammed into the steel beams behind which individual troops had taken cover, smashing the posts aside as if they were toothpicks. Screams and shouts punctuated the barrage of fire and the flurry of explosions as the men fought back.

A second massive shape came barreling out of the darkness, slamming into the Decepticon and knocking him off-balance. As Ironhide locked with Demolisher the frenzied barrage of human-directed fire slowed, the soldiers afraid to chance hitting their ally. With Ironhide clinging to his back, the Decepticon spun madly on his massive wheels, trying to throw him off.

As the pair whipped in wild circles, sending construction material flying dangerously in all directions, a third shape came powering out from the place where Demolisher had been hiding. Lennox got a line on it as it shot past him without even bothering to send covering fire in the humans' direction. Encased in the shape of a sleek European sports car, the Decepticon Sideways sped from the scene as fast as his engine and wheels could carry him. Such determined maintenance of its terrestrial guise indicated that he was intent not on fighting back as much as he was on preserving himself. Fighting could come later.

Right now, the smaller Decepticon's objective was escape.

Peering out from behind a still-standing steel beam, Lennox barked into his pickup. "Eagle niner, we've got multiple Decepticons! Track 'em—don't let 'em get away!" Not far away, Epps was shouting into his own pickup as he leaned over a moaning soldier whose legs were pinned beneath a chunk of broken concrete.

"Team members down, need medevac *now*!"

High overhead, helicopter gunships that had been patrolling the fringe of the search area began to close an aerial ring, tightening their range on the search. Keeping to as much cover as possible, Sideways tore through narrow alleys and beneath unfinished factory ceilings, all the while seeking a clear, clean exit from the scene of battle. Skidding sharply around a corner, he emerged into an area of open unguarded sky and accelerated. He had not much farther to go before it would find himself in among more densely human-populated areas. There, his sleek but unexceptional shape would allow it to slow, blending in invisibly with the rest of the nocturnal human vehicular traffic. Not only would the Autobots be unable to follow him, but even if one spotted his presence it would not fire in the presence of so many humans and . . .

There was a vehicle on his tail—a peculiar sort of blocky, unaerodynamic vehicle, brightly colored and much faster than his silhouette suggested. Sideways skidded around a steep curve, then angled sharply to his right, shooting down a much narrower roadway. His pursuer followed, but was ultimately too wide to negotiate the alley. Crashing, it split in two, each half rolling until it came to a halt. Pleased, Sideways roared onward, leaving the ill-considered pursuit in his wake.

Changing shape, the pair of identical seven-foot-tall bipeds that had comprised the ice-cream truck descended into argument and recrimination, shouting at each other via a series of electronic hums, buzzes, and squeals no human could understand. Responding to an especially pointed expletive, one half promptly punched the other, knocking it flat. By the time the struck half hit the ground, Sideways was already out of sight.

Ignoring them, the three sections that comprised Arcee came roaring around a corner to take off up the alley. Though no faster than the Decepticon they pursued, they were far more agile.

They caught up to the fleeing enemy as he turned down still another alleyway. Unfortunately, this one dead-ended in an ancient brick wall—one of several that marked the border of the industrial park and signaled a return to one of the district's original residential neighborhoods. Recognizing the barrier ahead, instead of slowing, Sideways accelerated—and changed shape.

Bursting through the brick, the Decepticon tore through the living room of a small house and exploded out through the far wall, changing back into his nimble terrestrial guise as he did so. One, two, three, Arcee shot single file through the ruined living area, closing on her quarry. Finally acquiring a clean line of sight, she opened fire on the fleeing target. Armor-piercing rounds tore into Sideways's steel skin, tearing off bits and pieces and slowing him. As soon as they drew close enough, the trio leaped on top of the wildly skewing vehicle.

That was enough for the frustrated Decepticon. Recognizing that at this point there was no way he was going to be able to slip unobtrusively into the still-distant flow of nighttime human traffic, he spun sharply. All three components of Arcee were flung off to smash into a nearby shuttered storefront. As glass and cement crumbled around them, the Decepticon shifted into his natural shape and brought his heavy weapons to bear, letting loose rapid-fire bursts in the direction of his unrelenting pursuers.

In a trice, Arcee's parts leaped acrobatically, combining into a single tall shape to return the Decepticon's fire. Not only was their new configuration more difficult to hit with weapons' fire, it also allowed them to shoot down at the cornered Decepticon. Before he could properly align his guns a new shape slammed into him from another side. Swinging one of his swords, Sideswipe slashed at Sideways, taking one of his legs out from under him. Lennox and his squad arrived just in time to see the target go down. Having lived through several similar seemingly optimistic scenarios only to see them turn nearly fatal, the major was not inclined to lie back and relax.

"Spread out! Triangulate your fire—pin him down!"

Confirming Lennox's caution, the cornered Decepticon let loose with a pulse blast from his primary weapon. Exploding outward, a bubble of highly compressed air rippled down the side street Sideways had just vacated. As the squad tried to avoid it, several of them were picked up, thrown forward by the force of the compression, and slammed into a flanking wall.

As far as the Decepticon was concerned, the injured humans represented only collateral damage. The pulse had not been aimed at them: the intent had been to take out the onrushing Sideswipe.

It failed.

Charging straight toward the target, Sideswipe demonstrated the agility for which he was famed. Leaping into the air at the last possible instant, the altered Autobot soared over a second pulse blast, landed with grace suggestive of a cross between a prima ballerina and a twenty-ton battle tank, and returned the Decepticon's fire. Moving to grapple with his attacker, Sideways found himself distracted by repeated sabot fire from the surviving humans. Several shells struck at weak points. They failed to bring the enraged Decepticon down, but they succeeded in slowing his reactions and forcing him to contend with damaging fire from multiple directions at once.

It was enough to allow Sideswipe to skate in beneath Sideways's weapons. Forcefully, the Autobot took his enemy's legs out from under him and flipped him into the air. Sideways was still firing as he came down—right onto one of Sideswipe's sword arms. The sharpened metal pierced the Decepticon's neck from front to back.

As their quarry writhed on the pinioning blade, Lennox was able to steal enough time to study his battlefield readout. What he saw made the hair on the back of his neck stand up.

"Air support!" he yelled into the unit's pickup. "Be advised—we've got one of 'em down and cornered. But secondary target is headed for the quarantine perimeter. Do *not* let it get past! Repeat, interdict secondary target at all costs!"

Grimly, he put away the readout and returned to the clash at hand. He could not be everywhere at once. The fight with Sideways was in hand and had been appropriately proscribed, but if Demolisher broke out of the containment area in the industrial zone, even at this hour of the night it would be difficult to keep the encounter under wraps in spite of the cautions that had been imposed on the local media. If anyone could keep the ongoing firefight under control, it was Epps.

At the moment, however, the sergeant was more concerned with avoiding the cloud of flying shrapnel that surrounded the other fleeing Decepticon. Some of it was a consequence of the fast-moving enemy's own heavy fire, while the rest was being generated by the clutch of Eagle gunships that were pouring fire on the target from above. Their shells did not appear to be having much effect on the heavily armored Decepticon.

As Epps looked on, trying to shoot and maintain cover at the same time, Demolisher leaped up onto an empty rail trestle. Did the Decepticon realize that the tracks offered a direct route not only out of the industrial zone but the quarantine area as well? If so, they needed to stop him, and stop him *fast*. Ducking back behind cover, Epps pulled his own battlefield com unit.

"He's found the rail access! Chopper fire's not slowing him enough and those of us on the ground might as well be throwing spitwads! We need something *heavy* over here!"

Fortunately, "heavy" was already on its way.

For such a big aircraft, the C-17 was surprisingly maneuverable. The few citizens out and about in the darkness who saw it come over low and slow paid it no special heed. Low-flying military and cargo aircraft were constantly shuttling in and out of the great city's airports at altitudes that would never be tolerated elsewhere. They ignored the big jet's thunder and went about their business. Doubtless it was coming in for a landing to disgorge some special cargo.

None of them had any idea just how special.

As the massive rear cargo door opened, exposing the interior of the aircraft to the gleaming lights of the city below, the jumpmaster checked his safety harness as he edged toward the windswept opening. He was waiting for control confirmation from his pilot. The instant he received word, he turned and yelled.

"Drop zone—go, go, go!"

It did not bother him that there was no one else in the expansive cargo hold to hear the command. That is, no other *human*.

Certainly there was no driver in the cab of the gleaming blue, flame-decorated semitruck that roared past him and out of the hold. As the truck plunged grillfirst toward the ground below, it began to change in midair. Three oversize parachutes popped open, each bearing a symbol familiar only to a select coterie of humans—and to the autonomous robotic life-forms it identified.

Landing softly, Optimus Prime immediately shifted back to his terrestrial guise to charge off in pursuit of the fleeing Demolisher. He did not even need to utilize his own perceptors to locate the ferocious Decepticon. All that was necessary was to lock in on the flock of choppers that were pouring fire, most of it futile, into a far corner of the industrial complex.

With every exit seemingly blocked and Autobots as well as hordes of irritating humans in pursuit, Demolisher searched for a possible way out. One presented itself in the form of an overpass. Leaving the train tracks, the massive Decepticon pivoted on a single massive wheel and flipped end-over-end to land on another roadway. As he rolled toward the city proper and potential freedom, the huge metal wheels that provided his terrestrial appellation crushed car after unlucky car.

He failed to identify the big semitruck that was traveling on another overpass and approaching from the opposite direction until it was too late. As Optimus prepared to hit the Decepticon from above, Demolisher burst upward to smash completely through the overpass bridge. The head-on assault neither slowed nor injured the leader of the Autobots. Changing shape, he leaped out and down to land hard on Demolisher's neck. The big Decepticon slowed but did not stop.

That changed when Ironhide arrived. Sliding beneath the Decepticon's massive frame, the venerable warrior took out one of his foe's wheels even as he grabbed on to the wildly swinging, hard-fighting enemy. Assailed from both sides by a pair of Autobots, even a Decepticon as powerful as Demolisher had only a slim chance of escape.

When those two Autobots were Ironhide and Optimus Prime, he had no chance at all.

Wobbling from side to side as he fought to maintain his balance while fighting back, Demolisher finally collapsed under the relentless dual attack. He crashed to a halt on his side, then made a few final useless thrusts upward until his spark flickered for the last time. Ready to shoot or lash out again should it prove necessary to strike one more blow, Optimus came closer. There wasn't much left of Demolisher's face. The rest of him had been reduced to scrap by the two Autobots' unrelenting assault. Gazing up at the one who had vanquished him, no longer able to shoot or strike back physically, Demolisher's last act of defiance took the form of sputtering, barely intelligible, and ultimately cryptic words.

"This is not your planet to rule . . . The Fallen—the Fallen . . . shall rise . . . again . . ."

The last glimmering of Demolisher's spark flashed once, twice, and then went dark. Forever, Optimus determined after a quick check of the motionless body. The great mass of metal lying before him now represented one more deluded Decepticon who would never again threaten the Autobots, the humans, or the enduring peace that Optimus and his brethren were fighting to bring to two worlds. His internal systems ran through the electronic equivalent of a resigned sigh as he turned to check on Ironhide.

There were too many times when the war seemed never-ending.

Underwear. Among the interminable problems of life, underwear was one that never went away. More specifically, it posed the great question that forever confronts every traveler: do I take more and wash less, or take less and wash more?

After helping save the world and coming within a poodle's coiffed hair of losing his life in the process, Sam Witwicky was more than content to contemplate his overstuffed suitcase and debate matters of considerably less import. Unable to resolve the momentous sticking point, he finally grabbed as many pairs of shorts as he could comfortably hold in both hands and shoved them into whatever corners inside the suitcase were still available. He was packing for college, after all, and while he could not begin to imagine how he might do academically, he could at least prepare as best he could to survive socially. Which meant having a modicum of clean underwear always on hand. Or rather, he thought as he tried to close the overfull suitcase, on butt.

Did Einstein, while he was at Princeton, ever have to do his own underwear? Sam wondered. Such profound reflection gave new meaning to the term "string theory." He shoved down hard on the suitcase with both hands. Trying to get the latches on a suitcase to line up with their receiving slots was an engineering problem with which mankind continued to struggle, something akin to successfully docking a spacecraft with an orbiting station. As Sam wrestled with the luggage, the voice of the CNN reporter speaking from the nearby TV drew his attention away from the frustrating work.

". . . Congress placed responsibility squarely on the secretive multinational tech giant Massive Dynamics."

"Massive Dynamics." At least someone was thinking with more than half a brain, Sam decided. The government's dissemblers had come up with a company name that suggested that it might manufacture anything from supertankers to swizzle sticks. The TV documentary switched to file video of recent congressional hearings.

". . . And this 'Automated Defense Initiative'—can you explain the program's purpose?" The congressman from Texas was plainly trying to contain his anger and frustration.

Not so the corporate representative for "Massive Dynamics," who replied with admirable composure. "We were building remote-operated, unmanned vehicles and other machines designed to evacuate and protect—I must emphasize *protect*—civilians in war zones. As you know, our government as well as others is always looking for ways to defend against large-scale terrorist attacks. Doing so requires the kind of mechanical ingenuity and technical development that can only be called cutting-edge. In order for new defense technology to respond as rapidly as possible to unforeseen situations of possibly cataclysmic scope, it is necessary that a certain amount of independence of action be integrated into the resulting equipment."

"Yet," the congressman continued relentlessly, "it was this 'independence of action' that resulted in an excessive amount of destruction when the technology you're referring to malfunctioned."

The "company" representative smiled vacuously. "We regret the damage incurred. One has to keep in mind that the technology being developed was designed to counter and prevent the kind of massive terrorist attack we never want to see again afflict this country. Countering that degree of incursion demands equally robust countermeasures." He shifted easily in his seat as he continued.

"The malfunction stemmed from a satellite blackout whose serious consequences were widely reported in the media. This induced a series of errors in the unfinished system that cascaded throughout the proposed defense structure, which I must remind you was and still is incomplete. Among the problems that took time to deal with was a severe GPS dislocation, which directed the defense vehicles away from their appropriate testing grounds and into Mission City."

Lips drawn taut, Sam could only watch the broadcast and shake his head in disgust. As governmental prevarication went, it was right up there with . . . with . . .

He put the thought aside. He was going to college, and right now that was all that mattered. Reinforcing that resolve was the sound of his father's voice rattling up the stairwell.

"Let's go, let's *go*. T-minus sixty, college boy!"

Slamming both hands down atop the suitcase, Sam evinced mild surprise as both latches clicked home. Locking the case before it could change its mind, he finished wrapping duct tape around a large box and began hauling it toward the stairs. He as much rode as pushed it to the bottom, then started dragging it through the living room.

His two legs got tangled up with four as he nearly tripped over Mojo. Convinced as ever that he was actually a downsized cross between an Anatolian kangal and a pit bull, the chihuahua came tearing through the room after Frankie, the family's newest addition. Equally bereft of long legs, the French bulldog was having a hard time staying in front of his yapping pursuer. Standing next to the disparate pile of taped and labeled boxes that had risen beside the front door, Ron Witwicky urged the two dogs outside. He was sweating from the morning's exertions, but happily so. His son was going to an Ivy League school, and the proud father was beaming widely enough to activate half a solar panel all by himself.

"Mojo, Frankie, outside, outside!" As he closed the door he saw Sam dragging the final box. "C'mon, kiddo, we're on a schedule here!"

With a grunt, Sam let the last box drop. "Dad, seriously, why're you trying to get rid of me?" His expression turned mock somber. "Tell the truth. You rented out my room, didn't you . . . ?"

His father looked as innocent as a handkerchief vendor at a wake. "Sam, that's a terrible thing to say! I wouldn't dream of renting out your space. How could I, when I have other plans for your room, and they rhyme with 'home theater.' "

Sam tried not to grin. "Hey, I grew up in there. Show some reverence. That room is crammed with all my childhood memories."

His father nodded vigorously in response. "Which I'm sure will leave plenty of room for surround-sound wide-screen reruns of the likes of *Red River* and *Yellow Ribbon* and *The High Country* and . . ."

"All right, all right. I'll be out. You can be as archaic in your video viewing as you want, Dad, without having to worry about sending me screaming into the street over your choices." Son and father smiled as one.

The brief instant of male bonding lasted the two seconds before Judy Witwicky joined them. Tears were streaming down her cheeks as she held up a pair of white baby shoes and declaimed in a voice that was an impregnable fusion of joy and sadness, "LOOK WHAT I FOUND YOUR BABY BOOTIES I'M LOSING MY BABY C'MERE MY BITTY BOOTIE BABY . . . !"

Sam would have responded, but the smothering hug in which he found himself suddenly enveloped temporarily restricted the flow of air to his lungs. Managing to half extricate himself, he looked over at his father and ventured a dejected sniff.

"*See?* This is how you're *supposed* to react when the fruit of your loins goes out into the cruel world to fend for himself."

Ron Witwicky smiled sardonically at the teen currently enshrouded in his mother's cephalopodian grasp. "Yeah, my heart bleeds for you. As for fruit, gimme an apple every time."

"I want you back here every holiday." Judy sobbed

softly. "Even Halloween and President's Day—*all* the presidents."

Gently, Sam began to untangle himself. "Mom, they don't let us off for Halloween. I don't even think that's an Ivy League–specific distinction."

She nodded sorrowfully. "Then we'll come to you."

The alarm in her son's reply rang throughout the room. "No, you will *not*."

Her eyes met his. Or tried to, as he started to turn back to the pile of boxes. "But I'm your *mother* . . ."

"My *mother*," he reiterated. "Not my 'smother.' Drop me off, go to Europe, see you at graduation. Remember? Europe? Museums, nice restaurants, where the family all came from?"

"They came from New York, as I remember." Ron eyed his tearful spouse. "Judy, let the kid breathe, okay? He's not eight years old anymore. And there's no way you're done packing for a monthlong trip. Let's all get a move on, shall we? Or Sam will be late for his check-in and we'll miss our flight." Turning, he lowered his voice dramatically as he passed his son.

"You'll always be eight years old to her, kid. Get used to it."

"What?" Judy Witwicky's gaze narrowed and her tear ducts shut down as she eyed her husband sharply.

"Nothing. I was just saying to Sam that he'll always be a little late. It's his nature. Do you want to catch that flight to Heathrow or not?"

She glared at him, but affectionately. "You'd think our first romantic vacation in eighteen years deserved a first-class flight, but I guess 'El Cheapo' strikes again."

Pivoting, Ron turned to confront her. "You know what first-class tickets for a month in Europe would cost? We could just buy a small hotel here instead. Besides, there's no first class within Europe. It's all 'business' or 'club' class, and the seats aren't even different. I did my homework. Now march, young lady, and finish your own packing." Reaching out, he gave her a fond pat on the butt.

She swung around gracefully, leaving a smile in her wake. "Ooh, I love it when you call me 'young lady.' So filthy."

For the second time in as many minutes, Sam looked distressed. "Guys, please, not in front of the kids. Save it for Paris." He grinned. "Don't worry about me, and you'll always have Paris."

"If we don't miss our connection," his father grumbled.

His mother nodded and headed upstairs. They could still hear her sobbing quietly from the vicinity of the bedroom.

"Y'know how it is," muttered Ron, his tone softening. "Hard for a mother to . . . ," he swallowed tightly, choking up a little himself, "send her only son off. Accept that he's all grown up." He faced the silent Sam. "That you won't be able to play catch with him on the weekends anymore."

His son smiled knowingly. "It's all right, Dad. When I've got my degree, when I'm working in another state, or another country, or wherever, we'll still be able to get together once in a while and play catch."

"Yeah, uh . . ." Turning away, Ron Witwicky rubbed at his face, gathered himself, and when he was ready, looked back again. "Anyway, uh, I'm real proud of you, kiddo. East Coast Ivy League school, fifteen hundred on your SATs." He shook his head, still remembering the disbelief with which he and his wife had read the official results. "How you did that is still beyond me. Not that I'm complainin', mind."

"Thanks, Dad. For the compliment, *and* for not complaining." He grinned anew.

His father shrugged. "Just sayin': you went from a 'B' average to straight 'A's' overnight. Then the scholarship on top of that. Everything I ever did in *my* life, I did to put together a future for you." He could have gone on in the same vein, building up his own contribution, but it wasn't necessary. There was no need to speak the pride that was plain to see in his expression. Sam heard it as clearly as if it had been voiced.

"Guess I did a pretty decent job." Now it was the father's turn to grin. "All the fun you're gonna have, friends you're gonna make. College life—closest I ever got was watching it on TV and in the movies. Guess the real thing will be . . ." His eyes widened as they focused on something taking place beyond his patient offspring.

Mojo was paying his respects to Frankie in a manner as calculated to finalize the canine pecking order in the Witwicky household as it was to embarrass any unexpected visitors.

"Mojo, no dominating! Frank, don't be so easy! Get off the couch, you debased mongrels!" The dogs complied, but at a speed that suggested that they were doing so as much out of boredom as from obedience. Coughing awkwardly, Ron turned back to his son.

"Uh, probably a lotta that in college too, Son. I just expect you to, uh, you know, be careful and . . ."

Sam hastened to relieve his father of an embarrassing moment even greater than the one the family pets had just engendered. "No reason to worry about that, Dad. I'm a one-woman kinda guy."

Though he nodded understandingly, Ron Witwicky was not about to shelve so important a subject so fast. "Look, Mikaela's the greatest, I'll grant you that in a minute, but you gotta give each other room to grow, to be honest about the fact that you'll end up seeing other people. That's just the way it is. Perfectly natural. It happens to every couple your age."

Sam's expression tightened slightly. "Most couples my age don't make the first contact with an alien race and save the world together, okay? Trust me. I know the odds." His smile returned. "Didn't you see my math score on the SATs? We're the exception that . . ."

His cell phone sang a familiar tune and the screen announced MIK. Proudly, he showed it to his father. "See? She can't get enough of me."

Ron Witwicky nodded knowingly, sighed, and turned back to the pile of boxes. "I'm gonna start moving these outside. If you can manage to be on the phone for less than an hour, you might consider giving me a hand."

Sam was backing rapidly toward the stairway. "Sure, right, no problem Dad—I'll be back in a minute." He put the phone back to his lips. "Hey, Beautiful, how's it goin'?"

The custom chopper shop was alive with quiet activity. Within the big open garage space, work proceeded much as it did in a hospital. Made of metal, the patients remained largely immobile while attendants bustled around them, working silently and professionally to get them in shape to go out into the world again.

Mikaela was putting the finishing touches on an airbrushed Bettie Page pinup that sprawled along the tank of a long-nosed bike. As she worked, she spoke into the cell headset riding atop one ear.

"I'm breaking up with you."

Back in his bedroom, Sam was checking to make certain he hadn't overlooked anything he needed, or wanted, to take with him. "Yeah," he replied into his own phone, "I don't know . . . gotta be honest, I'm not hearing a lotta conviction."

She hung up abruptly. Whistling softly to himself, Sam continued searching his room for anything he might have forgotten. Most of the posters that had decorated the walls and ceiling remained. At school there would be new posters, new pictures to hang, and it wouldn't do for a college freshman to paper the walls of his dorm room with relics from his adolescence. They would of necessity recede into the realm of fond memories—at least until his father got around to redecorating the old room.

The phone rang again and Sam answered with the same inflection as before. "Hey, Beautiful."

"I'm breaking up with you," the wonderful voice of his wonderful girlfriend insisted less than wonderfully. "So there's no point in me coming over to say good-bye. You'll just have to remember me the last time you saw me."

"Last time I saw you?" His grin widened. "Let's see, as I recall the last time I saw you we were . . ."

She hurried to cut him off. "Never mind that now. That's all in the past. Like our relationship."

He was checking drawers one last time. "Wow, you sounded almost serious that time. Guess what . . . ?"

The phone conveyed her sarcasm excellently. "You found your future wife in the freshman Facebook?"

He found what he was looking for. The cigar box held fragments of the recent past, each one replete with not only memory but also physical significance: a web-cam, mix CDs, a familiar and extraordinarily significant pair of old glasses scored with minute yet mathematically precise scratches, a battered old badge labeled SECTOR SEVEN, and more.

"No," he finally replied in response to her jibe. "I'm making you a 'long-distance relationship kit.' It's got a preset webcam so we can chat twenty-four–seven: all Witwicky, all the time. Some of our favorite mixes, a 'fragrance of love' scented candle, some poetry—not all of it rhymes, but it's from the heart." Even in the absence of an image on the phone he was sure he could feel her smiling.

"Lotta junk," she told him. "Anything worthwhile?"

"Just a few souvenirs from the event that cannot be mentioned when we're on cell phones. Badge, glasses—how 'bout my shirt? You want the infamous D-Day shirt?" Digging into the back of the drawer he pulled out the ratty, torn, folded shirt he had been wearing when he had helped to save the world. Her response offered something less than the ego boost he was anticipating.

"You kept your sweaty, dirty, shredded clothes?"

"You kidding?" he shot back defensively. "I *bled* in this thing. It's like my Super Bowl jersey."

In the restoration shop, the voice that called out to Mikaela was simultaneously businesslike and endearing.

" 'Kaela! Where'd you put the clutch covers?" her father inquired gruffly.

"Second shelf," she yelled back. "Next to the cam shafts. If they're not there, look on the floor by the softail."

Sam recognized the deeper voice in the background. He and Mikaela's father had yet to be formally introduced, but while the recent deportee from formal state incarceration had yet to give his approval of their relationship, neither had he objected to it. Sam had the distinct impression that as long as her father was able to drift contentedly in a sea of grease, oil, and assorted mechanical lubricants while plying his chosen trade, his interest in the outside world, including that of his daughter's future, verged on the minimal. While Sam didn't approve of the indifference, he had to admit that it made dating a lot easier.

"How's the old man holding up?"

"Y'mean my man-child father?" Mikaela's exasperation was unmistakable. "Fixing cars instead of stealing 'em, so that's a step up." She looked back over a shoulder as she spoke. "Right now he's humming the proverbial happy tune. One time I heard him say he wasn't going to go to heaven if there were no cars or bikes to build."

"Kinda like relationships," Sam segued smoothly.

"Which reminds me: I'm gonna say it again. Come with me, Mik. Just because the dorm's paid for with the scholarship doesn't mean I've gotta live in it. There's reasonable apartments near campus and . . ."

She interrupted firmly. "I told you, he's only been on parole four months. I gotta help him get on his feet. He's been clean so far, but with all that he's been through the past few years he doesn't have a lot of stabilizing influence in his life. There's just metal and me, and I'm the only one who'll talk back to him and tell him when he's screwing up. He listens to me, Sam. If he'll listen long enough, after a bit he'll get to where he won't need somebody to tell him when he's screwing up because he will have stopped doing it. Just for a little while."

She wasn't exactly pleading—that wasn't part of Mikaela's makeup. But in her own way, she was asking for his understanding.

It did not keep *him* from beseeching, however. "C'mon, Mik. Don't make me say g'bye on the phone."

"Did I say I was gonna do that? Big difference between me moving to the East Coast and wishing you a safe trip there. Lemme finish up, make sure there are no bubbles in this lacquer I'm working on, and I'll be over in twenty."

The connection went dead. He eyed the phone a moment before pocketing it. Could he stall his parents for another twenty minutes? If his mom maintained her slow packing pace he wouldn't have to find a reason to delay. And anyway, there were still a few last-minute details that required his attention.

First and foremost was the rag of a shirt. Holding

it up, he started to fold it as neatly as the embedded dirt and grime would permit. His expression one of mild disgust, he started brushing at the filthy fabric. As he did so, something that had been caught in the material of the inner pocket came tumbling out. He grabbed reflexively at what appeared to be a charred ember. There had been plenty of that during the battle for Mission City. Except—the splinter was not a charred ember, not a fragment of singed concrete, not a length of scorched wood.

It was a tiny sliver of the Allspark.

It shook him, and he staggered into memory.

Trapped in a hole in the street with metal titans battling above him. One of them falling to the ground. Slamming the Allspark into Megatron's chest and turning his face from the fiery, flaring, explosive consequences. Hundreds of alien symbols akin to those that had embellished the Spark shimmering in his mind's eye, threatening to overwhelm him, screaming at him to . . . to . . .

He stumbled backward, wildly waving his burnt hand as he tried to cool the tingling flesh. Reactivated by the contact and then flung aside, the sliver hit the floor of his room and promptly burned its way right through the hardwood floorboards, the intervening insulation, and the ceiling below. As it seared its way downward, it sliced through the wiring embedded in the floor. Momentarily overloaded, the circuitry running to his room sparked and began to smoke. The sliver landed in the kitchen, bouncing off the center cooking island as it emitted a small but unmistakable pulse blast.

Sam staggered toward the doorway as every wall

socket in his room spat sparks. Wallpaper above a couple of sockets turned black and began to curl upward. Only the fire retardant with which the material had been treated kept it from bursting into flame. He raced out the door, his tone frantic.

"Oh, no—*Dad!*"

Ron Witwicky couldn't hear his son's shouting. He was whistling cheerily to himself as he loaded yet one more of Sam's packed boxes into the car.

He also failed to hear—or see—what the pulse burst from the sliver of Allspark had done to his kitchen.

Not to the kitchen itself, but to its machines. A century or so earlier, in the absence of electronics, the pulse would have provoked little or no response. In contrast, the previously unoccupied room was now alive with a clashing of appliances that had been brought to frenetic life by the surge from the spark.

Heedless of what it might hit and indifferent to multiple targets chosen at random, the animated cappuccino maker sprayed small fireballs in all directions. Spinning on the legs that had sprouted from its underside, the toaster whipped what could only be described as mini-nunchucks in front of, around, and behind it, smashing to pieces everything from ceramic plates to an innocent set of salt and pepper shakers. Bashing its way clear of the prison beneath the sink, the now-multilimbed garbage disposal defended itself against all comers with a set of whirring blades only slightly slowed by remaining scraps of the previous night's meal.

A cell phone that had commenced ringing insistently at the first touch of the sliver's life-giving pulse found itself snatched up by the now fully animated microwave. Slamming the phone into its middle, the appliance turned itself on. The ringing from the trapped phone gave way to unsettling shrieks as it began to smoke, then spark, and eventually burst into flame. Disdaining its usual ring tone, the microwave clicked its door wide to eject the charred remnants of the unfortunate phone.

On the floor above, Sam's initial panic had swiftly succumbed to common sense. Halting his headlong flight, he located the upstairs fire extinguisher and raced back to his room. He turned it on one of the two electrical fires that had begun to creep up the walls of his room. Unfortunately, the extinguisher was both old and empty, regular checkups of such devices not being a part of the annual routine at the Witwicky household.

Cursing to himself he tossed the useless device aside, spotted a nearly full water bottle, and managed to douse the location where the fire had spread to the floor. Charred wood hissed as quenched flames gave birth to choking smoke, and the water that was not turned to steam ran down the hole in the floor.

The remaining trickle landed atop the agitated blender standing on the kitchen center island. Tilting back, it investigated the source of the unexpected drip. Within what moments earlier had been inert metal, rudimentary thought processes suddenly sprung to life processed this information and came to a decision. Leaping down from the kitchen island, the altered blender scrambled toward the stairs. It was followed by the microwave, the garbage disposal, and the rest of the ghastly mob of animated and armed appliances, including the now-hysterical cappuccino maker that was laying down a track of coffee residue behind it as it ran.

Gathering outside Sam's room, they alternately flailed and beat at the door. When it remained shut, they began to stack themselves one atop the other until the electric mixer's twin whirling limbs were on the verge of reaching the doorknob.

Downstairs and still oblivious to the mechanical carnage that was on the verge of attacking his son, Ron Witwicky entered the kitchen and immediately noted the trail of dark spots that had been left on the floor by the animate but now absent coffeemaker.

"Awww, no. Hey, Judy!" Awaiting a response from his wife, he crouched and tentatively sniffed at the markings. His brow furrowed, reflecting his confusion. "What the . . . ? Dogs're crappin' cappuccino?"

Equally ignorant of his father's current aromatic conundrum, Sam shook the last of the water from the bottle as the final remnants of the fire sizzled into oblivion. He had barely enough time to feel relieved when the door to his room burst inward as the hallway unleashed its horde of low-powered horrors. His eyes went wide and he threw up his hands defensively.

The gesture failed to keep him from getting nunchucked in one knee by the homicidal toaster. As he stumbled backward clutching at his bruised leg, the whirring blades of the advancing mixer changed into a pair of spinning turrets resembling the most mini of all mini-guns. Revolving at speed, they sent a fusillade of equally miniaturized bullets in his direction. As their intended target dove wildly to one side, they proceeded to shred the wall behind where he had been standing.

Meanwhile the advancing blender let loose with a newly morphed mini-cannon that missed Sam but blew the fish tank to fragments. As it and the maniacal blender swiveled their weapons in his direction, Sam upended his desk. It took the brunt of the second salvo and he climbed out the window, hung for a moment from the sill, and then dropped into the cushioning bushes below. Carefully nurtured and lovingly pruned branches snapped under his weight and he knew that his mother, the dedicated horticulturist, would Not Be Happy.

Struggling to his feet, he nearly ran into his father. Hearing the uproar, Ron Witwicky had come tearing around the side of the house as fast as his middle-aged legs could propel him.

"What's all the racket . . . ?"

Waving his arms wildly, Sam pushed his father and half dragged, half shoved him backward. As he did so, berserk altered appliances crowded the open window as each sought a clear line of fire. Equipped with more weapons than brains, they jammed the gap so tightly that none could get through.

That did not keep them from unloading a volley of tiny missiles in the general direction of the two fleeing humans. Taking cover behind the fountain that was one of Witwicky *père*'s pride and joys, divots of lovingly tended turf erupted around Sam and his father. Identifying a secondary structure as a smaller dwelling, two of the berserk appliancebots promptly blew the Witwicky doghouse to smithereens. Sam's shout of desperation just managed to rise above the clamor, confusion, and general destruction.

"BUMBLEBEE!"

Responding to this call with alacrity if not discretion, a yellow Camaro came smashing out the side wall of the freestanding garage. Halfway out, it had already begun to change into the brilliant black and yellow bipedal shape of the Autobot who had been charged by his colleagues with looking after the noteworthy descendant of Captain Witwicky. Appraising the situation with admirable speed, Bumblebee speedily unlimbered his own weapons and proceeded to reduce the pack of rabid appliancebots to scrap. Clinging to the awning above Sam's window, the altered microwave dared to return fire. Bumblebee's reaction was to unload the full fury of his weaponry on the remaining bot, obliterating it.

In the process, he also annihilated the second-story bedroom that had been Sam's refuge since preadolescence.

Rising slowly from behind the fountain, Sam and his father cautiously surveyed the house and yard. Nothing remained of the insane appliances to suggest to a casual observer that anything other than bits and pieces of secondhand domestic devices littered the ground. Side by side, father and son regarded the smoking debris silently.

Not so Judy Witwicky. Coming around the front corner, she halted in shock at the sight, mouth agape as she stared at the still-smoking top floor of her house.

"Holy mother of . . . !" Lowering her gaze, her eyes came to rest on an abjectly quiescent Bumblebee. "I am gonna melt you down into scrap metal, so help me *God*!"

The Autobot dropped his head as realization struck home that he might have been a tad overzealous in his defense of the young human still under his protection. It was just a wee bit conceivable that in taking out the last of the rampaging appliancebots, one missile might have sufficed in lieu of the several he had launched. Turning, he moped back toward the gaping hole that had assumed the physical location in the space–time continuum formerly occupied by the north side of the Witwicky family garage.

He remained there in silent terrestrial guise as several mobile representatives of the local fire department arrived and their personnel dispersed to survey and clean up the damage. As a stoic Ron tried his best to comfort an alternately angry and sobbing Judy, Sam slipped into the house in the wake of the diligent firefighters.

"Better stay out of here till the site's been cleared, kid." An officer gestured pointedly upward. "We've still got some heat on the second floor."

"I'm looking for my homework," Sam told him quickly. "I don't think my Economics prof will buy this excuse." When this met with a cold stare on the part of the professional, Sam added, "I'll stay down here and get out fast, don't worry."

This seemed to satisfy the firefighter. In any case, one of his colleagues was urging him upstairs. Sam was left alone in the kitchen. Not to seek nonexistent homework, but something smaller and far more important.

He finally found it glistening below the kitchen island. Having burned a path all the way through the thick oak and the linoleum flooring, it had finally come to rest on the concrete slab beneath. Sorting through his father's "miscellaneous" drawer, he found an ancient 35-millimeter film canister and carefully scooped the lifeless ember into the plastic cylinder.

By the time he returned to the yard, his mother had recovered from the initial shock and despair. As she stomped back and forth among the ruins of her garden, he listened while she unleashed a stream of verbiage the mildest of which was, "This *sucks*!" He looked around worriedly for his father, finally locating the old man deep in conversation with the local fire chief. As he approached the pair, his concern faded. Having dealt with the suspicious agents of the now-disbanded Sector Seven, Ron Witwicky had no difficulty allaying the unease of a local municipal employee.

"Y'know," Sam's father was saying, "we had a pretty old furnace in the attic up there."

The fire chief frowned at him. "You kept a working furnace in the *attic*? Where the heat would just rise? In a wood-frame house?"

Ron managed to look offended. "Hey, *I* didn't put it in. It was there when we bought the place. Gets damn cold on that second floor, but when that furnace was going even a little bit, it was nice and comfy." He turned aggressive. "This ain't Florida, y'know. If I could've afforded to redo the whole heating system with forced air I would've done it years ago. Always meant to." He nodded in the direction of the smoking second floor. "At least now the installation will be easier."

The sound of an arriving motorcycle drew Sam's attention away from the two men. As Mikaela slowed to a stop at the curb he hurried over to intercept her. She didn't offer a kiss. Instead, she just stared past him at the smoking house.

"What *happened*?"

Using his body to shield the transaction from view, Sam hastily passed her the film canister. "Do me a favor, keep this hidden, okay?"

She eyed him guardedly. "Am I not supposed to ask what's in it? Lemme guess—it's not your undeveloped baby pictures."

He looked anxiously over his shoulder. "C'mon, Mik—just do this, okay? I'll explain later."

She rolled her eyes and sighed heavily. "Why do those three words always fill me with dread?"

No one was paying them any attention, perhaps because Judy Witwicky had marched around the smoking remains of her home to once again confront her husband. Furiously, she pointed at the back of her head.

"I have a *bald* spot! And it's not from aging— though if I have to put up with any more of this the rest may fall out anyway. I want that talking alien car *outta* here—or I'm gonna have it towed to the junk-yard!"

"Excuse me a minute." Stepping away from the puzzled fire chief, Ron Witwicky took his wife by one arm and led her away. "Honey, shhh, okay?" He eyed her meaningfully. "National security, remember? Besides, as long as we stay quiet they'll take care of everything." He put on a happy face. "*Pay* for everything, too. You know how we've been waiting for years to redo the house? Well, consider this the official beginning of our remodel. And the worst of it can be done while we're in Europe." He spread his hands and smiled. "See? Everything works out for the best." Turning, he hailed his son. "Doesn't it, kiddo?"

She was less than mollified. "The *best*? I'll give you my 'best.' " As she turned to her apprehensive offspring, one hand flailed at the mutilated garage. "When you leave, *he* leaves. I have never been more serious, Samuel."

Considerably later, when the firefighters felt confident that the last spark (little did they know) had been extinguished and had taken their leave, and while Ron Witwicky attempted to explain to a dubious airline agent the reason he and his wife needed to change the departure time on their reservations, Sam and Mikaela made their way into the depths of the Witwicky garage. The damaged wall where Bumblebee had so precipitously exited had been covered with a tarp. As the two young humans approached, the Autobot again lowered his head.

"I'mmmm ssssoooo sorrryyyyyy . . ." His voice trailed off into a slow stream of electronic mush. Mikaela eyed him sympathetically.

"Still having voice problems, huh?"

The Autobot nodded sadly, perking up only when Sam drew near.

"Listen. Bee. Uh—about college . . ."

Music began to pour from within the great yellow and black entity. *"I'm so excited, and I just can't hide it . . ."*

"Bee . . ." Sam tried to take control of the conversation. It was hard enough to do with an Autobot,

even more difficult when the response consisted of
"... *I'm about to lose control!*"

"Bee, could you just . . . ," Sam implored as
Mikaela looked on.

"... *I think I like it . . .*"

"I'm not taking you with me."

The boisterous standard that until then had filled
the garage came to an abrupt and unnatural stop. The
resulting silence was as reflective as it was awkward.
A subdued Mikaela started to retrace her steps.

"I'll—be outside."

It was Sam who chose to break the uncomfortable
silence as he finally delivered the speech he had been
dreading for days.

"Look, it's not that I don't want you to come. It's a
university rule. Freshmen aren't allowed to have a car.
It's not allowed until you're a junior." He looked
away, toward the heavy tarp that occupied the space
where the garage wall had been. "It's a lame rule, I
know, but this isn't the local JC we're talking about."
His shoulders lifted and fell. "I suppose to the
school's way of thinking it's a way to keep new students focused on their studies at a time when they
shouldn't have any distractions. Makes sense—if
you're a sixty-year-old university administrator.
Maybe it makes sense if you're not—I dunno." He
turned back to his altered car—no, he corrected himself. To his friend.

"I can't do anything about it. I can't change the
rule, and as an incoming freshman I can't expect to
challenge it."

The Autobot looked away. While his face was ex-
pressionless, his posture was not. It was amazing how

much emotion could be conveyed through the subtle positioning of arms, the slight lowering of a head— despite the fact that they were made of metal. Only the most insensitive onlooker could have failed to grasp what Bumblebee was feeling.

Sam moved closer to his friend and protector. "Don't do that. Don't be like that. Think about it. You're suffocating in here. You deserve better than my dad's garage. You should be with your friends."

The Autobot's head came up. Though the lenses that peered into Sam's eyes were wholly inorganic, there was no mistaking what was going on behind them.

"Youuu are myyyy frienddddd, Sam."

The young man swallowed, struggling to contain his own feelings. "I know, I know. Man, don't do this, Bee. This isn't how I want us to part." He gathered himself. "You did your job, being my guardian. Even my parents don't get to do that anymore. But I've got to move on. We both have to move on." He forced a tight grin.

"And then there's this little overkill problem of yours. Makes me wonder if you've been hangin' with Ironhide too much. C'mon—blowing up my room just to take out some whacked-out kitchen appliances? You're an adrenaline junkie, you are. Half the time I come out here you're not around 'cause you're out doing your Autobot thing. That's cool, I get that. But as much as you're responsible for me, when you're operating undercover I'm kinda responsible for *you*. I mean, I don't expect you to sit here and sleep day after day, but there's gotta be a limit. Have you seen the pile of speeding tickets in the glove box?

They have *cameras* at stoplights now. Maybe they're not in the same intellectual league as Autobots, but they do their job, and I have to . . ."

Music erupted from the quietly listening Autobot: Sammy Hagar howling *"I can't drive—fifty-five!"*

"I *know*," observed the exasperated Sam. "That's what I'm saying. That's my point. I'm not the only one who needs space. You need your freedom, too." Reaching out, he placed a hand on the cool, gleaming exterior of the Autobot's cheek. "You should be with the others of your kind. Together you have a larger—purpose."

Excerpting from a multiplicity of available radio streams, each word enunciated by a different announcer or singer, Bumblebee cobbled together a response.

"What—is—your—purpose—Sam?"

It was not a question he had anticipated. Hoping to reserve deep contemplation for his initial classes, now here he was expected to consider such questions in the family garage. Out of respect for Bumblebee, he took a moment to ponder before replying. His answer was less insightful than he wished.

"Geez, Bumblebee—I don't know. I don't think I'm old enough to know. I *know* I'm not wise enough to know."

The Autobot nodded slowly.

"I want to be normal, I guess. To go to college, grow up a little, and figure out what I do want. I've got the rest of my life to work it out. And I gotta do that—alone."

"How do you mend a broken heart?" as warbled by Al Green, was Bumblebee's unfair response.

Sam refused to let himself be drawn in—either by the music or by Bumblebee's candid yet calculated riposte. "Bee, hey. C'mon. It's not like we're never gonna see each other again. I'll be back. I'll visit. Christmas, summers—you'll see me as much as my parents will. Maybe more. If I had," he had to catch himself and swallow before finishing the thought, "if I had a brother, I wouldn't see him any more or less often. You'll always be—my first car."

There was nothing more to say. Bumblebee knew it too. Silence settled over the garage's dim interior. Then the Autobot nodded sadly. One arm came up. Sam extended his own. Metal fingers that could crush concrete closed around the human's far more fragile digits with a gentleness that would not have roused a kitten from its sleep. Sam squeezed back, then withdrew his hand. Grinning, he presented his open palm. Bumblebee hesitated, then the flat metal of his hand slapped lightly against exposed flesh. With a nod and a last look, Sam exited the garage, not wincing and grabbing his stinging, reddening hand until he was well outside and halfway back to the house.

Like the best kisses, the farewell embrace between Sam and Mikaela in the front yard went on and on, the two of them oblivious to the neighbors or anyone else who might be watching. It lasted and lingered until interrupted by the decisive cough of the car starting up. Pulling his gaze away from Mikaela's face proved more difficult for Sam than separating their lips.

"Gotta go." His voice was barely audible.

"Say what? I can't hear you." Her fingers were in

his hair, tousling, her touch discreetly electrifying. He lost himself in her eyes.

"Um? Did you say something?"

She cooed softly. "Did you?"

Be strong, he told himself. Where's the Witwicky strength? The same strength that had allowed Archibald Witwicky to survive weeks of privation and freezing seas and howling storms in the Arctic.

With all due respect to Great-great-grandma Witwicky, Sam doubted that Archibald had ever found himself enveloped in the embrace of someone like Mikaela. Nevertheless . . .

"Jersey's only a cheap commuter flight away," he finally managed to gasp weakly. "You could come visit—anytime."

"Sure I could. On the money I take home from the shop. Or maybe I'll just jump in my Gulfstream. Can you make it through those East Coast winters? When I'll be back here laying out on the beach? In a bikini that weighs less than your imagination? All wet and sandy in the hot, *hot* sun . . ."

Her fingers were disturbing considerably more than just his hair. "Okay, forget school," he mumbled. "Just dropped out." She laughed lightly. "You're the best thing that ever happened to me," he finished.

Instead of replying she continued to lock his gaze. Waiting for the words he had yet to say. Waiting for the words that meant everything to a woman. Waiting for . . .

Well, he was a *man,* after all.

". . . And?" she prompted him gently.

"And," he murmured uncomfortably, "I'd do anything for you."

"*And?*" Not quite so gently this time.

He knew what she wanted him to say. And he wanted to say it as much as she wanted to hear it. Yet, still, however, nevertheless . . .

"Come on, 'Kaela. If I say it now, it'll be forced." He straightened slightly. "*You* never said it either."

She continued to hold him close. To hold on to him. "That's 'cause guys always run when you say it."

"So do girls. Especially girls like *you*, who can have anyone. And that makes guys like me, who look in the mirror and always see a dork looking back, really, really anxious."

She nodded thoughtfully. "I see. So all this—going to college, being the strong silent type—it's all your elaborate plan to keep me interested?" Her fingers had stopped moving, but it didn't matter.

"Basically, yeah."

Her knowing smile would have melted metal. "I hate that it's working."

Funny how sometimes even the nerdiest guy will know when to shut up. This time their kiss was more tender, though no less passionate. His father's voice, unusually compassionate, resounded from what seemed like a great distance but was in fact only the curb. With utmost reluctance, Sam drew back.

"Screw time and space. We're gonna make this *work*."

Stepping back, still gazing deeply into her eyes, he let her hands, her fingertips, slip away. Then he turned and walked hurriedly to the waiting car. As he climbed into the backseat, his father calmly restored reality with a murmured aside to his wife.

"Stop staring at the house. I already called the contractor. He can't wait to rip us off."

Judy Witwicky turned to her husband. "I thought you said the government was going to pay for the reconstruction?"

"Yeah, well, you know the government. There's gonna be . . . ," his voice dropped ominously, "*paperwork*."

Engine revving, the car pulled away from the curb. As it did so, a second vehicle rolled down the driveway to stop at the top of the sidewalk. Its engine generated only as much noise as was desired. Together, shapely Camaro and equally well-formed mechanic watched the Witwicky vehicle recede down the residential street. Mikaela could see Sam gazing at her out the back window until the car turned the first corner. Only when it had slipped from sight did she finally allow herself to wipe at her brimming eyes. Then she climbed on her bike, buckled on a helmet, and prepared to move on. Behind her, the Camaro hesitated, not yet in the street. Turning to peer over a shoulder, she regarded the sleek yellow and black machine.

"You need a place to stay, shop's always open."

With that she raced the throttle twice, then sped off in the opposite direction. Behind her the Camaro hesitated briefly, then headed off on its own course.

Neither of them paid any attention to the tiny truck that was parked at one end of the street. Wheels had observed the multiple partings in silence, his internal functions operating at the absolute minimum so as not to attract the attention of the garishly highlighted Autobot. As soon as the Camaro had driven out of the picture, the mini-Decepticon extended a single lens that was far more sensitive and efficient than any comparable human-built optic. It focused not on the departing enemy but on the single human who remained from the turgid confrontation that had taken place outside the wooden dwelling. Within the depths of Wheels's cognitive facilities, a simple phrase came into existence:

TARGET ACQUIRED

As she accelerated slightly, alternately checking for cross traffic while wiping at her still weeping eyes, Mikaela never detected nor did she have any reason to take notice of the nondescript little vehicle that trailed unobtrusively in her wake.

⚛ IV ⚛

The single passenger in the Blackhawk paid no attention to the exquisite turquoise and green waters of the lagoon that were flashing past beneath him. He had not come to the remote Indian Ocean island base of Diego Garcia on vacation. His purpose was as distinct and sharply etched as his manner. The latter had served him well as he had risen through the ranks in Washington. He was neither inclined nor in the mood to relax now. The sooner he delivered himself of the reason for his presence in this godforsaken corner of the planet, the sooner he could return to civilization.

As befitted the importance of its commuter, the chopper set down carefully and gently. Aware of their passenger's reputation, neither pilot had any desire to incur his disapproval. They were delighted to see that another soldier was waiting to take him off their hands. The sooner they were rid of him, the quicker they could return to the other side of the lagoon and more agreeable duties.

No one onboard the copter offered to help the passenger off, nor did he request any assistance. Stepping easily down the steep set of roll-up stairs, he acknowledged with a curt nod the solitary officer who was waiting for him on the tarmac. Lennox did not extend a hand in greeting. He did not have to, and he knew who the visitor was.

"Director Galloway: honor to have you on site." He gestured to his left. "It's been a rough day."

Galloway turned slightly in the indicated direction. Three "transfer cases," as the metal caskets were euphemistically known, were being loaded aboard a waiting aircraft. Two were draped in American flags, the other in that of the United Kingdom. As he guided the visitor across the tarmac, Lennox snapped a crisp salute in the direction of the three coffins.

"From Shanghai," he explained tersely. "I suppose you've seen the official report. Considering how bad it could have been, the general feeling is that the operation came off well." Once again he indicated the honor guard and its poignant cargo. "Except for those three guys."

Galloway's gaze was fixed forward. "All due respect, Major, I'm here with a message from the president. And that message is for the Autobot leader."

Nothing in Lennox's expression betrayed what he was feeling. The national security advisor's response had been as correct as it had been cold. However, the man could have phrased his reply differently. It was not as if he had been prying.

He hadn't been on Diego Garcia five minutes and already Lennox decided he didn't like the man.

The observation and relay satellite represented the best and most secure the military could put into orbit. It was huge, fully powered, and capable of transmitting many multiple streams of data simultaneously to dozens of points on the surface of the blue-white world below. Most recently, it had been employed to coordinate the action at Shanghai.

That was what had brought it to the notice of Others.

The second machine that was slowly and carefully approaching the satellite should not have been there. It had not been launched from Canaveral, Baikonour, Kourou, or any other place on Earth. Glistening lenses dominated its exterior, as befitted the Decepticon called Soundwave. Unlike Starscream or many of his brethren, his specialty was not fighting. It was listening. Observing. Recording.

Soundwave was a master spy.

The military comm satellite was designed to detect, report on, and if necessary take defensive action against other satellites. This primitive technology in no way equipped it to deal with an infiltration by something as sophisticated as Soundwave. The Decepticon did not counter the satellite's technology so much as he avoided or deflected it in such a way that his own presence was not even perceived.

Edging in close, he unleashed a plethora of undetectable tendrils. Penetrating the satellite's exterior, they neither caused it harm nor revealed themselves. Soundwave's intent was not to destroy or damage but to partake. Melding with the satellite's complex instrumentation, the Decepticon settled in patiently to listen, and to watch.

Whatever the satellite communicated, Soundwave would hear. Whatever it saw, the Decepticon would see.

And be in a position to relay onward to others.

*   *   *

Despite its size, the enormous hangar seemed hardly big enough to contain all the advanced electronic equipment and monitoring screens that had been crammed inside. Shunts and conduits crawled up walls like termite tunnels across wood paneling while operators fought for leg space beneath desks overflowing with instrumentation. The flashing of telltales, the flare of lights, and the subtle cacophony of electronic beeps and squeals would have been amusing save for the somber significance that lay behind them.

Noting the arrival of brass and bureaucrats as well as a cluster of driverless vehicles, Epps ceased chatting with the operators of two monitoring stations and ambled over to join the conference. He recognized all of them, including the recently arrived Galloway. For a "mere" NCO, Ray Epps's security clearance lay somewhere between Quantico and the moon.

As the high-hats gathered in one of the few open areas, the sergeant angled toward the national security advisor. Gathered around him were a couple of civilians in suits as severe as their expressions and several officers who between them boasted more stars than the average constellation. Epps settled in beside Galloway as his friend and superior Lennox greeted the chairman of the Joint Chiefs of Staff.

"Admiral." Lennox did not need to add anything else. The two officers, one battle-hardened and recently promoted, the other as senior as one could get in any service, had been working closely together for the past two years.

"Will." Morshower's lips tightened as he regarded

the younger man. "Heard you went up against a few tough customers out there. Sounds like it was a rough trip."

Lennox did not try to make light of his recent visit to the People's Republic. "Yes it was, Sir. I know protocol's to avoid direction communication, but something came up toward the conclusion of the Shanghai op that requires an immediate debrief. One that Security thought potentially too dodgy to entrust to regular comm networks, encrypted or not. With your permission, I'd like you to hear it from the leader of the Autobots himself."

Morshower nodded. "Proceed."

There was no need for Lennox to waste time with formal introductions. Words were inadequate anyway to herald Optimus Prime's smooth conversion from semitruck to towering metallic bipedal form. Having never been privy to the process in person, the awed Galloway let out a startled gasp as he took a reflexive step backward.

Epps was understanding. "Never really get used to seeing it, know what I mean, Sir?" Galloway said nothing; he just stood with his head tilted back and stared. Whether the viewer was a pipefitter or a presidential envoy, Epps mused, the reaction was always the same.

Optimus acknowledged the limited introduction with a brief nod in his friend's direction. "Thank you, Major Lennox." When he turned, it was to face the chairman. If this ruffled Galloway's personal pride or sense of official propriety, he kept it to himself.

"Admiral," the leader of the Autobots began solemnly, "our alliance has countermanded six Decepticon incursions this year, each on a different continent. But this last one was different. It came with a warning." Reflecting his abilities, Optimus did not simply repeat the last words of the dying Decepticon: he played them back as recorded.

"The Fallen—shall rise—again."

The mechanical intonation echoed in the silence that followed, until Morshower spoke for all of those present. " 'The Fallen' . . . meaning what?"

"We don't know, Sir." Like all truly great leaders, Optimus Prime was readily disposed to admit that he was not omnipotent. "It hints at something from our past, but we have no way of being certain of that. Much about our own history, the origins of our race, was lost with the destruction of the Allspark."

Unlike the typical pen pusher, Galloway had primed himself for his visit. The bureaucrat might not be likable, but he was certainly prepared.

"You also thought they'd leave the planet after this 'Allspark' was destroyed. But you were wrong. As of this past year, at least six times wrong. Clearly there's something *else* they want here."

Everyone present turned in the direction of the coldly confident speaker. It was left to Lennox to make the introduction.

"Director Galloway," he informed Optimus dryly. "National security advisor. The president just appointed him liaison." The leader of the Autobots eyed the just-arrived human wordlessly. Lennox studied the impassive alien face, but it was impossible to tell what the Autobot was thinking.

"Forgive the interruption, Admiral," Galloway was saying, "but after all the damage in Shanghai and the subsequent difficulty and expense of the usual follow-up and cover-up, I for one am hard-pressed to say the job's getting done." Turning from the chairman, he directed his attention to the silently watching Optimus.

"Under the classified Alien/Autobot Cooperation Act you've agreed to share your intelligence with us, yes? But *not* your advancements in weaponry. Advancements that would allow us to better deal with the Decepticons on our own. Advancements that would, need I spell it out for you, potentially save human lives."

Optimus replied heavily. "We have looked carefully at the human capacity for war. We have studied the recorded history of your entire civilization, which in its 'modern' form is less than a whisper on the wind. It is—ungainly. Releasing such information to you would bring more harm than good."

Give the man credit, Lennox thought as he observed the exchange: where many another would have been intimidated by the presence of Optimus, Galloway stuck to his guns.

"Excuse me," the security advisor responded, "but who're *you* to judge what's best for *us* when by your own admission your own civil war led to the destruction of your own planet?" When Optimus did not reply, Galloway added pointedly, "Might I remind you that you're here as *guests*."

"We have placed the lone remnant of the Allspark in your safekeeping, Director. In the spirit of trust between our races. No greater gesture of our cooperation can we provide."

Lennox had been quiet for as long as he could

stand. "Sir, we've been in the field together, fighting side by side for two years . . ."

Unintimidated by either the brass or the visitor's status, Epps felt similarly compelled to step forward. "They've never given us reason to question their loyalty or the alliance we've struck."

Galloway listened but otherwise ignored the two soldiers. His focus remained on the leader of the Autobots. "And these newest members of your team? More of your kind arriving here? I am given to understand that they arrived after you sent a message into space, an open invitation for any of your kind who received it and wished to do so to come to Earth, vetted by no one at the White House or the United Nations or any other earthly authority. As if you had the right to . . ."

Fortunately, Chairman Morshower spoke up before Lennox could do so. "Let me stop you right there, Mr. Galloway. The process was vetted right here."

"Really?" The advisor's brows rose as he regarded the admiral. "By whom? Not by you or by the Joint Chiefs, or I would have heard of it."

Morshower met the civilian's gaze without blinking. "The process was vetted by Major Lennox and his staff."

"You don't say." Galloway glanced in the soldier's direction. "By Major Lennox and his staff. I was unaware that the authority to render a decision that affects the entire planet had been so delegated."

"In my experience over the course of the past two years, the judgment of Major Lennox and his team has always been above reproach. Both on the battlefield and in discussion and debate over tactics and procedure their decisions have inevitably been proven to be correct."

Galloway nodded curtly. "Be that as it may, Admiral, it is the position of the president that when national, not to mention planetary, security is at stake, no one is above reproach." His gaze flicked in Lennox's direction. "No matter how courageous or successful their actions in combat." Clearing his throat, he continued in a less-confrontational vein.

"Now, here's what we know . . ."

High above and far way, the security advisor's words were automatically received and stored for forwarding and for archival purposes. Unbeknownst to anyone on the ground, human or Autobot, this process was tendered in triplicate. One set of recordings was relayed to NORAD Command in Colorado. The second was kept on an isolated speck of land in the middle of the Southern Indian Ocean. The third . . .

Instead of traveling many thousands of miles, the third was transmitted only a matter of feet, via undetected tendrils from the uploading military satellite to the shadowing Soundwave. While always on alert, the eavesdropping Decepticon took particular note of certain key words that were being transmitted from far below.

"We know that the enemy leader," an important human named Galloway was saying, "classified 'NBE—1,' is rusting in peace at the bottom of the Laurentian Abyssal, surrounded by SOSUS detection nets and full-time submarine surveillance."

Maps, charts, encoded military transmissions, visuals. History, development, previous communications, transportation manifests. Soundwave scanned, recorded, and within seconds made the apposite connections. Collectively they pointed to one particular place on the planet. Inferences were drawn. The conclusion was definite, the consequences profound.

He now knew Megatron's location.

Soundwave fought to control himself as he continued to monitor the transmission.

"We know that the only remaining piece of the so-called 'Allspark' is securely locked away in a special vault here on one of the most secure military bases in the world."

More maps, more charts, architectural drawings, construction manifests. Previous observations and information were correlated. One corner of the site from which the transmission was being sent pointed to a spot more heavily shielded than anywhere else. A single heavily guarded location. *By its defenses it shall be known,* a gleeful Soundwave knew.

The shard was there. It had to be.

Information was transmitted. Discussion was initiated. A decision was reached. It all took seconds.

". . . and since no one can seem to tell me what the enemy is *now* after, since NBE-1 has been neutralized and this Allspark has been virtually destroyed, the conclusion is inevitable and unavoidable." Galloway regarded the crowd, not all of it human, that had gathered around him.

"*You.*" His gaze roamed from Optimus Prime to the vehicles assembled on the hangar floor behind him. "You Autobots. They, the Decepticons, remain here in order to hunt *you*. You won the last round, but despite your best efforts and those of our own people they've persisted. They're still here; like yourselves they're continuously adding to their numbers—Shanghai showed that—and now we have this cryptic new threat. 'The Fallen shall rise again.' Sounds to me like something's coming. Like they're preparing to strike with something entirely new and unexpected." Raising a hand, he pointed undiplomatically in Optimus's direction.

"To strike at *you*. And while you're on our world we humans, who never heard of your war until you came among us, who never wanted and still don't want any part of it, suffer whatever collateral damage happens to occur. So far that's been—endurable. But who's to say this next, undefined, unknowable attack will not be ten times worse—or a hundred, or a thousand? The war is between you and the Decepticons. Isn't it possible that as long as you stay on this world so will they? Can you, in fact, prove to me otherwise?"

The roar of revving engines filled the hangar as the rest of the Autobots sounded their protest. They fell silent when Optimus raised a hand.

"No—I cannot."

Galloway looked satisfied, like any bureaucrat whose conclusions had been validated. "Let me ask you one last question, on behalf of the president, the Congress, and those members of the United Nations with whom we all have been in constant and close contact since you first arrived here. If we ultimately conclude that our planetary security is best served by denying you further, um, asylum on our world, will you leave peacefully?"

Lennox looked stunned. Epps bit back the response teetering on his lips, while others present who had overheard reacted with similar disbelief. But no one said anything. All eyes went to the looming, gleaming figure of Optimus Prime.

"Such a freedom is your right. If you make that request, we will honor it. It is not in our nature nor in our selves to impose our presence on those who do not wish it. But before your leaders decide, please ask them this." He leaned forward. Galloway did not flinch.

"What," the leader of the Autobots declared, "if we leave—and you're wrong?"

The decision had already been made. Whatever else the humans and their repellent Autobot allies concluded was now irrelevant, as was virtually everything else on the planet below. A panel on Soundwave's side opened, disgorging a small metallic pod. It hovered in place for a moment, orienting itself, preparing to navigate. Though it was part and parcel of Soundwave's body, it was entirely independent.

Settling its coordinates, calculating its drop speed, and fully equipped for the task ahead, it shot away from the compromised military satellite and the ominous shadow looming behind it as it fell toward the glistening blue and white surface below.

Morning dawned as brilliant as the students who were busily moving in and out of the entrance to the Gothic-style residence hall. Some of the luggage that was being hauled inside by troops of teens on the cusp of adulthood was battered, some was new, some bore the initials of overpriced and ingeniously marketed European manufacturers, but all pieces had one thing in common: they were stuffed to overflowing with bric-a-brac and paraphernalia that had nothing to do with research, academia, or future vocations. Instead, they were filled with life, much like their owners.

Several of the students had hired professional movers to shift their stuff, while others supervised the work of servants. These well-heeled few drew sideways glances from the less privileged that were both wry and wary. Though classes had yet to begin, the social pecking order was already starting to fall into place.

One of the vehicles that pulled up outside the venerable pile contained two adults and a wannabe, though judging from the enthusiasm of all three it would have been difficult to tell which was which. Climbing out of the backseat, Sam stood by himself and marveled silently at the building he had heretofore seen only in pictures. Helping her husband unload their son's belongings, Judy Witwicky was less restrained.

"Oh, my God, Ron. *Look* at it. *Smell* it." Closing her eyes, she inhaled deeply of ivy, tradition, recent grass clippings, and a surfeit of cologne and perfume. "I feel smarter just standing here!"

Being too occupied tugging at boxes and suitcases to partake of the academic bouquet, the father of the fortunate one spoke while manhandling a particularly awkward piece of luggage. "G'head, Sam, we'll bring the bags. Go check out your room." Though his tone was matter-of-fact, the pride that suffused the face of Ron Witwicky shone through.

Like the two below it, the third-floor hall was crammed with students, parents, and friends, all trying to find their way in a building that was completely new to many of them. The result was polite confusion spiced with excitement. Those freshmen who had arrived earlier and were now halfway moved in stood in their doorways and considered the less settled with studied detachment.

When he could, Sam stole sideways glances into open rooms. Each was sunny and neatly laid out, an example of the excellence and organization one would expect in the university residence that would be his part-time home away from home for the next several years.

Then he got to *his* room.

Taken aback by the spectacle within, he retreated. He checked the number above the lintel, looked inside a second time, was nearly swept up in the human tide that was coursing down the corridor, and finally, with reluctance stepped through the portal. He had seen similar panoramas before—on the news, usually from places like Oklahoma or Kansas, right after a tornado had passed through.

Open suitcases and boxes spilled their hastily unpacked contents onto floor, bed, and desk. Resembling termite mounds in Africa, clothes rose to form several cottony spires. The principal difference was that the termites were neater. One wall was almost completely papered over with posters that featured a wide and unvetted assortment of conspiracy theories. As the benumbed new arrival tried to take it all in and make sense of the mildly apocalyptic scene a closet door, squeaking appropriately if unexpectedly, swung wide to expel into the room another human male the same age as Sam.

"Hey. You must be Sam. I'm Leo. How's it goin', man?"

My roommate? Sam mused. *Surely not. Hopefully not. Please God, not.* But contact had been made. Precipitous flight would be impolite.

"Yeah, uh—what's up . . . ?"

"Hope you don't mind, I set up the crib." He indicated the two beds that were shoved against opposite walls. "You want this side or that side? I already chose that side. But if it's important to you I'm willing to debate the issue. You'll lose, though. I'm a hell of a debater. Come to think of it, you've already lost."

Fighting to stay abreast of a kind of conversation he had never encountered in high school, Sam could only shrug diffidently. "All yours, man. A bed is a bed no matter which side of the room it's on."

The two stared at each other, not speaking, long enough to become uncomfortable.

"So, this is that awkward moment, right?" Sam stated this as fact, rather than question. "You want to know if I'm a normal guy. I'm trying to see if you're a normal guy. Unmedicated, nothing in the crawl-space . . ."

Leo picked up, "Good personal hygiene, won't stab me in my sleep . . ."

Over to Sam, "No arrest record, won't steal anything . . ."

Leo now playing the net, "Including girlfriends . . ."

"Especially girlfriends," returned Sam.

That settled, Leo asked more amicably, if skeptically, "So you got a girlfriend?"

"Yeah, you?"

"Not a chance," Leo replied, though not as though it was an obstacle, simply a temporary state. "You a tech-head?"

Now on more comfortable ground, Sam replied simply, "I am."

Leo took this to mean that the ice was officially broken. "Sweet!" He then yelled over his shoulder, "Hey Sharsky! Fassbinder! How we doing in there?"

At this, two students poked their heads into view. Sam sighed and looked at the floor. These two represented the Platonic ideal of "Geek."

"Servers almost online, Leo," came Sharsky's enthusiastic reply.

"Got your network up and running," added Fassbinder.

"Uh . . . what is all . . ." began Sam.

"Welcome to my empire. 'The Real-Effing-Deal-dot-com.' You've heard of it, right?" Leo had the confidence of a true bloghead, daring Sam to claim ignorance.

Sam took the bait. "Uh, no."

Set atop the desk near Leo's bed, a recently installed computer suddenly beeped for attention. Leo spun to his computer, his active fingers on alert. Tentatively moving nearer, Sam peered over the other youth's shoulder.

The source of the viral video that was looping on-screen could be identified by the Chinese ideographs that ran down the right-hand side of the monitor. A stream of English subtitles supplied translations that were punctuated by an excess of exclamation points.

"*What's that?!,*" a voice on the video was saying. "*Are you seeing this!?!! . . . It's HUGE!!!!*"

Striving for a better look, Sam leaned closer. What he was able to make out caused him to stiffen. The hand-held pickup, probably a camera phone, that had been used to record the video was tracking a wild car chase, the object of which was enormous, metallic, and composed of several wheels that were rotating end over end. While he had never before glimpsed its like, Sam had a pretty good and equally unsettling idea of what he was looking at.

His attention focused on the monitor, Leo failed to notice his roommate's reaction. "See," Leo continued unabashed, "I'm more than a website, Sam. I'm a *brand*."

"The real deal," added Sharsky.

"Uncovering the truth," offered Fassbinder.

"Whoa," Leo reacted to what he was seeing on-screen. "Lotta traffic today. Half of Shanghai gets wrecked and China says 'gas leak.' Yeah, *right*.

"This is just like that tech snow job two years ago. You remember that, right? That top-secret 'corporate robotics' program that was supposed to have something to do with national defense? The one that went Rambo all over Mission City?"

"Um, I—just heard the rumors. Didn't pay much attention to it." Sam smiled wanly. "Pretty much buried in schoolwork, y'know? Tryin' to get into a decent college, family. Girlfriend . . ." His voice trailed away.

Staring hard at the screen, Leo hardly heard him. "Where's there's smoke, there's fire, man. 'Gas leak' my ass—so to speak. Those were *aliens* on that street!"

"I wasn't there, officially," Sam mumbled, "so I can't really speculate or comment on tha . . ."

" 'Speculate or comment'—what're you, the friggin' White House press secretary? Don't be suckin' the sack of mainstream media. You've seen all the allied pabulum for the public that's been put out there? 'Massive Dynamics'? It's a shell, man! A front! Three years ago it didn't even exist. I know; I checked every issue of *The Economist* for the past *ten years*. Ain't no mention of a Massive Dynamics. Massive *scam*, that's what it is. That 'CEO' they threw in front of Congress? *Baywatch!* Same guy got saved from drowning by Hasselhoff. Old show, old episode; the guy was a lot younger but you put the stills side by side and there's no mistaking it. Pam gave him mouth-to-mouth so hard her boobies almost popped!" He glanced briefly back over his shoulder. "Look it up—he's an *actor*."

Fassbinder broke in, the look on his face betraying frustrated disappointment. "Leo, bad news: we got scooped. The video's already up on G.F.R.!"

"Dammit, Fassbinder!" bellowed Leo.

Sharsky leaned in toward Sam, conspiratorially, and said, "G.F.R. Giant-Effing-Robots-dot-com."

"Guy's our main competition on conspiracy stuff. 'Effing' was my effing idea, he *stole* it!" Leo said, more to himself than to anyone else in the room.

Once again his fingers thundered over the keyboard. A site came to life: a treasure trove of amateur videos and conspiracy message boards spilling over with appropriately apocalyptic warnings and imagined scenarios. Eyeing it all, Sam wondered how many similar sites had sprung up on the Web over the past couple of years.

"Site's run by someone who calls himself "RoboWarrior," Fassbinder added for Sam's benefit.

Leo was in a state. "Crafty bastard's always linking to our site and thieving hits—the guy's taking food outta my future babies' momma's mouths!" Leo turned back to Sam. "By the way, I read your file—I'm poor, you're poor. We're gonna fix that. Tell you what: you work for me now."

"Uh-huh, sounds awesome," replied Sam. "Whole reason I came to college, so I can work for some dinky Internet firm . . ."

"You mocking my life's work? That's your one warning for 'trolling,' dude. Don't make me have Fassbinder hack your financial aid."

"Leo, I don't know how to do that," offered Fassbinder.

An exasperated Leo shot back, "Come ON! It's about perception! Nine-tenths of the law! What the eff am I paying you for?"

"You're *not* paying me," Fassbinder reminded Leo.

Sam slowly backed toward the open door. A fresh-faced dorm monitor was passing with tour in tow. Paying no heed to protocol, Sam intercepted her.

"Excuse me? R.A.? Are there maybe any other rooms available?"

Her retort was far too perky for the situation. "Oh, sad face! Sorry, Three-twelve. No switching, no trading. Let's turn that frown upside down!"

"Well, hello-hello." The voice that called out to him was more than familiar. "And here's Sam, and . . . oh . . . um . . ."

His mother's voice sank as she and his father arrived at the doorway, hauling boxes. Their expressions contorted as they took note of the condition of their son's room. An uneasy Judy Witwicky fingered the brownie she was holding.

"Uh, Mom, Dad." Sam summoned a smile. "This is Leo . . . and these guys—my roommates. For the moment." He fully intended to continue and, if possible, explain, but the brownie caught his attention.

"Mom? Where'd you get that?"

She held up the dark brown square. "Oh, down the hall," she explained breezily. "These extremely conscientious boys are having a bake sale for their environmental group. They said their brownies were pure Hawaiian green."

Father and son reacted simultaneously.

"Uh, Mom—don't eat that," Sam mumbled.

"Judy, drop the brownie." Ron Witwicky reached for the chocolaty square.

His wife pulled it away from him. "Oh, c'mon, it's my cheat day." She turned back to her son. Her college student son, she reminded herself proudly. Her Ivy League student son. "You just relax here. We'll get the rest of your stuff. Make friends, make friends." Before husband or son could intervene further she gobbled down the remnants of the brownie, licked her fingers, and headed back down the hallway. Ron hurried after her, his expression conflicted.

Having moved up to stand beside Sam, Leo was now ogling the girl who was moving in directly across the hall: a fresh-faced clone of numerous television blondes. Mega-cute. In spite of himself, Sam could not keep from staring.

Leo whacked his arm. "*Es la casa del chicas en fuego*. Sharsky hacked campus housing and we stacked the dorm with pretty bettys . . . you're welcome. She's tied for number five on my to-do list. So do *not* birddog my quail. You hear me?"

Sufficiently loud to penetrate the general noise and confusion, Leo's voice caused the subject of his observation to turn and regard them curiously.

"Uh—hi." She was careful to keep close to her room and not step across the hall. Conversation would be conducted at a safe distance.

Leo straightened to his full height. "Leo Ponce de León Spitz, The-Real-Effing-Deal-dot-com."

Her return smile was understandably guarded. "Alice."

"I'm Sam." No harm, he told himself, in being polite. Especially to a new neighbor. Especially to a new neighbor who looked . . . who looked . . .

She was staring directly at him, interdicting his thoughts. Blocking memories with sparks. Spitz picked up on the instant rapport between the two like a hound scenting blood from a stuck javelina. His voice deliberately rose and deepened.

"Leo," Leo felt the need to remind her.

"Hi, Sam." Her gaze and her tone suggested that Señor Spitz had ceased to exist as a physical reality in the current quadrant of the known cosmos.

"He has a girlfriend." More than a hint of desperation was beginning to creep into Leo's voice.

"Lucky guy," smiled Alice.

Leo persisted. "Plus he's got some gastrointestinal issues, this guy. It's like a butt died in his pants."

"Leo's in a boy band," Sam countered.

Flashing a smile only a few watts short of melting glass, she picked up one of her move-in boxes and turned toward her room. "Nice to meet you guys . . . Sam." All golden-blond hair and curves that had no place in a trigonometry text, Alice took her box and vanished into her room.

Leo turned to Sam with a scowl. "It's *on.*"

"I *have* a girlfriend . . . ," protested Sam.

Leo pointed a finger at Sam's chest. "I'll cut you."

Sam swallowed hard, but not in reaction to Leo's threat.

Sam was intent on following when he noticed something out a hallway window. Down on the quad, Judy Witwicky was hugging a man who was not her husband. To his credit, the man looked startled rather than engaged. Releasing him, she moved on to a middle-

aged woman and embraced her with equal enthusiasm. A wide-eyed student was next, followed by . . .

Uh-oh. Grasping that his mother was deep in the
throes of brownie-inspired sociability, Sam bolted for
the stairs.

He arrived in the vicinity of his highly exuberant
parent approximately the same time as did his father.
Spinning gaily away from her husband, she pirouet-
ted across the lawn. As she did so, she drew amused
stares from arriving students and the occasional look
of horror from their parents.

"Welcome to the dorm!" She was shouting at no
one in particular, with the possible exception of the
clouds scudding past overhead. "My son is Sam
Witwicky—W-i-t-w-i-c-k-y. He's a student here, too.
He's a nice boy. These are his baby booties."

Sprinting out of the main ground-floor entryway, a
horrified Sam located his mother just in time to see
her dancing with the mini-shoes in question as if they
were a pair of pale blue castanets.

"Mom! What're you *doing* . . . ?"

"Oh, hi, Sammy." Following this brief acknowledgment of his presence she resumed speaking to the
crowd. Those adults nearest to her picked up their
pace, while the other new students she was addressing smirked or giggled according to their gender.
"He'll be homesick, so *please* be nice to him; don't
tease him, he's very sensitive . . ."

"Mom, you need to stop *right now*." Short of
lasso and gag, the increasingly desperate Sam could
envision no way to put an end to the continuing embarrassment his mother had become. He looked frantically toward his father, who was likewise standing

nearby looking alternately mortified and helpless. "Dad, *do* something, this is *not* okay."

"I'm trying," Ron Witwicky protested. He strove to gently but firmly get a grip on his wife's arm as she continued to boogie energetically out of his grasp. "Help me get her outta here."

His more-than-happy wife proceeded to intercept a well-dressed couple who were on their way toward the residence hall entrance. This precipitated a little jig as they tried to go around her and she kept moving to block their path. While the man only looked irritated, his wife was growing increasingly nervous.

"Did you know," Judy Witwicky murmured with the air of one imparting a mystery of great gravity, "that his car is a talking robot?"

"*OnStar!*" Having managed to secure a grip on his mother's right arm, a frantic Sam was trying to guide her in the direction of the curb and the car waiting there. "She means I have OnStar! And I have no idea who this woman is!"

His mother exploded in hysterical laughter. "Onstar, on-star—don't know which star they're on, on-star!" Lapsing into a moment of sudden silence, her lips parted as she gasped in delighted surprise at something across the lawn. "Frisbee!"

Breaking free of husband and son, she raced across the grass to intercept a game of Frisbee. As one of the participating students bent to pick the disc off the lawn, she got to it before him. A tug-of-war ensued: young student trying to politely but forcefully retrieve his toy, middle-aged homemaker growing increasingly bellicose as she clung to it with both hands.

"Leggo! It's mine!"

"Look, Miss, I don't know where you came from or what you think you're do . . ."

Father and son arrived before the confrontation could turn serious. Putting an arm around his addled spouse, Ron managed to break her death grip on the disc as he aimed her in the direction of the street.

"Whoa-kay, that's enough fun for one day. Let's go, Grace Slick."

Once again she twirled out of his arms. "How 'bout you show me around the library, professor?" Bending forward, an inviting silly grin on her face, she crooked a finger at Ron. "I'll do *anything* for an A."

"Sounds good. You're walking on the moon, Judy," he murmured as he caught up to her. Resistance suddenly folded as confusion fogged her thoughts. Not to mention her stomach. He was finally able, with Sam's aid, to guide her to the car. As she slid into the front passenger seat, suddenly docile, it was clear that she had sunk deep into thought. Neither man cared to know the subject of her meditating. All that mattered was that she was safely in the car, which her husband thoughtfully locked from outside using the key-chain remote. He turned to his son.

"Wish me luck getting her past the dogs at the airport." With his spouse now safely secured, he felt able to bestow a last proud smile on his offspring. "You're a free man now, kiddo. And I do mean 'man.' This is gonna be a great time for you. Just use your head and make us proud. I'm sure you'll do great. We'll call you from our trip." He glanced back into the car, to where his wife had chosen to focus her full concentration on the palm of her left hand. She was tracing the lines there. Hopefully they would be of sufficient complexity to keep her occupied until they reached the airport.

"Love you, Dad," Sam replied simply. There was no need for further elaboration.

"Love you too, Pal. You're gonna do great things, I can feel it." Ron nodded in the direction of the looming residence hall. "And no brownies. I *mean* it."

Sam grinned back. "Not hungry, Dad. Gotta watch my figure anyway."

They hugged as fathers and sons do: briefly, with a touch of embarrassment, but hard. Then Ron Witwicky hurried around the front of the car so that his son would not see the moisture that had begun to form at the corners of his eyes. As he climbed in behind the wheel, his wife rolled down the window on her side.

"Okay, good luck! Good grades!" Raising her right hand, she formed a "V" with the middle and index fingers. "Peace out!" As the car drove off, pulling away from the curb as fast as her husband could safely manage, Sam's last glimpse of his mother was of her staring at her forked fingers as if she had never seen them before.

The smile stayed on his face all the way back to his room. Where Leo was waiting.

"I like your parents. They're good people."

As evening descended, something else besides the arc of the burning tropical sun set over the edge of the Indian Ocean and disappeared beneath the surface. No one saw it; no one recorded the rapidly dispersing cloud of steam that erupted briefly in its wake. Sinking through the clear, warm water, it began to change shape. Limbs of varying size and function sprouted from the skin of the cooling orb. Propelling itself through the water, it paused occasionally to inspect a variety of growths and other native life-forms as it advanced in the direction of the atoll that was its target.

Nothing if not agile, Ravage did not need to find a way through or under the metal fencing that barred his path: relying on his tightly wound strength, he simply leaped high over the barrier in a single bound. Keeping low to the ground, he made his way toward a line of concrete structures that featured sloping, windowless sides. Alongside signs warning of the presence of ambient radiation, others replete with garish color suggested the presence of far more deadly devices. The Decepticon, however, was interested in something far more important than mere nuclear weaponry.

The last bunker in line bore the simple, innocuous designation "E-7." Ascending the inclined white wall, Ravage maintained his low profile as he examined the roof. It was as solid and featureless as the walls save for a couple of air vents. These were so slim and hightech as to preclude entry by anything larger than a worm. Furthermore, they did not run directly into the interior of the bunker but instead deliberately twisted and turned to foil any attempt at entry by a probing tentacle or wire.

The intrusion Ravage had prepared was nowhere near so primitive.

Like miniature versions of himself, the cloud of tiny ball bearings the Decepticon fed into the vent sprouted minuscule limbs of their own. Little bigger than bird shot, they scrambled downward with a malign col-

lective intelligence that was frightening to behold—
except that there was no one to witness their incursion. They moved in total silence, communicating
with one another on a wholly unique and completely
secure frequency.

Pouring into the vault below they swirled about a
common axis, gathering themselves together like a
rising dust devil. The shape they collectively assumed
was roughly bipedal and thin as a reed. Ignoring the
explosive elements, radioactive materials, ignition devices, and other primitive weapons material stored
within the vault, the newly arisen shape advanced
without hesitation toward the far end of the chamber.

A single tank stood there. Composed of quartz
whose molecular structure had been altered, it was
capable of defeating any drill. But it could not resist
the sophisticated laserlike beam that formed out of
the body of the swirling shape now standing next to
it. As the intense light sliced through the container,
nano-thin wires embedded within the otherwise
transparent material began to set off one alarm after
another. Ignoring the outbreak of flashing lights and
reverberant sounds, the shadowy figure concentrated
on the precision work at hand.

As soon as it had made an opening large enough to
permit the extraction of the tiny, softly glowing shard
inside, a thin tendril of the reed-thin figure made its
serpentine entrance, curled around the singular object, and withdrew it from the case.

Outside the bunker, heavily armed troops dismounted from a clutch of vehicles and surrounded
the structure. A grim-faced noncom punched the access code into the door lock, then stepped back to let

an officer enter a second code into a parallel lock. As soon as the heavy barrier swung aside, crack troops rushed in.

Spreading out on the doorway end of the vault, weapons parallel to the floor and fingers on triggers, they scanned the interior with eyes and instruments. Neither revealed anything amiss, though the holed tank at the far end of the chamber put the lie to the tranquility they were seeing. No one noticed the reed-thin figure. Compacting himself, he was so thin as to be virtually invisible. His actuality was more solid—and far more deadly.

Leaping forward, he sprang toward the door. One unfortunate soldier happened to be standing in the Decepticon's way. The threading of perfectly aligned, tightly entwined mini-bots went right through his chest and out his back. As he crumpled to the floor, blood spreading beneath him, several startled colleagues raced to his aid. Their eyes continued to search the chamber for the source of whatever had taken down their comrade. Portable instruments revealed nothing.

What the hell was happening?

For one thing, they were now looking in the wrong direction. Racing out the open doorway, the virtually invisible creature quickly scrambled up the side of the bunker. It was met at the top by Ravage. Opening wide, he proceeded to inhale his horde of malevolent auxiliaries. Released by the dispersing reed-thin figure, the precious shard fell into the grasp of Doctor. Clinging like the symbiote he was to the front of Ravage, the smaller but exceedingly advanced Decepticon held the shard reverently in one of its small, sleek, highly specialized limbs.

Below, someone was shouting and pointing toward the roof of the bunker. Fanning out around the structure, troops aimed lights upward and began to open fire. Sprouting rapid-fire weaponry of his own Ravage took off, leveling those who were unfortunate enough to find themselves in his way. For the second time that evening, he easily cleared the high fence that surrounded the "secure" area.

Fanning out behind him and to both sides, soldiers in a variety of vehicles sped to where the compound's boundaries met the edge of the island. They had the intruder cornered now. Notwithstanding his speed and weaponry, there was nowhere left for him to run.

The roar that sounded from a slight coral promontory underlined the soldiers' hubris as plainly as it did Ravage's liftoff. All they found of the invader as they closed in on his last known location were some uneven lumps where old coral had been melted into calcium carbonate slag by a sudden surge of tremendous and inexplicable heat.

✦ VI ✦

The noise was deafening. It thundered not from exhaust or enigmatic engines but from the speakers that pounded out the latest top-ten hits by singers who couldn't sing and musicians who couldn't play instruments, but who by dint of artful aesthetic deceit and elemental prehistoric rhythms had succeeded in convincing a large proportion of the under-thirty population that the sounds they generated were worthy of approbation.

A dubious Sam trailed Leo, Fassbinder, and Sharsky through the frat house as his confident roommate hacked a path between fellow celebrants, the majority of whom were at once older, more experienced, more confident, and more attractive than any of the incoming freshmen.

His roommate's assurance was unassailable. Like a select few, Leo Spitz traveled within a cocoon of self-confidence blissfully invulnerable to the assaults of reality.

"First frat party's the game-changer. We're hunting in the wild now, boys. This is where freshman reputations are *made*."

"Okay . . . we're huntin' . . . we're huntin'," replied Fassbinder.

Sharsky added, "Fuel the jet, baby, fuel the jet."

"Hey, *I* say 'fuel the jet,' that's my signature," an affronted Leo replied. "Everything I say is copyrighted. Don't infringe."

Sam said, "Probably shouldn't stay long. Got a webcam date with my girlfriend."

Despite secretly wishing he had any kind of date with a female, Leo feigned contempt. "Well, while you play smoochie-poo with your MacBook, I'm gonna be gettin' my Spitzy-freaky-freak on."

A reluctant Sam allowed himself to be pulled along, a two-liter plastic bottle of adolescent insecurities swirling helplessly in the wake of the wildly weaving boat that was his bombastic roommate.

Space for a dance floor had been cleared upstairs. The deejay was busy, the room was rocking, and the place was packed. Here too, Sam followed his fellow freshman through the crowd. The music, the color, the sights, the lights, the veneer of sophistication that was so different from his hometown and from high school kept him pinned in the place like a magnet. He was an anthropologist who had discovered a fascinating new tribe, only it was not the tribe that was lost: it was him.

"College," Leo was saying, "gotta love it. Set your intellect aside, bro. This is nighttime, when all the goodies come out. It's like a giant petting zoo, only restricted to one species. L-Spitz gonna get his freaky freak on."

Spotting a member of the opposite gender who might or might not be dancing by herself, he abandoned his roommate to his own devices as he made his way out onto the dance floor. Set free, Sam let the tide of music and youthful humanity push him in the direction of a table laden with drinks, food, and a large punchbowl. The latter contained a neon greenish liquid whose garishness lacked only the presence of three witches muttering over its semi-metallic surface to fulfill a promise of impending gastric dissolution.

The music had begun to numb not only his hearing but also his consciousness. Both began to echo and fade, intensify and rebound. He felt—odd. Had he sipped or consumed something packing an unadvertised surprise? He had assiduously avoided anything that resembled a brownie, but in the course of the evening he had already nonchalantly availed himself of a number of other snacks. Who knew what might have been hidden therein?

Take the plate of cupcakes laid out in front of him, for example. What pharmacological mysteries might they contain? What exotic ingredients foreign to his gullible digestive system? Reaching out, he found himself tracing shapes in the frosting. Symbols that might mean nothing—or might be of significance only to those whose origins were far more alien than those of any of the unknowing celebrants presently partying in the room.

A voice cut through the trance into which he had fallen. Had he been daydreaming?

"Huh, lemme guess. You wanna be an art major."

Blinking as he turned, he found himself unsettlingly close to a vaguely familiar and exceptionally attractive face. It belonged to his newly arrived neighbor from across the residence hallway.

"Oh—this—no," he mumbled with a distressing lack of finesse. "I'm just—getting punch." He looked meaningfully at the green liquid. "Probably liquid kryptonite. Maybe a little antifreeze for taste. Lime juice," he concluded weakly.

She paid no attention to his feeble chemical analysis of the inscrutable fluid. "It's 'Sam,' right?" She looked away, toward the center of the dance floor. "So your roommate, he seems really—popular."

Following her gaze, Sam saw that Leo had staked out a piece of hardwood in the vicinity of the deejay and was attempting, with notable lack of success, to grind himself up against several of the more attractive girls. Creeped out by his antics, they shuffled quickly clear of his self-proclaimed zone of influence as fast as their dancing feet could gracefully carry them. Alice leaned closer to the quietly aghast Sam.

"We should get out there before he chases *everyone* off the dance floor."

Sam hesitated, his overstimulated brain struggling to ensure that it was correctly interpreting every conceivable nuance contained within her suggestion.

"Oh, you mean—out *there*. You and *me*. As in you *and* me. The two of us . . . Like a pair? Like a duo? Please stop me . . ."

She laughed softly. "Wow, you've got some serious game."

He fought to recover. "No, that'd be great. I mean, hypothetically. Presuming you're a good dancer—not that it matters. To me." He knew he was drowning— hypothetically. "It's just that I kinda, sorta, technically . . ." He took a deep breath. It helped—a little. "I have a girlfriend. Not, y'know, *here*."

She shook her head as she locked eyes with him. "I've got a boyfriend back in Orlando. He's a prince."

Some of the tension oozed out of him. "Ohhh, cool. That's where you're from?"

"He got accepted to Stanford. Now he's three thousand miles away."

His unease was giving way to sympathy. "So then you know what it's like."

"Sorta. I mean, I thought we'd stay together, but— now that I'm here talking to you—I dunno. Do we really know what life's about in *high* school, Sam? Do we really know, at seventeen, what we want for the rest of our lives?"

The party atmosphere suddenly seemed less all-enveloping as the conversation turned heavy, and from a source that caught him completely off-guard. He tried to come up with a response that would sound mature and not trite. He was not sure he pulled it off.

"I—like to think we know enough."

She nodded slowly, evidently pleased with his reply. "Fair enough. Hey, I've got an idea. How 'bout you pretended I was your girlfriend and I pretended you were my boyfriend? Like we're still kids. Adults aren't allowed to pretend, but kids are, and we've got the rest of our lives to be stuck being adults. Just pretend girlfriend and boyfriend. That wouldn't be against the rules, would it?"

He considered. Was it the noise, the music, the laughter that was making him dizzy? "A little role-playing. Hard to say. Might have to get the lawyers in on that one."

Flirting in college, he reflected, was actually not all

that different from how it had been conducted in high school. Except that he'd never met anyone like Alice in high school. Did it ever change? She was smiling, he was smiling; it was all harmless, wasn't it? Just play, that's all. Nothing serious. This wasn't an ethics seminar and there would be no surprise quiz next week. Was he at a party or what?

She was staring at him, a touch of impatience in her expression. "So are you dancing with me or what?"

He tried to stammer something clever. Clever and demurring. But before he could do so, she grabbed him and with strength as unexpected as her forwardness pulled him out onto the dance floor. The music caught him there—the music, and her smile, and the rest of her. His mind might still be confused, but his body was not.

Leastwise, his legs and arms were not.

On another part of the continent, an I-chat screen announced emotionlessly: *Sam Witwicky NOT CURRENTLY ONLINE.*

Mikaela checked her watch. It was almost time to close up the shop and there really was no point in lingering after dark. The day's work was done.

The day's enjoyment would, it appeared, have to wait until sometime tomorrow.

Sam did not so much check his watch as incidentally catch sight of it when his flying arm happened to cross in front of his face in perfect conjunction with the glare from one of the overhead lights. Otherwise he might not have noticed the lateness of the hour. Not that the time mattered, except that—except that . . .

Oh crap. Dropping his arms, he started to mouth an apology. At the same time Alice, for whom the time clearly held no significance, playfully threw her arms around his neck. At the same instant the raucous blare of a vehicle alarm succeeded in rising above the pounding of the music.

"Alice," he mumbled, "I gotta go. I'm sorry, it's been a blast, but I really have to . . ."

Beer in hand, one of the frat house seniors shoved open the second-floor door. His tone was cross and his visage matching.

"WHO BELONGS TO THE FREAKIN' YELLOW CAMARO?"

Slipping free of Alice's embrace, a stunned Sam rushed to the nearest window. An all-too-familiar coupe was parked outside—on the frat house's row of decorative bushes. Its alarm wailed plaintively. Also rather louder than was legal. Spinning, Sam rushed toward the stairs. The senior's glare he ignored effortlessly. Alice was not so easily avoided. He found himself having to dodge.

"Sorry, I—I'll see you. I mean, you're right across the hall, how would we not see each other—I mean, visually—eventually."

"Sam, I . . ." Her expression confused, she reached out for him, but he was already past.

Charging down the stairs he half ran, half tumbled past the line of students and the milling crowd on the floor below. Once outside, he found a small but rapidly increasing mob clustered around the Camaro. One of the frat officers was cursing as he tried and repeatedly failed to open the hood. Banging on it with a fist caused it to pop open a couple of inches. The would-be mechanic's smile of satisfaction turned to one of shock as the edge of the hood swiftly slammed back down on his probing fingers, sending him yelping backward in pain and surprise.

"Hey, what kind of motor . . . ?"

Rounding on the driver's-side door, Sam leaned in the open window and hissed, "What is this? What're you *doing* here? I thought we . . ."

"FRESHMAN!"

Looking up, Sam saw a cluster of frat guys heading his way. Several of them were disconcertingly large, probably not from engaging in regular workouts at the chess club. A couple were gesturing at the ruined landscaping. Nothing in any of their various expressions hinted that they were in an especially forgiving mood.

"THAT YOUR CAR ON OUR BUSHES?"

"Me?" Sam protested. "No way—a friend of mine . . ."

The extent of inebriation among his approaching antagonists varied considerably, but the one who was addressing him at the moment was sufficiently in possession of his cognitive faculties to Not Buy It.

"Don't give me that." He indicated the smashed and torn-up landscaping. "Does anything over here say 'Parking Space'? How 'bout I park my *foot* in your *ass*?"

"Uh, nothing on my pants says parking space, either. Says Levi's, I think. Sorry about the dama— hey, I'm gone, I'm outta here."

Wrenching open the door, he slid behind the wheel and gunned the engine. He reached for the shifter, but the Camaro was already spewing dirt from its rear wheels as it spun into reverse. Quick as the car was, it couldn't quite elude Alice. Yanking open the passenger-side door, she leaped in. Her eyes widened as she got a good look at the immaculate interior.

"No way! This is *your* car?"

"No—yes—sort of." Gripping the wheel even though he knew any control he tried to exert over it would be superficial at best and could be taken away from him at any time, he leaned forward and declared with becoming determination, "So I'm *gonna drive it now*—away."

Obediently and with a responsiveness that would have made a retired Detroit engineer proud, tires squealing and engine racing, the car reacted with precision to every twist of his hands.

As they sped away from the overamped building, leaving a mob of angrily gesticulating frat members receding rapidly in the rearview mirror, Alice ran her hands over the dash. Slowly, seductively. Watching her actions out of the corner of an eye, Sam could not keep from wondering what it might be like to be the recipient of a similar caress.

"I *love* Camaros!" Her voice had dropped, the tone now huskier than it had been at any time all evening. "My first car was my dad's '92 Z-28, fuel injected. The roar of the engine—it's so *throaty*. It just *tickles* me." Snuggling back into the curving seat, her hands dropped from the dash to her lap.

It required a considerable effort on Sam's part to keep his eyes on the road. "Maybe," he declared, swallowing with some difficulty, "this isn't the best time for—stories. Or for sharing—ourselves."

She whipped around to meet his gaze so sharply

that he twitched a little in his seat. "C'mon, Sam, live a little. One ride. That's not too much to ask, is it? Cheaper than dinner and a movie." Slipping off her lap, one hand slid down her thigh. "It's just pretend, remember? The relationship lawyers'll never know."

To his very great credit, Sam blushed. At the same time, the radio suddenly sprang to life.

"*Your cheatin' heart,*" it began to croon.

Sam hammered a fist on the dash. "Okay, no. That is *wrong.*" Realizing that such a violent physical reaction to a brief snatch of song might strike his passenger as a trifle odd, he hurried to explain himself. "Incorrect, I mean, uh, wrong radio station there. I'm not into country." His tone sharpened. "Especially country that *interferes.*"

The engine revved threateningly. While the noise may have given Sam pause, it only seemed to further inspire his passenger.

"Whoa, it's so *powerful*! The feeling is just—it makes me want to . . ."

Without warning, her seat fell all the way back to near horizontal. Startled, she fought to recover her balance—just as it whipped forward and slammed her face-first into the dash. The impact wasn't hard enough to break anything, but it was no love tap, either.

A stunned Sam panicked. "NONO—that is *so*— uncalled-for!"

Pulling over to the side of the road, the car skidded sharply to a stop. As a dazed Alice tried to recover her equilibrium, the air-con vent on her side flared to squirt a stream of bright green antifreeze, dousing her with the pleasant-smelling but decidedly unsolicited fluid. Sam's panic intensified.

"Alice, oh God, I'm so sorry! There was," his mind churned frantically as he improvised, "a recall on this model. Had to do with a special booster for the climate control—I forgot all about it—meant to take it in to get it fixed before I came up here. That's why I . . ."

She was holding her nose. "I'm—I'm okay—I'm fine." She didn't look at him as she reached for the door handle. "I think I'll just walk from here. Probably safer."

"Are you sure . . . ?" Leaning over, he looked after her. She was wobbly, but stable. One hand rose unsteadily as she stuck out a thumb in the direction of passing traffic. He slumped back in the driver's seat, both hands gripping the wheel, and spoke through clenched teeth.

"That was so way out of line. Giving a girl a ride is not cheating, and WHAT THE HELL BUSINESS IS IT OF YOURS ANYWAY? What're you doing here? Are you spying on me?"

The radio crackled. A news excerpt further excerpted, or possibly a line from an old radio show. *"The situation on the ground has changed—a soldier's duty is to follow orders . . ."*

Sam blinked, and his knuckle-whitening death grip on the steering wheel relaxed slightly. "Orders? What're you talking about?"

This time he thought he recognized the voice of the actor from the old war-movie clip that played back through the car's speakers. *"The commander has requested to see you, sir. There's no time to waste."*

Sam's anger gave way to confusion as he frowned. " 'Commander'? What 'commander'?"

The Camaro did not answer. Not directly. Not in words borrowed or new. Instead, after first taking care to check for oncoming traffic, Bumblebee pulled away from the curb and accelerated into the night. Very soon they were exceeding the speed limit by a considerable amount. Sam pondered pointing out that the speedometer was now registering velocity in the triple digits, but decided against it. He had warned Bumblebee on numerous occasions about radar and speed cameras, and presumed that by now, the Autobot had managed to devise a means to avoid such inconveniences.

After all, he reasoned, anything that could run circles around a Decepticon ought to be able to find a way to beat a speed trap.

He did not expect their destination to be a graveyard. The Autobots tended to favor abandoned industrial zones and empty manufacturing facilities. There being none in the immediate vicinity, the cemetery had been singled out as the place least likely to suffer an accidental incursion while the meeting was taking place. Effortlessly, Bumblebee decoded the electronic lock on the main gate and rumbled through, letting the metal grilles swing shut behind him. A short, slow drive brought them to a hilly one-lane road flanked by large stone and concrete crypts. Probably nineteenth or maybe even eighteenth century, Sam thought as he studied the disquieting surroundings.

Without a word, Bumblebee slowed and stopped. The driver's-side door popped open. Sam started to say something, hesitated, then climbed out. Immediately, he saw the reason behind his car's silence. Additional explanation was not necessary and anyway, when among themselves the Autobots did not waste words. Even in the darkness, the figure that towered above the trees was instantly recognizable.

"Hello, Sam." Optimus Prime inclined slightly in his direction.

Sam nodded back. "Just in the neighborhood?"

The Autobots did not waste words when among humans, either. Especially when among knowledgeable ones.

"A fragment of the Allspark was stolen."

It was as if the events of the past days, as well as this night, vanished like a drop of water on a hot iron. Everything else was blotted out. Nothing else mattered. Not school, not relationships, nothing. Such was the power of Optimus's terse announcement. Where moments ago Sam had been tired, even sleepy, now he was fully alert.

"As in 'by Decepticons' stolen?"

Optimus looked away, out into the night. Toward the distant horizon, Sam found himself wondering— or toward the stars? "We permitted it to be placed under human protection and surveillance as a gesture of good faith. The risk was high, but considered worthwhile. It was a means of showing how much trust we place in your kind. Your military is on high alert. And now I am here—for your help."

"*My* help? Why?"

"There are those in your government, as well as in others, who believe that by our continued presence here we have brought vengeance upon your planet and your species. We cannot convince them otherwise. They must be reminded of the truth, and of the reality. Of the trust and the common goals we share. They must be reminded by one of their own kind. By a human. By you."

Sam felt his throat constricting. "What—what're you asking me to do?"

"Speak for us. Stand with us. You have done both before, with great success. You know us as no other human does. Despite your youth, your words and experience will carry weight where those of an older but less intimately involved individual of your kind may not."

A small laugh escaped from Sam's lips. "You're kidding, right? You want me to go somewhere else, *now*? To leave college? I just *got* here."

As always, Optimus formed his reply carefully. "Fate rarely calls upon us at a moment of our choosing. I know this personally."

"I bet you do—but you're *Optimus Prime*. This—this isn't our war. It isn't *my* war."

"There was a time, long past, when it was not my war either." The leader of the Autobots paused meaningfully before continuing. "Until I lost everything. What you would call a—'family.' I learned a painful truth: that fighting for what we believe in begins with those we care about." Huge reflective eyes met Sam's own far smaller, softer ones. "What do you care about, Sam?"

He licked his lips, then tried to reply as firmly and convincingly as he could. "Look, I wanna help, I *do*—but I'm not that person, okay? I'm not the kind of statesman or orator or interlocutor that you're looking for. I'm just a normal, average kid from Burbank who still gets zits. There's a *reason* I got cut from the football team. It kinda all became clear to me when I was falling off that *twenty-story building* with a giant evil alien robot trying to rip my head off. I'm just not that guy—not the guy you want, anyway. And by the way—it *hurt*. It still hurts, sometimes. Like for instance when I'm dancing. You're not supposed to have back problems when you're *eighteen*." His voice lowered. "I mean, it's not like I didn't give at the office, y'know?"

"And of those eighteen years I have known you for barely two," Optimus replied evenly. "While brief, I feel that that has been sufficient time to render a reasonable assessment of any human."

"Yeah?" Sam shot back challengingly. "And what's your 'reasonable assessment' of me?"

The leader of the Autobots spoke quietly. "That your only shortcoming is your lack of confidence in yourself."

Sam paced back and forth, shaking his head. "Look, you're a forty-foot alien robotic life-form. If the powers that be won't listen to you, they're sure not gonna listen to an eighteen-year-old incoming college *freshman*."

Optimus continued to differ. "There is more to you, Sam Witwicky, than meets the . . ."

Sam whirled on the Autobot, not realizing as he did so that while nearly anyone else would have been intimidated by Optimus's presence and afraid to confront him so forcefully, he was comfortable enough to do so without hesitating. It was significant that the fact did not register on him.

"*Stop* it! Enough. I can't help you!"

The Autobot leader said nothing and Sam was immediately regretful.

"Look, I'm sorry. You changed my life. In ways I'm still not sure I entirely understand. But *this* is my life now. I belong *here*. I did what I could when I had to. But now I have—a choice. I gave a lot to you—people. Now I owe something to myself, and to my parents, and to—others." He looked up at the shadowed, silhouetted shape. "Nothing I do or say is gonna make a difference. Where all this is concerned, I'm outta my league."

Optimus nodded once. "If that is what you believe, then it is already true."

Sam didn't know what more to say. What *could* he say? His response had come from the heart. Could Optimus Prime understand that?

"You'll convince 'em, okay? You will, I know. You're Optimus Prime. Me, I gotta go now. I got—I have class in the morning. My first class. Don't wanna miss it."

Turning, he walked deliberately down the winding path that led to the main gate, passing the altered Bumblebee without a word. Standing beside each other, the two Autobots watched him go.

"I believe there is greatness in you, Sam—even if you don't," Optimus murmured after him.

Bumblebee followed his friend with his eyes until the small human had disappeared from sight. "What he does not realize is that, in so many ways, he has already graduated . . ."

* * *

The freighter hauling containers and construction equipment was plowing through the North Atlantic a safe several nautical miles from the zone that had recently been designated on all marine navigation maps as RESTRICTED—MILITARY DROP SITE. Despite the proximity, there was no reason for the captain to alter course. The modern freighter's GPS and autonav would keep it well clear of the forbidden zone. He relaxed in his cabin, secure in the knowledge that with a good crew, an experienced first mate, and advanced automated steering equipment they would make landfall on the East Coast of the United States right on time. Rolling over in his bunk, he prepared to get some well-deserved shut-eye.

Out on deck, a member of the night watch was enjoying a relaxing stroll among the cargo. It was hardly necessary to check the straps and bolts. If one of the containers or big construction machines was going to break loose, it would have done so in the course of the brief squall the ship had endured several days earlier. But orders were orders, an assignment was an assignment, and it was nice to be out on deck anyway. One couldn't watch DVDs or read books all the time. Besides, the deck watch was known to occasionally spring a surprise. A flying fish flopping on board, roosting seabirds, a dead body . . .

The sailor pulled up sharply. On a cargo ship at sea there were no strangers, and he recognized his colleague immediately. How or why the man had died the sailor on watch did not know, except that the amount of blood oozing from the corpse combined with the awkward and unnatural position of the dead man's limbs suggested that he had not perished from a heart attack or some other natural cause. Alarm—he had to sound the alarm. Or at least alert the others, and quickly . . .

He never saw the enormous hand that struck him down from behind.

The ship's radar and other instrumentation were programmed to look forward for obstructions and the occasional unexpected floating object—not aft. So it did not detect or record the object that was presently speeding toward the ship. Nor did any of the onboard security gear perceive it as it changed shape and landed on deck among the stacked cargo containers—or the quartet of construction vehicles that had altered form to greet the newcomer. No longer forced to squat on wheels or treads, they stood revealed in their true shapes—as did Ravage.

Rapid communication was exchanged among them. None paid the slightest attention or so much as acknowledged the two slain humans at their feet. Each following close upon the other, they launched themselves over the side of the ship.

Oblivious to the twin deaths among his crew, the captain of the vessel slept soundly as it continued on course. Below and behind his vessel's powerful props, four large bipedal shapes and a singular sphere sank swiftly into darkness.

Following its regular patrol route, the sub stayed deep. Alert at their stations, the sonar team on the bridge tracked and ticked off the usual signatures: mountainous projections, known wrecks disintegrating with incredible slowness, the occasional whale . . .

The technician sat up a little straighter and hastily

double-checked the readout he was getting. No, he corrected himself—the multiple readouts. They were clear and sharp, and he didn't hesitate. A single such signature might be attributable to a thermal anomaly, but not five of them. Not when each was as distinct and well-defined as these. He spoke with confidence into his pickup, as well as loud enough to be heard throughout the bridge.

"Conn, Sonar. We have five unidentified contacts, bearing two-four-one, range two hundred and dropping fast. Confirmed on course for Project Deep Six, Blacksmith drop point."

Coming over, the captain bent to have a look at the screen for himself. "That's on the bottom at ninety-three hundred feet. Only our unmanned surveillance vehicles go that deep, and we don't have any on station here right now." Straightening, he barked commands. One order all commanders had received with regard to Project Deep Six was that if an abnormality was detected, they should not hesitate.

"Right full rudder, all ahead flank, sound general quarters!"

Klaxons rang out, underscoring the command that was relayed the length and breadth of the great ship. *Now, general quarters, general quarters, all hands man your battle stations.*

Magazines were flung aside, DVDs ejected, meals left unfinished, and letters being composed for future Internet transmission hurriedly saved as the crew sprang into action. All crew members rushed to their stations, absorbed in their own thoughts. Each wondered, as they always did on such occasions, whether this was just another drill.

Four Constructicons came to rest on the floor of the abyssal deep. Primeval mud billowed around their legs. A few ghostly white, wholly blind fish shot away as fast as their wriggling, eel-like swimming movements could propel them. Around the new arrivals, all was blackness save for the occasional bioluminescent life-form.

Indifferent to the immense pressure, they switched on their internal beams. Light, an utterly alien presence in such surroundings, illuminated their position. All around was nothing but mud, drifting deep-sea detritus, and a single gigantic, chain-wrapped figure, silent and unmoving. Silt obscured the scene as the four of them spread out, checking the area, making sure it was secure.

A sixth shape, the Doctor, detached from Ravage to skitter spiderlike up the enormous body of Megatron. While the other five kept watch he performed a swift, thorough examination of the inert form. Disappearing into one shattered leg, the smaller Decepticon was gone for several moments before popping out again.

"Incomplete! Need parts! Replacements!"

Have regrouped to watch the Doctor at work, the four Constructicons stood in the cold silence. Then three of them turned to the fourth—and began to tear it apart. There was no one to hear the electronic screams in the language of an impossibly distant planet that rippled through the abyss except those who were doing the violent disassembling.

Work proceeded rapidly and without unnecessary conversation. When the repairs had been completed to the Doctor's satisfaction, the arachnoid Decepticon extended a tentacle outward.

"Ravage—the shard!"

Accepting the precious fragment, the Doctor turned back to the dark hole in the center of Megatron's chest. Delicate tendrils went to work, sealing, repairing, and reconnecting. Then the shard was carefully inserted. Finished, the Doctor moved back. So did Ravage and the remaining Constructicons.

Nothing. Silence, darkness, cold. And then . . .

The enormous body shuddered slightly. A giant metal hand rose, then fell. Fingers clenched, opened, and clenched again. Slowly at first, then with increasing speed, a bright blue light began to spread throughout the body from the vicinity of Megatron's chest. The hole that had gaped there began to close up, the metal epidermis to reseal itself.

Eyes opened, blazing with crimson life. Reanimated, Megatron straightened. Communication ensued—flickers of consciousness and enlightenment that passed silently among the assembled Decepticons. Their leader tilted back his head to regard the blackness and watery weight above him.

Trailed by his jubilant minions, he started upward.

Aboard the sub, warning lights began to come alive in rapid succession. Not quite able to believe what he was seeing but unable to deny it, the sonar tech raised his voice sharply.

"Captain! Contacts have changed heading. Constant bearing, range decreasing rapidly and . . . ," he checked his instrumentation one last time to assure himself that he wasn't imagining things, "there's something *big* in the middle of them."

"Sound collision alarm! Hard left rudder, all back emergency!"

The sub slowed as its reactors poured power to the propellers. Something huge roared past its bow, so close that it all but scraped the titanium nose. Seconds later, the shock wave generated by its passing rocked the ship. On board there was no panic. The crew was well trained in the handling of such emergencies.

But if not panic, there *was* a good deal of concern.

High, high above, a Navy P-3C long-range Orion surveillance aircraft was circling a section of ocean that had suddenly become a scene of greatly heightened interest. On board, the usual phlegmatic attention to work had given way to a flurry of activity.

One of the scan operators turned to look forward and call out to the pilot.

"Sir, SOSUS nets detect unauthorized activity at Deep Six drop point. We're monitoring comms with the *Los Angeles*. Something going on; they've sustained some damage. Standing by for assessment."

The pilot considered briefly, then nodded. "Raise Lanfleet, flash precedence."

On the bridge of the carrier crossing toward Hampton Roads, the commanding admiral turned in the flag chair as his CO arrived to brief him.

"Admiral, Lanfleet's ordering us to change course and steam at flank speed to investigate an irregularity at Project Deep Six, restricted zone."

"Very well."

Orders were dispersed, commands relayed. As a precaution and just as they had been on the sub, battle stations were sounded throughout the carrier task force group of more than twenty ships. Battle stations were always in order whenever Project Deep Six was involved.

In this instance, however, no one on any of the course-changing vessels realized how relevant that particular order was going to prove.

☒ VII ☒

Ennui filled the lecture hall like gas at a tailgate party. Students sat and stared blankly at the new textbooks they had been compelled to purchase in order to take the current class. Some texted. A few surfed the Net. A great many had their Netbooks or other recording devices programmed and ready to record the lecture in its entirety so that they would be spared the arduous process of actually taking notes.

The oversize and old-fashioned blackboard was covered with complex equations. Flanking the auditorium, posters of the ancient constellations exposed the knowledge of the ancients to both admiration and ridicule. Striding to the podium down on the floor was the class instructor, the natty and eminently self-satisfied Professor Colan. He had chalked up the opening day's selection of equations himself. They were as familiar to him as his scarf and fedora, and the closest he could come to actual art. Simply seeing them up there, on the board, filled him with the contentment that is known only to the long happily married, those who have inherited large sums of money, and professors who have achieved tenure at institutions famed for the size of their endowments.

He opened with a grand sweep of his hand that encompassed the entire auditorium. "The constellations. Leo, the Lion. Orion, the Hunter. Early mankind's first crude yet in their own artistic way admirable attempts to bring order to a cosmos they could not comprehend. The first glimpses of the infinite and ever-expanding universe that lies beyond this small, out-of-the-way, unimportant world. A vastness so profound, so immense, that the best minds of every generation have quailed before its beauty and mathematical precision. The universe is a clock whose workings we have only just begun to comprehend and which none of you could possibly understand at this larval stage in your educational process. It is this profound ignorance that this class hopefully will, in some small measure, seek to ameliorate." Looking back, he indicated the equation-filled board.

"Behind me, a sampling of the work of Albert Einstein—once a professor, like *moi,* in these very same hallowed halls. His famous equation $E=MC^2$ defines the formation of energy throughout the universe—as most of you doubtless already know but will be reminded of yet again when you open your new textbooks to page—one."

Sighs filled the room like steam from an old radiator as the somnolent mob dutifully complied. Inside the cover was a photo of the book's author—Colan himself. Sam glanced at it only briefly. He was doodling in a notebook, but his efforts were not the typical male teenage obsessions; rather, they were an assortment of symbols that almost seemed to make sense. Absently, he flipped the textbook open to the second page, glanced at it, then flipped to the third.

And the fourth, and the fifth, and . . . the nine hundred and third, featuring the last of the book's footnotes, whereupon he let the book fall closed.

"Fourteen billion years ago, when infinity's infiniteness began . . . ," Colan was saying. He never finished the sentence. Instead, he found himself gazing perplexedly at an arm attached to an otherwise unremarkable-looking student in the approximate middle of the auditorium. The arm, astonishingly, was vertical.

Seated at Sam's right, Leo gawked at his roommate. "Man, are you out of your freakin' mind? What're you *doing*?" As he delivered himself of these questions, Spitz was also trying to shrink as far as possible down behind his own desk.

"You." Colan had the manner, if not quite the voice, of an annoyed tax inspector. "The one with your hand up. Have you any idea how much I despise having my stream of consciousness interrupted? Especially on the first day of class?" He smiled humorlessly at the offender. "As I have spoken but few words and proposed no questions, I shall be fascinated to hear the nature of your inquiry. As I am sure we all will. Please do not keep us in suspense."

A few nervous laughs greeted the professor's speech, none of their progenitors quite certain whether they were giving in to honest amusement or to sucking up. Regardless, every face in the room was now gazing in Sam's direction. Aware of the attention he had drawn, he lowered his arm. But despite his roommate's warning he felt oddly, *forcefully*, compelled to follow through.

"Sorry, sir, it's just that I—I just read your book, Mr. Colon."

More laughter, this time without any thought toward sucking up. The professor was not amused.

"It is Col-*an*," he corrected dryly. "At the risk of wasting yet more of this class's precious time, young man, I must ask—what do you mean you 'just read my book'? It's a brand-new edition, just out and available a few hours ago at the campus bookstore— fortunately for you all—in time for this school year. Unless you happened across a set of publisher's galleys, which I strongly doubt, you could not possibly have 'just read' it."

Sam found himself nodding assuredly. "Yeah, just now, the whole thing. Found one little problem. You forgot to mention: Einstein was wrong."

This time the laughter that filled the hall was suffused with giggles. Unable to reduce his physical exposure any further without actually sliding beneath his desk, Leo had covered his face with papers.

"You're killing me, man . . ."

Colan regarded the youthful speaker calmly. The young man appeared quite cool—or more likely, quietly stoned. The professor pursed his lips. "I must admit that your assertion does indeed present me with a bit of a dilemma. To wit: should I simply fail you now, and save us both the weeks yet to be wasted? Or would you care to elaborate? Those being your two choices, since your impolitic interruption is already too late for apology."

"Sure, yeah, no sweat," Sam replied blithely. "I mean, Einstein's not a *total* idiot. Energy does equal mass times the velocity of light squared—in *this* dimension. But your book doesn't address the physics and mathematics of the *other* seventeen dimensions, which if entered can provide access to physical energies that operate according to entirely different formulae. Nobody ever talks about the other seventeen—what's that about?"

Fearing further loss of time, not to mention a potential swing in the focus of amusement, Colan interrupted. "Young man, you have entered *my* sanctuary. We have not gathered here for your amusement, but to try and learn something." His crocodilian smile returned. "Of course, if you have a bit of *actual* knowledge you would care to impart, I am sure the rest of us poor deprived souls would be delighted to share it." More laughter, this time unquestionably directed at Sam.

It didn't faze him in the slightest. Leaping to his feet, he rushed down the nearest aisle and up to the board. Picking up the chalk stylus and the eraser, he began obliterating the professor's carefully reproduced Einsteinian equations and replacing them with alien symbols. As one line of higher mathematics after another fell to the student's energetic efforts, Colan's expression grew less and less amused.

"No problem," Sam was saying. "Okay, clear example for you. If you break down the elemental components of Energon, assume a constant decay rate, and extrapolate for each of the fourteen galactic convergences it took for the Sentinel Prime expedition to receive an echo on its signal, you end up with a formula for interdimensional energy creation that mass and light alone can't possibly explain. Even if you throw dark energy into the mix, the figures still don't zero out. I mean, c'mon. Guys, we learn this in the drone stage—am I alone here?"

Colan's eyes widened. It all made sense to him now. The young man standing before him was not actually a student, seriously intent on taking the class. He was a—fan. Of certain movies and television shows. Probably not even enrolled at the university. And he, Colan, had let it go on too long already. He had been suckered, and on the first day of class, too. His face reddened.

"Young man, I will not be pranked . . . I will not be 'punked.' Not by a freshman. You mock me! Einstein, *and* me. Well, this is my universe, understand?! I am Alpha and Omega here! And you, young man, are nothing but a statistical insignificance. You are banished, sir. Banished from my classroom and, if you find it further amusing, from my *galaxy*! Get *outtttt!*"

Colan's tone, if not his words, was sufficient to shake Sam out of the daze into which he had fallen. He blinked, glanced at the stunned, amused faces of his fellow students, and then looked back at the professor.

"Did I—say something?"

"BANISHED!"

Another series of blinks. Reality clashed with memory in Sam's brain. He was not merely confused, not just embarrassed—he was *scared*. When your thoughts aren't your own, and when those thoughts impel you to do things and say things that likewise aren't your own, then—where are *you*? Whirling, he bolted up the aisle, past the row where he had been sitting, and out the nearest door, not even bothering to recover his class materials.

Leo Spitz watched until the door finished swinging shut behind his departed roommate. Then he turned to the attractive and equally thunderstruck girl sitting next to him.

"I do *not* know that guy. He just sat down here and started talking to me, that's all. *Total* stranger."

The girl was trying to see past him. "He's kinda weird, but cute."

"However," Leo continued, clearing his throat as if something stuck there had now been dislodged, "he *is* my roommate. Hamilton Hall, three-twelve. Stop by, I'll introduce you. And if he's not there, well . . ."

There were not as many students in the library stacks as there used to be. The Internet was too easy to use, the Web too full of information to ignore. But not everything had been digitized, not every book put online. Especially older material of little apparent significance. There were so many books, so many tomes devoted to obscure topics. Doubtless they, too, would in time appear online. But scanning and recording required labor and money, and there was much yet to do.

One such volume that had yet to be put up on the Web was of particular interest to Sam Witwicky.

Pulling *The Arctic Grail: An Expeditionary History* from its shelf, he found an empty, isolated reading table, set the dusty tome down, and began to flip through entire chapters in less time than it would have taken someone else to peruse the entirety of the first page. It took seconds to locate the short section he sought. The heading said it all:

ARCHIBALD WITWICKY:
TRAILBLAZER OR CRACKPOT?
Tales of the "Mega-Man"

Sam speed-read avidly. It was all there: the falling through the ice; the discovery of the mysterious "Mega-Man," né Megatron; the glasses. Reproductions of his institutionalized great-great grandfather's "lunatic" writing. Sam knew those symbols as well as he knew the rest of the story.

And he had just inscribed them on his physics professor's auditorium blackboard.

"Oh, my God . . . ," he mumbled under his breath.

Somewhere.

The world itself was dead. Frozen, uninhabited, isolated, a planet circling a cooling star no longer able to give light or life to the worlds held in its orbit. The surface of the planet was torn, shredded, convulsed by gravity, and forgotten by tectonics. Its core had likewise cooled, leaving behind little save an ice-covered, twisted mass of rock tormented into splintering mountains and winding gorges.

It was into the depths of one such chasm that Megatron plunged, following ancient memory as well as the seemingly endless fragments of torn metal and composite that lined the bottom of the rift. The metallic trail terminated at the stern of an immense ship partially embedded in the solid stone that had finally put an end to its forward momentum. Like the rest of the planet save the lonely wind, the ship was motionless.

But it was not empty.

A huge rip in one side allowed Megatron entry to the hulk of the *Nemesis*. Deep within, he came to the chamber he sought. One wall boasting nothing but sarcophagi towered high. Each sarcophagus contained a single inert cohort. Each an individual, silent and immobile. They would wait thus, if necessary, until the end of time.

As Megatron stood waiting, the deck before him began to shift and flow. Millions of tiny mechanisms rose to form a single visage: the Decepticons' own death's-head. It was at once a symbol and a face.

The face of The Fallen.

In all the known cosmos, before this image and this image alone would Megatron himself stand contrite.

A voice that conjured visions of great expanses of time and space echoed in the chamber: "So . . . my apprentice has awoken. Now reunited with my ship. While I assemble forces in other dimensions . . ."

"I have failed you, Master."

"No. Our race may yet survive," intoned the voice of the millions of components. "There is another means of creating Energon—one that was stolen from me long ago. The Allspark knew where it was hidden."

"But the Allspark was destroyed—by Optimus . . . and his pet insect."

"Ah, but was it truly?" came the reply. "Were *you*?"

Megatron's eyes brightened. "The Allspark—lives still?"

"Its essence can never be lost. Its power, its knowledge will under circumstance and stress only change form, to be absorbed and retained elsewhere. In this instance, on the human planet." The voice became a hiss. "By the insect child who bested you. I have felt this."

Megatron's contempt was mixed with astonishment. "The *boy*? Let me avenge myself, Master. Let me strip the very flesh from his body . . ."

"Patience, my apprentice. First he must be found. And when our war is won, as I have promised, I shall bestow upon you the powers of The Dynasty. You will have what you have always sought. For you, too . . . shall be a Prime. Only one boy stands in your way."

The encounter was at an end. Silent once more, the face of The Fallen melted back into the hull of the *Nemesis*. Not until the last vestige of the ancient visage had vanished did another figure dare to appear. Powerful in its own right, in the immensity and chill loneliness of that place, the new arrival seemed reduced and uncertain.

"Forgive me, Lord Megatron," Starscream began, "but in your absence someone had to take command. I have deployed spy drones to the insect planet. They have already located the child who—bested you."

It was not the wisest choice of words. A whirling Megatron slammed a fist into the subservient Decepticon and knocked him skidding across the deck. It felt good to strike out again.

"Even in death," he roared, "there is *no* command but mine. My words ring truer in my absence than do yours when you are present, self-server!" He started toward the recumbent Starscream, who scrambled to recover his footing. If this was to be the final battle, then . . .

But Megatron halted. The cosmos was vast, and the all-powerful had a need for servants. Even the inadequate and inept. Leaning toward the apprehensive Starscream, the leader of the Decepticons lowered his voice.

"*I want the boy.*"

"The boy, Lord Megatron? We are already watching . . ."

Turning, Megatron issued an electronic command. No terrestrial monitor would have understood it, but it was received and acted upon by the great ship. The *Nemesis* was grounded, but it was not dead.

Across from the two Decepticons, the covers of thirteen immense sarcophagi began to open.

As was her practice, Mikaela beat sunrise to the shop. Light was just brightening the horizon when she punched in the code to disarm the alarm and keyed the lock. The interior was quiet and calm, populated by bikes in various stages of disassembly and repair. Marching in, she dropped her purse on the front desk and headed for the custom job that had commanded the bulk of her attention and skill for the past week. Several parts remained to be installed, and she pondered which to begin with this morning.

She did not notice the toy truck lurking in the shadows. Wheels tried to draw farther back as she started in his direction, but was saved from the need as she was diverted by the ringing of her cell phone.

Picking up the phone, she checked the ident. "Sam"

was all it said. Mouth set, she answered without hesitating.

"You stand me up on our first I-chat?"

The voice that replied was unquestionably that of her erstwhile boyfriend—yet somehow different. There was something in his tone, a quality that she recognized from a previous occasion: Mission City. It took only an instant to put a name to it.

He sounded scared.

" 'Kaela, listen—something's happening to me!"

Not only scared, but dead serious. She was immediately alert. She knew him well enough to realize that this was no joke, no attempt to put her off guard or turn the subject away from his failure to respond to her previous call. Something important was up. Where Sam Witwicky was concerned, that could mean anything.

"What's wrong?"

He replied without hesitation, talking way too fast—and way too freely. "My great-great-grandfather's arctic mission, he got zapped by Megatron, started seeing symbols in his head and . . ."

She cut him off as fast as she could. "We're on cell phones. You're aware of that, right?"

Her warning had no effect as he rambled on, hardly pausing for breath. "I'm seeing them too! And there's more—more that I don't understand. Like I just read a nine-hundred-and-three-page astrophysics book in thirty-two point eight seconds and then had a full-scale mental meltdown at the beginning of class! I all but called the professor an idiot and he threw me out. I would've thrown me out, too. It's like some part of my brain's going haywire ever sin—ever since . . ."

He stopped in mid-sentence, reflecting on the sudden thought, deliberating over the realization.

Mikaela stared at the dead phone for several seconds before deciding to prompt him. "Since *what*?"

"Since . . ." His voice seemed even farther away than it actually was. "Since I touched that splinter of the cube."

Seeing that the young female human was preoccupied with the conversation taking place on her primitive communications device, Wheels began to move, changing shape as he slid off to one side. He could have waited longer, but the likelihood of other humans arriving and further forestalling his work motivated him. He was anxious to be finished and away before that happened. Driven by the urgency to complete his assigned task, he felt that he could brook no further delay.

It was *here*. He could sense it. But where, precisely?

"Oh, God," Sam blurted in sudden recognition. "You still have it, right? It's still secure?"

"Yeah," she assured him. "It's in the shop safe. Been there ever since you handed it to me before leaving town."

Humans! Wheels mused as he stopped dead and spun toward the safe. It was not necessary to confront them directly. One had only to wait for them to provide the means of their own destruction.

"Listen to me," Sam said earnestly over the phone. "Do not *touch* it."

"I already touched it," she shot back, "when you gave it to me."

"Well, then, don't touch it again." His confusion came through clearly over the connection. "Maybe you didn't have contact with it long enough for it to affect you. It was on me for a long time. And I carried the whole cube around with me during the fight at Mission City, right up until the end when I—look, just don't touch it again, okay?"

"Whatever you say, Sam. You know more about . . ." A noise made her pause. An odd sound, like a metallic tickling. She turned, every sense alert. "Hold on," she murmured as she brought the phone close to her lips and moved off into the shop.

Focused on the safe, Wheels discovered that he was not quite tall enough to reach the lock. That deficiency was easily remedied. Espying a nearby box that was just the right height, he turned to pick it up and . . .

Snap! As primitive a mechanical device as could be found in the confines of the shop, the rat trap slammed shut around one of the Decepticon's feet. More surprised than inconvenienced, the startled Wheels stumbled backward. Attuned only to "advanced" mechanical devices that boasted at least a minimal electronic signature, he had not perceived the presence of the simple spring-activated mechanism. For exactly the same reason, he did not note the presence of the rodent glue trap into which he had just stepped.

Ever resourceful, he discovered that the addition of both traps raised him just high enough that he no longer needed the box. Straining, he put an auditory receiver to the lock on the safe and began adjusting the dial. Had the lock been of the electronic variety, he could have picked it with a simple electrical override. It was its very simplicity that thwarted him—but only momentarily. His sensitive instrumentation could discriminate between each mechanical tick of the internal tumblers as clearly as if they were hammer blows.

The whooshing sound that suddenly became audible, however, had nothing to do with the safe containing his objective. Nor did the sudden heat that accompanied it. Turning, he observed that the young human, displaying unexpected stealth, had managed to come up quietly behind him. In one hand she held a pair of industrial tongs. The other gripped a blue-flamed blowtorch firmly by its handle.

As Wheels attempted to react, Mikaela jammed the tongs against the upper part of his body just below his head and thrust the torch's flame, thoughtfully set on MAXIMUM, directly into his face. Her shouted query as she did this was characteristically straightforward.

"What're you doing here, you little *freak*?" Adjusting her larynx, she further startled the intruder by shrieking in passable Decepticon. "English! Speak English!"

Trying to fight, with little success, clear of the flame, Wheels struggled to babble an intelligible insect response. "Stop—hurt—stop! STOP! Talk!"

Warily, Mikaela inclined the point of the flame slightly to one side. "What're you *doing* here?" she repeated tightly.

"Seek knowledge from Cube!" the pinioned Decepticon babbled. "Any piece! Every piece! All contains much and little contains all. Secrets of ancients must be reclaimed!"

Faced with hellish demolition, the little alien made an admirable quisling. Keeping the flame close, Mikaela put all her weight behind the tongs. "What 'secrets'? What 'knowledge'?"

Hacked by a blowtorch, Wheels began to spill information freely. "The Fallen commands! Whatever form the knowledge has taken, we must recover it! Show mercy, Warrior Goddess! I am merely a lowly salvage and scrap surveillance drone!"

"And I'm merely your worst nightmare," she growled.

Gripping the trapped machine with the heavy tongs she wrenched him sideways, lifting as she did so, and shoved the struggling Decepticon into a metal storage bin. Withdrawing the tongs, she slammed the lid closed and flipped the latch shut. There was no lock handy, but the crankcase she heaved on top of the bin was sufficiently weighty to keep the lid down against the imprisoned alien's frantic banging and shoving. As soon as she was satisfied that neither the bin nor its frenzied contents were going anywhere, she picked up the phone again. Sam was still on the line, more frantic than ever.

". . . the hell was *that*," he was saying as she caught the tail end of an anxious sentence.

"Something that's not for an open phone line. I'll tell you in person tonight."

"In person? Mikaela, what . . . ?"

"Tonight. I'm getting on a plane." Before disconnecting, she added, "Sam—*be careful*. Something's—up." She switched off.

Behind her, the storage bin continued to jiggle and shudder, but the crankcase proved too heavy to dislodge. Taking a deep breath and readying herself as best she could, she picked up the tongs and started toward it once more.

Still buttoning his shirt, Lennox nearly ran over Epps as the two men converged in the hallway leading to the Command Center. A glance was exchanged, but no words were spoken. There was nothing to be said; not yet. Both men had been woken by the alarms in their rooms. Around them, the hall was alive with technicians and soldiers on the move. No one was talking. Without exception, the expression on the face of each man and woman reflected grim purpose.

Guards stepped aside as the two soldiers hurried into the Center. Lights were alive on a series of consoles, and every monitor was active. Lennox led the way toward the central console, arriving just as the senior technician turned to report.

"Major! Incoming SOS from the Autobots! They have multiple Decepticon contacts, vicinity Eastern United States!"

Damn, Lennox thought rapidly. Not the Sahara, not the Himalayas, not even Rome or Shanghai this time. It was going to be hell to keep a lid on whatever was happening. And whatever was under way, if multiple contacts were involved it was liable to be big. The conceal-and-obscure guys were going to be pissed.

"Autobots are on the move," declared the officer seated beside the tech, "splitting into teams."

That clinched it, Lennox knew. Anything that required the Autobots to separate into groups was bigtime. "Full weapons deployment, all teams on duty. Wheels up in twenty minutes." Whirling, he saw that Epps was already pounding for the exit.

"Let's *move!*"

☙ VIII ☙

The check-in counter was only moderately busy. Waiting in line, Mikaela did her best to blend in with the rest of her fellow travelers. There was no reason for her to feel as if every eye was on her, as if she was being singled out. But why was that old man constantly looking over his newspaper at her? And why were those two women peering in her direction and whispering?

Paranoia, she told herself, fighting to stay calm. The old man was looking at her because he was an old man and she was young and attractive. The two women were peering at her and whispering because they probably didn't approve of what she was wearing—or because she was young and attractive and they weren't.

Stay calm, she told herself. *There's nothing to worry about. Nothing to single you out.*

After what seemed like half an hour the traveler in front of her finally concluded his business, took his ticket, and moved off. Stepping forward, she presented her electronic ticket and smiled. Fortuitously, the ticket agent was young and male. He responded instantly to her deliberately engaging smile.

"Uh, good evening." He smiled back as he took the

ticket, glanced at it, and began working his keyboard. "Any bags to check?"

"One," she told him as she lifted the metal box off the baggage cart and placed it on the scales. "You might tell Security that it's full of expensive, sensitive tools. I'm a mechanic."

"Oh, you don't say?"

She fastened her eyes on his. "I've locked it, but I can unlock it if you think it's necessary." Her voice turned meltingly husky. "I'd hate to have anyone going through my things."

He swallowed slightly. "I'm sure it'll be all right. Did you pack your own bags today?"

"Of course."

He recited by rote and necessity. "Have any strangers given you anything suspicious to carry on?"

"Nope."

On the conveyor belt the metal box quivered slightly. Lifting her leg, she gave it a firm kick, as if to send it farther along its way. The internal jiggling stopped. Busy checking her in, the agent barely noticed.

"You said your luggage was full of mechanic's tools?"

She nodded. "X-ray might look funny. I suppose they can break the lock if they have to."

He smiled back at her. "I'll put an appropriate label on it. I don't think there'll be any problem—as long as there's nothing explosive inside."

She leaned forward over the counter as far as she could manage. "Not inside *that* box," she murmured.

*   *   *

Alice tried to avoid Leo, but in the narrow hall, and considering that their rooms were opposite each other, it proved impossible. In addition to his school gear he was laden with a large, flat box whose contents, at a distance, were unknown but whose aroma was unmistakable.

"Aliiiice—can I interest you in part of an eighteen-inch Zookeeper's special?"

Slowing, she eyed the enormous pizza box guardedly. " 'Zookeeper's'?"

He grinned conspiratorially. "An extra-large triple cheese with bits of every known hoofed mammal as toppings. Basically I've got like eighteen inches of meat." He contemplated the box. "Unless you're a vegetarian. Then I am too."

She looked past him. "Uh, is Sam home?"

"Sam . . . Sam . . . remind me who that is again? Oh, he's out, he left school, he died. No seriously, it was kinda brutal. But automatic A's for me!"

"Uh-huh, maybe I'll just check," came the skeptical reply.

He waited for her to step in front of him. She waited for him to open the door first. Which he did, whereupon all previous thoughts including those relating to pizza and girls evaporated from his mind. To erase notions of both from the brain of Leo Spitz required a substantial shock indeed.

Sam Witwicky had provided it.

He was standing on his bed, finger-painting symbols on the walls. Leo gaped at their room. All of Sam's posters had been taken down, to be replaced with arcane symbols and ideographs whose origin was as alien to him as the content of the several textbooks he ought to have been reading. The indecipherable, inexplicable drawings covered every flat surface as high as Sam could reach. Which was why he was presently standing on his bed, struggling to inscribe the last vestiges of unmarked wall. While Alice stared, her gaze roving over the esoteric imagery, Leo tossed the pizza down on his own bed and confronted his roommate—though he was careful to keep his distance.

"Dude—what the *eff*? You're going all 'Beautiful Mind' on me! *Please* tell me that's not your feces you're writing with!"

It was Sam who replied, but in a voice that was oddly distant, as if one part of him was furiously scribing symbology while the other serenely responded to the interruption.

"D'you ever have a song? Stuck in your head? And it's like the worst song ever, but you can't not whistle it or sing it and it repeats and repeats and *repeats* over and over again? A mnemonic with music? Like 'It's an itsy-bitsy-teeny-weeny yellow polka-dot *bikini*'— only with calculus and physics?" Straining on tiptoes, he filled the last remaining unmarred corner with lines and circles and diagrams that had no evident relationship to any known script.

"I have to find out what it all *means*. There's gotta be a *reason*. It's like some kinda code, like a puzzle. I put it together, maybe it *stops*. Like a jigsaw puzzle. Put all the pieces together and the picture finally makes sense, and then you can turn out all the lights and go to bed."

Pizza forgotten, Leo took a step back. "Oh-kay, Section Eight. Whatever you say. Alice, I'm *horrified* you had to see this; let's go. I'll try to explain my 'friend' here as best I can. I know a quiet place where we can . . ."

She cut him off. Politely but firmly. "Actually, I came to talk to Sam alone."

Leo finally achieved the physical contact he sought, but not in the form he wished for. She was determinedly pushing him toward the door.

"But it's H.Q.! My office!" he protested. His gaze traveled longingly to the pizza, cooling on his bed.

"I know." She smiled encouragingly as he darted past her just long enough to recover his meal.

He was not quite done. "Can't I just stand in the corner and watch?"

"No," she informed him firmly as she closed the door in his face.

His voice filtered in from the hallway, plaintive and hopeful. "What if I just sit and eat quietly?"

She shook her head, muttering to herself. "What a perv!" Then she turned back to the room's remaining occupant. Sam had stepped down from the bed and was rapidly, almost desperately, connecting the symbols he had drawn with crosshatched lines. Mesmerized, she came up behind him.

"Sam, you're like a genius. I knew there was something special about you." Raising a hand, she gestured at his efforts. "I don't know what all this means, but it clearly means something. I think I'm smart enough to know that much."

She was very close to him now. Straining, she whispered in his ear. "Y'know what they say when two smart people get together?"

Half of him was able to respond while the remainder continued to work with the painted symbols that now dominated the décor. "What's that?" he mumbled absently.

"They're genuinely amazing in bed."

Given the depth of the trance he had fallen into, there was very little that was capable of shaking him out of it.

Her words succeeded.

The dorm lounge was occupied by a number of hall residents. Some were chatting softly while others, oblivious to conversation, were studying hard. Both activities were interrupted as Leo kicked open the door, strode to the empty couch that fronted the flat-screen TV, dropped his pizza box on the nearby table, picked up the television remote, and switched the unit on. The channel he finally selected was not one to inspire quiet contemplation, nor was the noise he made as he began to chow down on the huge circle of faux mozzarella and meat. Sparing an idle glance for the room, he noted that everyone was looking in his direction.

"Hey, can you guys keep it down?" he barked challengingly. "New episode of *Cribs* is on."

Bor-ing, Leo decided. Pizza dripping tomato sauce down one hand and remote in the other, he flipped through several channels until the image of an especially appealing (i.e., hot) girl caused him to pause and lean back contentedly on the couch. It took him a minute to realize that the girl was animatronic. Not that he had anything against animatronics. They were as synthetically stimulating as the ivory-white cheese substitute that was currently forming a satisfying if barely digestible ball in the pit of his stomach. He didn't even care that the sexy image was featured in a theme park ad instead of a movie.

". . . with Mickey the friendly mouse," the screen voice chirped. "And experience the magic and mystery of our new Alice in Wonderland animatronic ride. Sponsored by Honda Motorworks, the most innovative robotic technology on Earth!" The smile the mechanical pitchwoman was flashing was beguiling, in a deliberately pseudopedophilic way.

So beguiling that he felt that he had encountered it before.

Letting the remnants of the pizza slice slip from his fingers, he sat up straight on the couch and leaned, openmouthed, toward the screen. The girl was a pretty, barely post-adolescent, almost-familiar blonde. With a matching, more-than-almost-familiar name.

In the dorm room, Alice gave Sam a shove that sent him backward onto his bed. Deciphering haunting alien symbology had suddenly become the furthest thing from his mind.

"Whoawhoawhoa, stop! I have a *girlfriend*. We're like, almost nearly semi-engaged! Or going steady, anyway."

She sat down on his legs, grabbed one hand, and moved it onto her skirt. "She'll never know; we're only human. C'mon, Sam—relax."

He moved to pull his hand back and was startled to discover that he could not. "What the . . . ? Wow, you're strong . . ."

Trying to twist away, he caught a glimpse of something bright on her neck. At first he thought it was part of a necklace, or maybe a wayward earring. But it was flat, and bore some kind of inscription, and—it didn't seem to be moving against her neck.

It looked as though it was screwed *into* it.

He squinted, trying to get a closer look even as he struggled to fight her off. "What is *that*? Does that say—Honda?"

Moaning, she thrust herself forward against him and shoved her tongue into his mouth. At the same time, a second protrusion emerged from the back of her head. Thin, metallic, and quivering with a life of its own, it flicked upward. The tip of a hypodermic needle snapped out of the end as it snaked around in a wide arc, aiming for the back of Sam's neck. Preoccupied with Alice's tongue and other animated body parts, he didn't see it.

At which point the door swung wide to admit the just-arrived figure of Mikaela, carrying the now-securely locked metal storage bin by its handle. Before the portal could open fully, the probing tendril swiftly retracted into the back of the skull of the female figure on the bed. Mikaela's stunned reaction to the sight that greeted her was summed up in few words.

"*Great!* Perfect, thank you, Sam . . ."

"Mikaela!" Fighting his way out from beneath the blonde, Sam struggled to get off the bed. "Okay, wait, this is not what it looks like. We were *talking*. The rest was just . . ."

Alice regarded the intruder coolly. "Your girlfriend?"

"Ex." Pivoting, Mikaela stomped out the doorway.

"Mikaela, wait, I . . . !" Sam started after her.

Something thin, powerful, and unyielding whipped around his neck, cutting off the rest of his words. As he reached up to try and dislodge it, it yanked him backward toward the bed, spinning him around in the process. Trying to force his fingers beneath the metal coil, he saw that he was being held back by—her tongue. His eyes widened and he tried to shout, but all that emerged from beneath the choking cable was a desperate croak. Whipping him around, the coil slammed him into the far wall as a dainty hand at the terminus of an arm that had suddenly become ten feet long shoved the door shut behind the recent arrival.

Or tried to. Having heard the noise, a frowning Mikaela had turned back to investigate. Another girl would have simply walked on, but Mikaela had heard too many similar noises in the past to let this one pass unnoticed. Of course it was probably nothing, just Sam's new slut hammering him into the bed, but just in case . . .

She pushed the door wide just in time to see the blonde's flashing tongue-tentacle hurl Sam across the room. Reacting instinctively, Mikaela threw the only thing that was handy—the metal box. It struck the girl-thing's head a glancing but hard blow, sending it swiveling around 180 degrees so that the creature was now staring directly back over her shoulder blades at the human female who had dared to interfere. Bouncing off the skull, the box went crashing out the window. An instant later and slightly out of breath, Leo arrived.

"Sam, check it out—that Alice chick? Something is seriously . . ."

The sight of the girl in question brought him up

short. Perhaps it was the fact that her head was presently on backward.

". . . weird," Sam's roommate finished as "Alice's" face exploded into a mass of Medusa-like tentacles.

The tentacle tipped with the hypo jabbed straight at Sam, who ducked just in time and made a dash for the doorway, yanking the door shut behind him. Following the needle a handful of spikes shot forward, again just missing him as they exploded all the way through the wood. Shoving Mikaela and Leo ahead of him, Sam stumbled out into the hallway.

Adrenaline replacing the oxygen he had already sacrificed in his dash from the common room, Leo screamed at his friend as they ran.

"*It's a frickin' metal she-beast robot monster!* What the hell's *happening*, Witwicky?"

"She's an alien robot!"

His roommate's eyes grew even wider. "What? WHAT? They're here? They're *real*?!"

Sam nodded once as he tried to lengthen his stride, keeping pace with Mikaela. "They're all *real*."

"Oh, God," Leo moaned, "I can't believe I almost had sex with her!"

Behind them, the door to their room blew off its hinges as "Alice" strode through. There was no sign of flailing hypodermics, no hint of grappling metallic tentacles. Alice's appearance had returned to normal— if one discounted the killer look in her eyes.

She most definitely was not a transfer student from Wonderland.

Instruments far more sensitive than human eyes and ears scanned the hallway in both directions. A girl approaching from the other stairwell looked askance at the destruction of the dorm room door. Encountering the gaze of the feminine creature standing among the debris, she started to stutter something, then very sensibly dropped everything she was carrying as she turned and ran screaming in the opposite direction.

Her attention occupied elsewhere, Alice started off the other way, progressively increasing her speed.

Out on the quad, the three escapees sprinted across a parking lot in the direction of the library. A glance over his shoulder revealed to the increasingly anxious Sam that his new girlfriend was still in pursuit. Her embrace was one he had no desire to relive.

He and Leo flashed their student IDs so fast that the monitor at the library entrance had no time to check to see whether Mikaela had one. The youth started to protest, then shrugged and returned to the video game he was illegally playing on the hacked entryway computer.

Leaving Security behind, the trio secreted themselves as far back in the book stacks as possible, ignoring stares from the occasional curious student. So unsettled was Leo that he did not even react to his proximity to Mikaela. For once, instead of trying to hold on to a girl he was struggling to hold on to his sanity.

"Man, I just saw her on *TV*, she was a frickin' Alice-in-Wonderland android! I mean, not like a *close* resemblance, but an *exact* double!"

Mikaela nodded knowingly. "It's called 'trans-scanning.' "

He blinked at her. "Say what?"

"They scan our machines," Sam explained as he

crouched low and kept his attention focused on the far end of the aisle where they had taken refuge. "And adopt their shape and external characteristics. They prefer to use vehicles, but they can imitate anything."

Leo stared at him. "Dude—you have *so* been holding out on me!"

From where she was settled in among Early European History, Mikaela glared at the man she had come to warn. "I see you're really *missing* me."

"Hey," he protested, "she—her huge tongue . . ." He broke off and with great deliberation tried hard to throw up. "Couldn't get her off," he finally protested, wheezing. "Metal-strong. *I'm* the victim. Her breath," he swallowed hard, his face screwed up in a look of utter disgust, "it was like jet fuel! I think she might've pierced my uvula. Check it out."

He spit, sputtering as he felt his tongue and the back of his mouth.

She was only partly mollified. "You deserve it."

A touch of righteous indignation was beginning to replace Sam's initial anxiety. "Hey, she *tricked* me." He looked over at the half-paralyzed Leo. "Didn't she trick me?"

Shaking his head tersely, his roommate kept his gaze fastened on the far end of the aisle. "She violated your orifice with her nasty alien probe?"

Sam turned back to Mikaela, arguing as much as pleading. "That's why they're called *Decepticons*. Because they thrive on *deception*."

Her mouth twisted into a smirk. "*That's* convenient."

It finally penetrated Leo's terror that the being

standing very close to him was not only warm, but possibly soft. He looked her up and down. "Wait, *you're* a real chick, right?"

Mikaela eyed him as if he was something foul that had suddenly been ejected from beneath the body of Wheels. "Who the hell're you?"

"I'm Leo Ponce de Léon Spitz. I'm the key to this! The aliens tracked me," he was moaning. "They know I know too much, they want me silenced. I'm dead."

Mikaela's disgust turned to pity, if not quite understanding. "They're not after you, idiot." She nodded at Sam. "They're after *him*."

"Could we just hide *quietly* for a second?" Sam pleaded, a moment too late.

The stack behind them exploded, sending books flying in all directions as the now full-metal Decepticon known as Alice smashed her way through. Covering their heads, the trio fled around the back and down the next aisle as the relentless Decepticon came after them. Screaming students raced from the floor as Sam and his friends dove under reading tables in a desperate scramble to protect themselves while they tried to reach the exit.

Behind them, Alice was picking up the heavy wooden tables and flinging them aside like cardboard as she pursued. Emerging from a graceful shoulder, a deceptively small barrel let loose with a plasma charge in the direction of Sam's companions. It singed the air above their heads and blew a hole in the solid stone exterior wall. As the Decepticon took fresh aim, Sam scrambled to his feet and led the way through the still-smoking opening.

Chaos dominated the parking lot as frightened students ran in all directions. Hastily started cars and pickups burned rubber as their panicked drivers ignored barriers, signs, and every traffic law in the state of New Jersey in their haste to flee the scene.

As they ran, Mikaela tried the handle of every unoccupied car they passed. When one finally responded, she yanked open the door and threw herself behind the wheel.

"Get in!"

Sam piled in on the passenger side and joined her in ducking while Leo did a belly flop onto the rear seat and tried his best to bury his face in the upholstery.

They stayed low for several minutes, listening to the cries of the slowly thinning crowd outside. Tentatively raising his head, Sam sneaked a cautious look back the way they had come. Some students continued to dash about aimlessly while others, newly arrived, only added to the confusion as they struggled to make sense of what was happening.

"I think you're clear," he muttered to Mikaela.

She nodded and began to inspect her immediate surroundings. While the glove box offered no help, she found what she was looking for in the center console. Using the small screwdriver she found there, she popped the cover panel off the ignition and began to strip the interior. Wires were pulled clear and shoved together. A spark, another, and then the engine rumbled to life.

From the rear seat, Leo was prompted by the noise to look up. "You know how to hot-wire a car? That is so *hot*! Sam, how could you cheat on this girl?"

Sam looked back. "Leo, *shut up!* " 'Kaela, *drive the car!*"

A few experimental revs indicated that it was not going to stall out on them. Putting the sedan in gear, she headed off slowly. As they cruised the edge of the parking lot past the damaged library, something on the lawn off to one side caught the light and her attention. Surrounded by broken glass, the metal storage bin lay on the lawn where it had landed. Its lid was still secured. She nodded in its direction.

"Sam, grab that."

Another time, another place, he might have protested. Might have sought explanation. But knowing Mikaela well enough to realize that she had to have a good and sound reason for making the request at this risky moment in time, he complied. The box was heavier than he had expected and he had to struggle to wrestle it back into the car.

"Got it." He studied it curiously. "What's insi . . . ?"

A metal tendril smashed through the windshield and began to coil venomously in the space between them, seeking a fleshy purchase. Sam and Leo screamed at her to drive, but Mikaela was already flooring the gas pedal as metal claws emerged in front of them, digging into the front hood.

"Hang on!" Holding the wheel with one hand, she handed Sam the screwdriver.

Sam's eyes widened as he stared first at the small tool, then forward. " 'Kaela, *are you out of your . . . !*"

He concluded the sentence on a rising *"mind!"* as she slammed the car straight into a light pole. The impact dislodged the creature who had been clinging to the front of the vehicle. It also set off the driver's- and passenger-side air bags, providing Sam with the reason she had passed him the screwdriver. As she threw the car into reverse, he jabbed first at his air bag and then at hers. Gas escaped in a rush, stinking up the interior of the car while flattening the two safety balloons.

Her view ahead now restored, Mikaela once again gunned the engine.

"Kiss this, bitch!"

The twin jolts were more severe than expected as she drove over the battling Decepticon. Damaged but indefatigable, it struggled to rise and pursue.

Sitting up in the backseat of the car, a seriously frazzled Leo stared out the rear window as the crumpled monstrosity receded rapidly behind them. Only when it was completely out of sight and they were well down another road did he manage to collect himself sufficiently to give voice to the thoughts that were crashing around inside his head.

"All right, Sam—start talking! From the *top*. Why are you guys so calm? Are you from the future? Did I send you back in time to save me? Well, save me!" His gaze fell on the car's driver. "And I wanna know how you got a girl like *that* to look at *you*."

Eyes and attention locked on the road ahead, the subject of his inquiry still found time to respond.

"Will you please . . . shut up!"

Sam seconded the motion.

Leo nodded to himself. "I'm just scared, okay?"

Sam explained, "Okay, Leo, here's how it is. There's like ten terrible things they can do to you. Let's start with death. That's the first thing: death. And it just gets worse from there. They open up buses like a bag of chips. They blow through buildings. They take down planes. And if you ever hear one of them coming, I'm telling you, it's already too la . . ." Sam's words trailed off.

Peering out the punctured windshield, Sam found himself squinting at something in the sky ahead. Reflection off the shattered glass, or . . . ? Then it was gone. He sat back, relieved. Just a reflection.

The car went into a forced skid as the huge Russian heavylift chopper dropped out of the sky straight toward them. Mikaela's desperate attempt to avoid crashing into it was followed by a deafening ripping sound as a steel talon the size of a couch smashed through the center of the roof and the car was lifted into the air. The impact popped the passenger-side door, and a frantic Sam had to wrap his arms around his seat belt to avoid being thrown out. It was impossible for them to maintain any kind of stability, because the perforated vehicle kept swinging wildly from side to side as well as rotating in circles around the grasping metal hook.

When it finally straightened and slid clear, the car dropped like a stone through a yawning hole in the roof of a long-shut foundry. Intervening beams and projecting walkways that had not echoed in years to the percussion of busy footfalls helped break their fall. As the car banged and rattled its way downward, Sam finally lost his grip and slid out of his seat belt, rolling to a halt on a second-floor landing.

Amid a cloud of rising dust and splinters, the car finally came to a stop—only to be split neatly down the middle by a scything blade the length of the car itself. As both equal halves of the vehicle fell over in opposite directions, the two remaining occupants unbuckled themselves and managed to stumble clear.

Retracting the shining blade that had cut the car in half, Starscream needed only half a stride to cut off their escape. His worst fears far exceeded, a paralyzed Leo could only stand and stare. Mikaela, on the other hand, started to bolt to her right—only to be brought up short as another shape rose before her. Recognizing it, she stumbled backward until she bumped into Sam's unmoving roommate. Leo was sufficiently shocked at seeing his nightmares become real that he did not even react to the contact.

The sight of the gigantic figure looming directly in front of them was more than enough to choke off anything even faintly resembling a sophomoric double entendre.

Ignoring them, the metal colossus turned back toward the opening through which the car had fallen. Its attention was focused on the only creature on the entire planet who actually mattered.

"Come here, boy!" Nearby, Starscream raised a threatening fist above Mikaela and Leo, who unabashedly cowered behind her.

Sam came running down the stairs from the floor on which he had landed. "Don't hurt them, please!"

The giant's response was to reach out with a hand and flick the oncoming Sam into the air as easily as if he were an errant ant. Flying, tumbling head over heels, Sam landed hard on a cement slab. The impact stunned him. As he tried to rise, taloned fingers slammed into the concrete to pin him in place. An enormous, glaring face, all hard edges and sharp angles, descended to within a foot of his own.

"Remember me? I remember *you*," Megatron snarled.

☒ IX ☒

Barely able to move, with nowhere to run and no chance of escape, Sam could only gaze up into eyes that blazed back into his own with an inhuman ferocity.

"You will pray for a sudden death, insect . . . while I . . . shall take my time."

Sam was in a panic. "No no, look, I know you're pissed—I killed you, I'd be pissed too, you're not in the wrong. It's a valid point, but let's work it out, clean slate, fresh start—I don't know what I know, but I know you need to know what I know, you know?"

A microscope on the table suddenly changed into a small, evil-looking robot, the Doctor. Multiple legs skittering along the concrete, the Doctor climbed up onto Sam's chest and commenced a detailed, forthright, and indelicate inspection of the prisoner. There was little the subject of the small but highly evolved Decepticon's examination could do to forestall the poking, probing, and scanning.

Metal fingers clicked together as the Doctor signaled to the waiting pack of insectlike robots. A flock of tiny winged machines came forward to hover above Sam's upturned, pinioned face. As he looked on in horror, they deposited what looked like a worm on speed onto his upper chest. Instantly, it came writhing and humping its way upward. Clenching his jaw muscles so hard they throbbed, he shut his lips tight. As a gesture of defiance the effort proved futile. Approaching the sides of his head, a pair of menacing little machines reached out with small but powerful tendrils. Each one gripping the sides of his mouth, they pried it open enough for the worm-thing to slip inside. Then they released his face.

Immediately he began gagging and trying to throw up. Once, the tip of the worm-thing's tail waved from a nostril, only to disappear back inside. When he finally spat it back up, its emergence was due more to it having completed its assigned task than to any successful muscular convulsions on the part of his outraged gastrointestinal system. In actuality, its fact-finding mission had focused on areas considerably farther north than his stomach.

Recovering the worm-probe, the Doctor fastened it to his own body. Images began to appear in the air before the specialized Decepticon: scenes from Sam's life, recent distractions, imaginings that would have greatly embarrassed both him and Mikaela had they not been too terrified to pay attention, recently acquired alien symbols . . .

The excited Doctor played these back repeatedly, his hyperactive commentary scarcely intelligible. *"Traes itresea, voluminta, Brain kazeezei inspecta!"* Multiple limbs flailed, gesturing variously but in some kind of crazed alien amalgamation. Listening, watching, Megatron plainly approved of the result.

"Yesss—the Cube's knowledge is eternal, even

though freed from its metal membrane—into *yours*. Now you have become its vessel. Even an insect such as yourself must know how one obtains the contents of a sealed container." The implication contained in the Decepticon's words sent a shiver down Sam's spine. "We're going to *squeeze* it from your brain. But first, of course, the stoppered vessel must be— opened."

As he stepped back, the end of one of the Doctor's limbs altered shape. The razor-toothed blade into which it had changed positioned itself carefully over the top of Sam's head. Held immovable in the grasp of the Decepticon who was restraining him, Sam could only kick and scream as the Doctor lowered the surgical edge toward his skull and . . .

The Doctor paused, his attention having been distracted by a small red dot that had suddenly appeared in the center of his body. As he stared and tried to make sense of the bright crimson pinpoint of light, the dot quivered imperceptibly—just before the Decepticon blew apart, erupting in an explosively expanding sphere of metal splinters.

Accompanied by torn steel beams, crumbling chunks of reinforced concrete, and crumpling sections of metal roof and gangway, Optimus Prime descended feetfirst into the open foundry chamber, both of his cannon arms blasting away at his startled enemies.

While shells and energy pulses and missiles and everything else in the Autobot's inventory of heavy ordnance slammed into and around them, Megatron and Starscream shot off in opposite directions in order to regroup. As they did so, a second new shape came sprinting onto the factory floor. Reaching down, it picked up Mikaela and Leo, one in each hand, and raced for the nearest exit. Separated from his friends by the ongoing battle of giants, Sam couldn't see what was happening to them as Optimus yelled for him to run.

Once outside and clear of the last structure, Bumblebee changed back into his terrestrial guise with the two young humans safely inside him. Too shaken to faint, his senses too heightened for him to scream, Leo fell to examining the interior of the seemingly ordinary vehicle in which they were now rocketing away from the abandoned factory complex. As they roared into the greenbelt of a nearby forest, he sat up straight in the front passenger seat.

"What—no, *who* the hell's *this*?"

Seated behind the wheel, hands at her sides, Mikaela buckled up as the car drove itself. "Your new best friend," she explained tersely.

Unable to cover enough ground to get away, Sam found himself dodging fire just as Optimus scooped him up. Under pressure from both Megatron and Starscream, the leader of the Autobots fought his way outside and toward the surrounding forest.

Roaring back down in jet form and firing as he came, Megatron slammed into Optimus with hands as well as weapons, knocking his opponent off his feet. As he went down, Optimus reached up to grasp his adversary in an unbreakable body lock. Hitting the ground together, they rolled over and down a steep embankment, mowing down tall pine trees as they descended. Somehow Optimus managed to keep Sam safely within his grasp—until the three of them hit the bottom. With Megatron on top, the leader of the Autobots had no choice but to let the human roll free. Sam scuttled clear of the battle, banged up but very much alive and still mobile. Once Sam was in the clear, Optimus's arms morphed into a pair of huge, metal-rending scythes, causing Megatron to back off. Crouching defensively, the Decepticon leader eyed his opposite number in disbelief.

"*Prime*. You risk it all—for an insect *child*?"

Cutting arms held out in front of him, the Autobot glared back at his foe. "For a *friend*."

Though confronting his principal opponent both in body and word, Optimus was not so inattentive that he failed to note Starscream slipping in behind him. Pivoting sharply, he countered the attack, grabbing hold of the enraged Starscream and spinning him around so that the contained Decepticon was between him and Megatron. An instant later the heavy chopper Decepticon arrived to join the fight.

Optimus took everything they could throw at him and still managed to hold them off. As the battle raged, Megatron could not keep from taunting his old opponent.

"Your 'friendship' will not sustain you. More than pleasant thoughts and feelings of satisfaction are required. Energon is our lifeblood, Prime—and the Allspark was *not* the only source!"

"You're lying. As for sustaining, I'll choose my friendship over your lies anytime."

"Fool! There is another way. One that was hidden on this planet long ago. Think of it, Prime! Another source of sustenance for the future. Another font of life for our kind. Within him the boy unknowingly contains the means to lead us to it. Is the future of our entire race not worth a *single* human life? Not even one to which you have become unaccountably attached? Has your ability to crunch numbers and follow logic been so totally corrupted by the short time you have spent on this world?"

"More lies. You thrive on lies, Megatron. I know you. You speak of a single human life, but I know that you'll never stop at one. Sooner or later all of Earth would share his fate, or be bound forever into the slavery that sustains your ego."

"Then you will share his fate as well!" Frustrated, the furious Decepticon hurled himself forward.

Three to Optimus's one, they charged simultaneously. Ducking, blocking, returning blows and fire, Optimus continued to hold his own even as he noticed a mesmerized Sam standing nearby, looking on from behind a wholly inadequate tree.

"Run! Go now!"

Sam reluctantly complied, but only until he reached a denser stand of vegetation. There he lingered, keeping under cover as best he could while continuing to monitor the titanic ongoing battle, unable to tear himself away. As he watched, he remembered seeing Bumblebee arrive to snatch up Mikaela and Leo and carry them off to safety. Where was the yellow-and-black fighter now? For that matter, where were the rest of the Autobots?

They were coming, and coming fast. Led by Bumblebee, Arcee, the Twins, Ironhide, Ratchet, and Sideswipe were closing in on the foundry site. They would be there in minutes.

But where Autobots and Decepticons are concerned, a minute can become a very long time indeed.

As the conflict raged, the forest in which it was taking place was being shredded by the fall of massive bodies and the detonation of a host of explosive elements. Fires broke out and began to spread among the trees. Only a series of precoded warning signals broadcast by Optimus kept unknowing human authorities well clear of the scene of battle. Had they arrived to "help," ordinary police and firefighters would instantly have become collateral damage. As for more experienced and better-qualified NEST operatives, there were none in the immediate vicinity. They were now on the move, but it was unlikely their advance forces would be able to arrive in time to affect the outcome of the clash.

A powerful kick from Megatron sent Optimus flying backward. He had hardly struck ground when he was up again. Gripping the grappling Starscream with one powerful hand, he flung him aside as the copter Decepticon charged in, blade-arms spinning. As the infuriated Starscream rose and took aim, Optimus ducked under the chopper Decepticon's howling blades, picked up Starscream, and spun him around. Instead of striking their intended target, Starscream's multiple blasts slammed into his startled blade-wielding collaborator. With his opponent momentarily stunned by the effects of his own ally's shots, Optimus launched himself onto his enemy's shoulders. His arm cannons changed into a pair of hooked scimitars as he did so. Slicing down and in, they cut the giant's head in two. The big Decepticon tottered, lurched once, and fell forward, leaving the leader of the Autobots ready and poised to take on his next opponent.

That would be Starscream, who, alone and confronted by Optimus, started to back off and change shape into his aerial terrestrial guise. Determined not to let him get away this time, Optimus reached out for the retreating Decepticon.

As he did so, twenty feet of pure Cybertronian metal blade punched completely through his body from back to front.

Impaled, he tried to turn. But this blade, this weapon, was too well formed, too strong, too eternally forged. It belonged to Megatron, who had risen silently behind the leader of the Autobots to run him through from behind. Stunned, unable to bend or snap the blade that had pierced him, Optimus stood almost motionless.

Damaged but not destroyed, Optimus Prime's Spark sent out an internal distress call, redirecting all remaining energy toward healing. The injury was extensive and Optimus began to fade, subsiding into a state of suspended animation while all internal processes turned to a single task: survival.

Eyes wide, Sam screamed his anguish and helplessness from behind the tree where he had taken cover.

Megatron held his stance for a moment and then for longer, not taking any chances, wanting to be sure. The light dimming from his eyes, Optimus Prime slowly keeled sideways like a felled redwood to smash through a cluster of pines, splintering them on his way to the ground. The sound of his falling echoed through the trees as his head landed barely ten feet from the bewildered Sam. Just before slipping into complete stasis, Optimus uttered his last command, "Run . . . boy . . ."

Looming behind the body, Megatron glared down at the unconscious Optimus Prime. He raised his blade for the final, killing blow, the blow that would extinguish Prime's Spark. Now all that remained was to . . .

A sleek yellow-and-black shape came sprinting toward him, dodging in and out among the trees, firing as it approached. Megatron regarded it out of pitiless eyes. One more Autobot to dispense with. One more misguided entity to reduce to its elemental components. Taking aim at Bumblebee, the leader of the Decepticons elevated his primary weapons. Off to one side, Starscream was doing the same. Caught in their withering cross fire, the brave but absurd Autobot would not survive more than a moment or two.

A pulse blast of surprising strength caught Megatron in the chest and knocked him backward. Startled, he turned sharply to his right. Not one but two of the cursed miscreants were coming at him from another direction—and they were a lot bigger than the foolhardy Bumblebee. His moment of absolute triumph now set aside, Megatron gauged the firepower and determination of Ratchet and Ironhide as they charged in his direction. And there were others behind them.

"Get him out of here!" Ratchet yelled at Bumblebee.

Swiftly shifting to terrestrial guise, the yellow-and-black Autobot skidded to a halt beside Sam. Still in shock, Sam let himself be pulled away by Mikaela as she sprang from the side of the Camaro.

"Sam, run, c'mon!" Tears were welling up in her own eyes as they swept over the prone, unmoving form of Optimus Prime. "You can't do anything here!" Stumbling, staggering, he let her drag him into the waiting car as bursts from Megatron's weapons detonated around them. Accelerating rapidly and using the trees for cover, Bumblebee sped them away from the fight.

Already battered by their struggle to subdue Optimus, neither Decepticon was prepared to take on half a dozen fresh Autobots. Shifting to terrestrial aerial mode, both blasted off into the sky, the injured Starscream trailing smoke. Now that Optimus had been dealt with, there would be plenty of time to finish off his inferiors.

Not that they really mattered any longer in the grand scheme of things, Megatron thought with satisfaction as he climbed toward the eastern horizon.

They gathered quietly and in disbelief around their fallen leader.

Sam could barely bring himself to speak, but at last uttered the impossible words: "Is he—is he dead?"

Ratchet's response was surprising, if not overly reassuring. "No, at least not in the human sense of the word. He is, however, in complete stasis lock, and will remain so until his internal systems can repair the damage. If we were back on Cybertron, and I had access to the right equipment, I could speed the process. But here, now, there is little I can do. He will remain in this state for a long time, long even as Transformers measure time."

"Then there's nothing we can do?" asked Sam.

"We can hope," came the reply. But of all the things Sam had in his heart at that moment, hope was not one of them.

Hours passed, then days. It was such a simple thing, a quietly fuming Megatron thought. It was not even a large planet. Yet here he was, having to chastise his supposed assistant again for yet another failure.

The island on which he met Starscream was isolated and cold, unobserved by the humans and unwanted even by the simple life-forms that inhabited this thinly populated top of the planet. As driven snow swirled around them, he confronted the other Decepticon.

Starscream did not hesitate. There was no point. He knew all too well Megatron's disdain for prevarication. Especially, the Decepticon thought, when it was ineffective.

"We've lost the boy, Master, and cannot locate his track."

Megatron's contempt was so great he did not even bother to strike his inferior. "I can't even rely on you to swat a simple insect."

While Starscream was subordinate, he did have his limits. He was emboldened by the knowledge that pointing out an irrefutable fact could not be construed as defiance.

"One insect among seven billion," he replied forcefully. "By this time he could be anywhere. There are no signals, nothing to indicate his present whereabouts. The electrical impulses generated by human bodies are too slight to be individually identified at a distance. And the Autobots are hiding him."

Megatron considered. "Then we will force the insects of this world to find him for us. Sometimes insects are better at locating and identifying their own kind than are superior beings." He turned thoughtful. "Contemplate, for a moment, the potential usefulness of these absurd emotional relationships they form among themselves."

High above, Soundwave received the orders of his Master and set to work. Scanning abilities only dreamed of by the creatures on the world below allowed him to monitor and examine millions of communications in minutes. Television, radio, even gaming instructions were noted and scrutinized for the kind of link the Decepticons sought.

Until one was found.

Unsurprisingly, it came from a cell phone. Shifting his position in emptiness, the Decepticon spy zeroed in on the contact identified as "Witwicky, J." How easy the humans in question made the task, Soundwave reflected. Had the identifier he had been seeking been labeled "Smith, J." or "Garcia, J." or any one of thousands of other far more common names, identification and isolation would have taken considerably more time. Even among the seven billion, there were a limited number of Witwickys.

Even so, the initial identifier by itself was not enough. Soundwave speedily ran a side-by-side comparison with another brief, innocuous message he held securely in internal storage banks that operated on the atomic level. Every inflection, every tone had to match precisely in order for him to pronounce the communication he had intercepted a successful match. Elation succeeded confirmation. He was not known as Soundwave for nothing.

Once verification was complete, he positioned other tracking instruments to pinpoint the source. This took virtually no time at all.

Even though in human terms, Paris was a fairly crowded place.

After making the short call to a friend back home, Judy Witwicky set her phone down on the table. The device looked out of place against the stark white linen cloth, not to mention the fine dining ware. Nearby, the restaurant's strolling violinist was dutifully sawing away at a classical tune that was popular and romantic, striving Franckly for a tip while wishing that he was practicing Brian's concerto instead of vapid late-Romantic melodies. But a job was a job, and one still had to work when the orchestra season was over.

Neither of the two Americans ensconced at the corner table were paying the bored performer any attention. The Eiffel Tower in view behind them, they were concentrating on their meal. Leastwise, Ron Witwicky was concentrating on his. His spouse was more focused on her degree of consternation.

"*Really*, Ron," she murmured disapprovingly while

eyeing the thin trickle of oily liquid that was tracing a glistening path down one corner of his mouth. "A *cheeseburger*?"

Mouth half full of ground sirloin and masticated bun, he looked up and blinked. "What? Hey, it comes with *French* fries." He gestured at the gastronomic gastropods artfully arrayed on a dish in front of his wife. "You think I flew across the ocean to chow down a plate a snails?"

Judy drew herself up slightly in her chair. "They're called 'escargots.' "

Holding his burger possessively with both hands, Ron shrugged. "What's the difference?"

"They're high-class snails; they come from good families."

She continued, "C'mon, what is it with you, Mr. Grumpy?" She gestured at their surroundings. "We're in *Paris*. Candles, violins, ratatouille—you can even get béarnaise sauce with your burger. Lighten up."

Turning away, he looked off into the distance—and not at the nearby nineteenth-century iron architectural marvel that dominated the horizon, either. As opposed to him simply eating something, something was clearly eating at him.

"What is it, Ron?"

He hesitated, eyed his sandwich, and put the next bite on hold. "Y'know how sometimes you take dinner out of the oven too early? And it *looks* like it's done, but then when you take a bite it's kinda like—a breaded ice cube?"

Her expression hardened. "Are you criticizing my

cooking just 'cause we're in Paris? Ron, what the hell're you talking about?"

His concern dismissed her attempt at humor. "I just hope we didn't let Sam out of the oven too early. I hope he's ready to—find his own way."

Seeing that neither her kitchen nor her parenting skills were under attack, she relaxed. "Oh, Ronald— it's the sign of a real man when he can admit that he misses his child. I miss Sam, too." She turned wistful. "His voice, the way he always used to ask for a second glass of milk, the sound of his feet coming down the stairs to dinner, the way he would look at girls and then hurriedly look away if he thought you noticed—so many things! Maybe—maybe we could have another one. A girl, this time."

"What? Nah, they're *way* too much of a pain in the ass." He indicated their surroundings, his response showing that in actuality he was not *totally* oblivious to them. "Can you imagine being here, like this, with a little kid in tow? Not me. I'm done. It's *Ronny's* playtime now."

Beneath the table, her foot rose and came to rest on the seat of another chair. One that was already occupied by her husband. She settled it into the warmest, most comfortable nook available. This caused him to pause yet again with his burger half- way to his mouth.

"Judith . . . ?" He stared straight back at her, only a few sesame seeds threatening to interrupt his sud- denly laserlike line of sight.

"Ronald . . . ," she murmured, leaning forward and resting her chin on the back of one hand.

"What're you doing?"

She smiled innocently. "Just—admiring the Eiffel Tower. It's even bigger than I imagined." Her smile segued into a wide grin.

He responded in kind, looking around and calling to their waiter.

"*Garçon?* Check, *por favor.*"

The man smiled a response. "Immediately, *monsieur.*" Americans—linguistically inept, with table manners and appetites that would make Obelix look stylish, but they always tipped well.

Judy Witwicky's cell phone rang. Someone returning her previous call, she wondered—or another friend interested in vicariously sharing her vacation? She answered merrily.

"*Oui? Bonnnn-jourrrr . . .*"

An eerie and decidedly unsettling electronic howl caused her to pull the phone away from her ear. Some kind of serious intercontinental interference, she decided. Then the whine resolved itself into words that were more disturbing than the drone.

"WHERE—IS—YOUR—SON?"

The pleasure of the previous moments dissolved under the weight of the unsettling query. "What? Who is this?"

"WHERE—IS—YOUR—SON?!" The reiteration was both a question and a demand.

She stared at the phone as if it had suddenly turned into a toad. Who could it be? What was behind it? Her catalog of experience dredged up the most likely explanation.

"Your heavy breathing is not impressing anyone, pervert—and I will report this call to the French foreign legion." Disconnecting, she turned off the power to the phone. Across the table, her husband eyed her uncertainly.

"What was that all about, hon?"

She summoned back her earlier smile. "Wrong number."

The pair of huge metal orbs came screaming down from space, tearing through the atmosphere so fast that their arrival barely had time to register on a few scattered monitors and telescopes. Not that anything could have been done to stop them even if their presence had been recognized and their respective vectors plotted sooner. They were moving far too fast.

The first came down over the open Atlantic, but it did not plunge into the dark green waters. It slammed straight into the flight deck of the U.S.S. *Lincoln*, traveling so fast that no one even saw what had struck the ship. Torn apart by sheer kinetic force, steel, aluminum, alloys, and carbon fiber were shredded like tinfoil. A series of explosions ripped through the guts of the huge vessel, sending planes, equipment, and personnel flying.

Hulled completely through, the carrier began to inhale ocean at a rate no shutting of watertight doors could forestall. Total destruction had overcome it so fast that there had not even been time to sound the Abandon Ship. As the two halves sank beneath the waves, men and women fought to surface, struggling to attach themselves to hastily inflated life rafts, preservers, or anything that might float.

One figure needed no such puny artificial support. Standing on the screws of the rapidly sinking stern of the carrier, Megatron surveyed what he had wrought with cold satisfaction.

Ron Witwicky was holding his wife's right hand and staring into her eyes when the glasses on their table began to shake. The vibration intensified, spilling her wine and his beer.

"Earthquake?" She eyed him uncertainly.

He was openly doubtful. "In Paris? Never heard of an earthquake in Paris." The shaking grew worse, and he gripped the sides of the table to keep the remnants of their meal from sliding off. "Never heard of an earthquake in *France*." A bright light made him look up and to his left.

The sky was screaming.

Coming in at a much less acute angle, the second metal orb streaked past the Eiffel Tower and without slowing, sheared off the top of a building before splashing into the Seine.

More identifiable screams filled the surrounding streets and shops and cafés as pedestrians and diners surrendered to panic. Cars crashed in the streets as gaping drivers forgot what they were doing to gawk at the destruction. Gendarmes stared, then fumbled for their phones to report that they were witnessing the impossible. The boulevard and side streets began to fill with fleeing, terrified residents and tourists.

Ron grabbed his wife's hand as they ran from the restaurant. But to where? What might happen next? Was there a safer place to be?

Their hotel. It wasn't far, just a few blocks around the corner. As good a place as any. In any event, the only place they knew. But the street was packed, and drivers were beginning to accelerate in defiance of every law. Trapped, some motorists started driving on the sidewalks, heedless of the danger this posed to those on foot. Better, Ron decided, to get away from the increasingly treacherous traffic.

He turned down an alley he was convinced ran straight to the back of their hotel. Surely there would be at least a service entrance there, and the narrower passageway was devoid of vehicles as even those on scooters and bikes sought to get away from the city center. Here there was nothing to impede their flight, he saw, except garbage bins, Dumpsters, and the occasional stray cat.

Funny how much noise a stray cat could make, he thought as he searched for a sign that would indicate the location of their hotel.

The noise grew louder. Footsteps, and not those of a cat, not a cat of any size. Judy Witwicky looked back and screamed. Her husband would have screamed, too, except that he was too busy cursing helplessly as enormous metal hands reached down to pluck them from the pavement.

Confusion enveloped the Pentagon, but there was no panic. One of the benefits of repetitive training is that it ceases to be boring only when it becomes necessary. Individual fears were set aside as everyone rushed to their assigned posts.

At Central Command, the head of the Joint Chiefs of Staff was on SatLink viewer with the general in charge at NORAD. They were discussing, succinctly and professionally, the unthinkable.

"Is it possible the *Lincoln* had a nuclear reactor failure? Sufficient for containment to prevent release into the atmosphere but inadequate to prevent her from going down?"

On the monitor, the general in Colorado replied while simultaneously sneaking brief glances at something offscreen. "Negative. We're just getting initial reports in from our facility on Haleakela. They confirm the entry and final touchdown right where the *Lincoln* battle group was steaming of an extra-atmospheric projectile traveling at approximately thirty thousand knots."

The chief considered this briefly. "Meteoric in origin, or possibly a small asteroid?"

On the monitor, the other general officer shook his head. "Last-minute—no, last-second—ranging indicates that it was a perfect sphere and externally at least of apparently uniform composition. No way it's natural." His voice dropped meaningfully. "*Or* manmade. Other readings suggest that . . ."

His voice vanished along with his image. The senior officer started to turn to the nearest technician but caught himself as the monitor cleared. Another visage had appeared on it and was now looming over the conflict room. Whether seated or standing or rushing between stations, everyone else, from the highest-ranking official to the lowliest message carrier, stopped what they were doing to stare at the image onscreen.

It was not human.

"Insects of the human hive," Megatron intoned, "now you know what your leaders have hidden from you. *We* are here. Among you."

In a restaurant in a small town in Nebraska elderly retirees, stoic farmers, busy waitresses, and housewives whose children were now safely at school halted in their conversation and dining to stare in shock and fear at the alien face that had without warning appeared on the screen of the small television above the single counter.

"We can destroy your cities at will."

Cards, mah-jongg tiles, and electronic gaming machines all ceased motion as gamblers and bar girls and employees of the huge casino in Macau stopped what they had been doing to turn their full attention to the bizarre yet threatening face on the giant monitor suspended above the ranks of roulette tables.

"If you wish them to remain standing—if you wish to remain standing *yourselves*—you will search for, find, and deliver to us at a place of our choosing—*this boy.*"

The contrast between the overawing, terrifying alien visage and that of the ordinary, slightly geeky Caucasian male that replaced it was stunning. For a moment, the face of Sam Witwicky dominated every active television and computer monitor on the planet. Then that of Megatron returned.

In a shop window not far from the Kremlin a mesmerized, frightened, and growing crowd fought for a clear view of the oversize new TV monitor on sale in a shop window.

"Your military leaders have just witnessed and can attest to the destruction of your largest and most powerful warship. This constitutes a demonstration of but a small part of our powers. There is no valor for those who try to resist, and no future for those who fail to comply. There is only annihilation. Our demand is a simple one. Find and deliver to us the one human in question. Delay, and more destruction will be visited upon you. You have one solar day."

At which point every monitor on Earth went to black.

They brought Optimus Prime in to McGuire Air Force Base in New Jersey slung between a pair of turbocharged Chinook helicopters. Autobots and NEST team troops stood side by side, shoulder to leg, watching. The Chinook pilots tried their best to ease the setdown, but sudden gusts of wind and the awkwardness of their hastily strapped load made it downright dangerous. At a command, the slings were released and the Autobot leader crashed unceremoniously to the ground.

Lennox and Epps had not even begun to approach the motionless mountain of metal when a convoy of Air Force security vehicles came rumbling out onto the tarmac, heavy machine guns raised and at the ready. Instinctively, the Autobots activated their own weapons. Splitting up, the two men hurried to put a damper on any possible confrontation.

"Whoawhoawhoa!" Lennox danced in front of the lead vehicle. "Everybody stand down! We're on the same side here!" Off to one side, Epps approached a soldier he knew.

"Yo, Mike—what's goin' on here? Put the guns down, man."

The tech sergeant's sincerity left the security officer

unimpressed. He nodded toward where Ironhide stood glaring at the encircling soldiers.

"Them first." The two men regarded each other calmly, but neither was prepared to back down.

Slipping out of a Jeep, a smug Galloway drew Lennox's attention.

"Your NEST team is deactivated, Major. From this moment on you are to cease all anti-Decepticon operations forthwith and return to Diego Garcia pending further orders."

Repressing the emotions rising inside him, Lennox regarded the advisor coolly. "Sir, we get our orders directly from Chairman Morshower."

Reaching into a pocket, Galloway produced a carefully folded piece of stationery. "I'll see your chairman of the Joint Chiefs and raise you a president of the United States." Opening the paper, he brandished it in Lennox's face. "His National Security Directive to me, on official stationery with his signature. *I* have operational command now."

Having wandered over to listen, Epps commented with his usual tact and delicacy, "Are you outta your *mind*? You got no idea what we're dealing with here, and . . ."

Galloway broke in on the sergeant, his tone that of a man used to having access to the highest levels of power and unafraid to employ it.

"I know *exactly* what we're dealing with here, Sergeant. An enemy ultimatum and a public on the verge of national panic. And that's just here. You should see the communiqués we've been receiving minute by minute from the French government. Not to mention every other administration on the planet.

An alien blood feud has been brought to our shores for which our soldiers—and now a number of European civilians—are paying the price. The secret's out. It's *our* war now. Not a private quarrel that can be dealt with by a couple of covert agencies operating on their own and undercover. We'll win it as we always have: with a coordinated military *strategy*—not through actions carried out by a motley collection of bounty-hunting rogues and rejects from other services."

Epps leaned forward. "Yeah, and while you're 'planning' a strategy, they're out executing one."

With a gesture, Lennox indicated the integrated mix of Autobots and humans standing behind him. "This is the best fighting force we've got. We need to make use of it."

"What we *need*," Galloway shot back unrepentantly, "is to draw up battle plans involving the entire world's military forces while we buy time by exploring every possible diplomatic solution."

Though he knew he should not have been surprised, Lennox was taken aback. "You mean by handing over the kid."

Ironhide's growl was low enough to rattle the fillings in the teeth of the men standing near him. "You think you can negotiate with *Decepticons*?"

To his credit, Galloway did not flinch from his commitment. "I will not say it again. You'll all follow orders to the *letter*. Stand down, or we are going to have a *problem*."

Reaching over, Sideswipe put a hand on the bigger Autobot's scarred and oft-repaired left arm. "Ironhide—this isn't what Optimus would want."

The huge weapons' master contemplated the available options. Then, grudgingly, he lowered his cannon arms.

"Autobots," he muttered, "we have our orders."

Lennox glared at the advisor. "Whatever the Decepticons are after, whatever their ultimate goal is here, this is just the *start*." He nodded at the executive order. "You can bet every line in your paper-pusher's arsenal on that."

Having been insulted by far more articulate adversaries than the officer standing before him, Galloway merely sniffed derisively. "Get your 'assets' back to base, Major." Looking past Lennox, he nodded in the direction of the unmoving mass that occupied the center of the runway. "And be sure to take all that scrap metal with you." Turning on a heel, he climbed back into his waiting Jeep. At a nod to the driver, they turned and sped back the way they had come. Abandoned on the tarmac, a cluster of humans and Autobots stood side by side in shared fury.

Epps nodded solemnly at the rear of the receding vehicle. "One thing I can tell you for a certainty: that guy's off my Christmas list."

Lennox refused to be baited. "We'll get him back." Tilting his head, he contemplated the sky. "We'll do as directed. We have no choice. But I have this feeling we'd better get in all the sun and sand we can, because we're not going to be back at base for very long."

People understandably tend to shun prisons, even abandoned ones. They're unpleasant places at the best of times. They're also as unlikely a hiding place as can be imagined for one wishing to avoid the attention of the law.

The abandoned prison was also the only place the three teens could suggest that was large enough to allow them and the Autobots to move about freely while at the same time concealing them from normal police patrols.

They had no television, but Leo's phone supplied a steady stream of terror alerts. They crowded around him as yet another update appeared on CNN. It reflected the confusion that had surfaced in the wake of Megatron's transmission.

". . . conflicting reports about the recent 'robot' broadcast continue. No world government has yet confirmed that an 'alien race' is behind the attacks. We're hearing everything from a communications satellite–hacking prank based in remote northern Sweden to terrorist fear tactics. There is no confirmation as yet that the sinking of the U.S.S. aircraft carrier *Lincoln* and the destruction in France might in any way be connected. In some circles the former is being attributed to a nuclear accident that the U.S. military is seeking to cover up, while the damage in Paris is being called by others the result of the inevitable weathering and rusting of century plus–old iron . . ."

Knowing more of the truth than he wanted to know, Leo stared at the tiny screen as Sam looked on beside him. "Official dissembling. Public might buy it, might not. Take it from someone who's spent plenty of late-night hours studying this kind of stuff. One thing I do know for sure."

"What's that?" Sam wondered.

"Dude, our lives are *so* over."

A pair of Autobots joined them: Skids and Mud-flap. Although it would stretch the human definition of the word, these were the Twins. Having abandoned their combined alt-mode of an ice-cream truck, they now sported the guise of sporty, albeit compact, cars.

"We twied to contact the rehth of the Autoboth, but their frequenthieth are currently nonoperational," said Mudflap, his thick lisp making him difficult to immediately understand.

"They got orders to stand down!" his counterpart barked. "Gov'mint won't let 'em bust any heads! It's outrageous, bro!"

Sam couldn't believe what he was hearing. "But that's—*insane*. Are you telling me that the Autobots are taking the fall for this?"

Mudflap nodded. "Yup. My geth ith they're being ordered back to baythe . . . againtht their will."

"Then what?" A fretful Sam looked from one identical Autobot to the other.

"Lockdown in the crib, baby," declared Skids solemnly. "It's what happens when the Man steps on you."

Leo directed their attention back to his phone. "*Hey!* Check it out."

The steady drumbeat of confused reporting was interrupted as the channel broke into a live FBI press conference. Sam winced as his picture filled the screen. The shot had been lifted from his college application. Though such a thing did not seem possible, it made him look even geekier than usual. Drawing back from the image, the screen shot made room for additional photos of Mikaela and Leo. The current director of the FBI was standing beside what must have been the country's least-imposing trio of mug shots.

". . . all we're prepared to say at this time is that we believe they may have information relating to the tragedies. It's for their own safety that they be found. The FBI, the CIA, and Interpol are seeking the cooperation of law-enforcement officials worldwide . . ."

A sudden realization caused Sam to reach out and snatch the phone away from its owner. A startled Leo tried to take it back, only to see Sam slam it to the floor.

"Hey! What's the idea?"

"They can track us." Unwilling to trust the impact, Sam proceeded to use his heel to stomp the components out of the phone's case.

Throwing up his hands, his roommate rolled his eyes skyward. "Oh, great—they can track us!" Lowering his head, he stared back at his friend. "Look, I—I'm not with you guys . . . you forced me into that car . . . technically I'm a hostage—this is kidnapping!"

Observing the verbal exchange between the two humans, Mudflap was moved to comment. "Doth thith guy ever thut hith twap?"

"Let's pop a cap in his ass," suggested his counterpart. "We do it fast, he'll feel nuthin'."

Frustrated and fearful, Leo turned on the two Autobots. "Yo, bumper cars, I'm *hearing* you. No one's popping any caps in *anybody's* ass." He buried his head in his hands.

Sam had had just about enough of his friend's wailing. "*Hey! You're* the one who wanted 'em all to be real. Well, are they real enough for you? Kinda different from pushing captions around on a webpage, huh?" He nodded toward the nearest way out. "You wanna run? No one's stopping you." Turning, he stalked out the corridor doorway without looking back.

Leo watched him leave, started to follow, then stopped. It was bad, all bad, but it wasn't Witwicky's fault. With the Twins watching him, he sat down and let his head fall forward.

Planning on computers was all very well and good until it turned out that the computers were trying to kill you.

In an open area around a near corner, Mikaela was tending to Bumblebee. One panel and its covering armor had been snapped open to reveal the interior of a portion of his left arm. Having followed his directions and extracted the necessary sealing hose from the interior, she was working to close the gashes on his left hand. An electrical interrupt that would have to be fixed later had prevented the internal healing and repair tube from doing its own work. The human, the Autobot reflected as he silently watched her work, was a very adequate and extremely flexible substitute for a jumper line.

"Try and hold still," she was telling him as he twitched slightly. "I'm good, but I can't fix a coolant line if somebody's jiggling it, either." Obediently, he froze in place.

"There—that's the last of it, I think." Rising, she let the tube rewind into his arm. Flexing the damaged fingers, he nodded appreciatively. Movement caused

Mikaela to turn as Sam entered. His expression was anguished, and she did her best to try and reassure him.

"Don't take it to heart, Sam. There's nothing you could've done."

His gaze met hers, his tone downcast. "I could've *listened*." Continuing on past her, he stopped as close as he dared to the silent Bumblebee. He started to say something only to find that he could not. He could not look his car, his friend, his guardian, in the eye—even if it was only a flat plane composed of inorganic optical sensors.

"I'm so . . ." He tried to find appropriate words, gave up, and found himself rambling helplessly. "I'm so sorry. I messed up. I thought I was doing the right thing. Seemed so important." He laughed humorlessly. "Being in college, being normal. Important, yeah—for who? For me? Talk about selfish! I thought—I thought I deserved it." His throat started to constrict and he swallowed, trying to control his emotions.

"Optimus fell. Because of me. He came back here to protect me. To look out for one lousy, immature, self-centered human *child*. And on top of that, now the rest of the Autobots are getting blamed for what's happening."

The yellow-and-black Autobot listened to all this without comment. Now his radio crackled with the voice of a familiar television character intoning a brief snippet of dialogue from an old film.

"I have been, and always shall be, your friend."

That said, even if it was not in his own voice, he

shifted shape back to his sleek, four-wheeled terrestrial guise. Sam looked over at the idling car.

"I let you down, Bee. I let all of you down. And I gotta make that right. No matter what the consequences. That's part of growing up, too, right? Dealing with the consequences of your actions? Taking responsibility? I can't let you guys continue to take the blame for something that I might've been able to prevent." He looked toward the exit. "I gotta turn myself in."

Bumblebee responded in a different radio voice this time, harsh and insistent: *"No, no, no!"*

Sam smiled affectionately at the car. "We don't know that there's anyone else left but us. You, me, 'Kaela, Leo, and those crazy Twins. We can't stop Megatron alone. How can you deny that my life isn't worth saving the planet?" He paused, waiting, until the silence had run on long enough to make his point. "You can't, can you? *Say* something."

The car radio finally responded, utilizing bass so deep that the speakers shook the interior. Because it was speaking in the voice of Optimus Prime.

"I believe there is greatness in you, Sam. Even if you don't."

The words didn't affect their intended recipient half so powerfully as did the expertly reproduced voice of the Autobot leader. Mikaela came up behind Sam.

"If Optimus hadn't saved us, do you really think the Decepticons would have just taken you and then left the rest of the world, the rest of humankind, alone? I don't know nearly as much about this rivalry as you do, Sam, but from what I've seen of the Decepticons and how they function, I think you'd be the last person on Earth to trust them to leave us alone after they have you—and I'd be the second to last."

Bumblebee followed her observation with another broadcast of his own. This time the radio's speaker was unidentifiable, but the words were immediately familiar.

"It is for us, the living, to resolve that these dead shall not have died in vain."

Old words, Sam thought. Words that he and every one of his fellow students had been forced to memorize in high school. Words that had to be correctly recognized on one of a seemingly infinite number of written tests. How boring they had seemed at the time! How archaic! And now, suddenly, how relevant.

Much subdued and perhaps also a little matured, Leo confronted his angst-ridden roommate. "You're the leader now, bro. So? *Lead.*" He gestured at their grim, silent surroundings. "If it comes to it, I'd rather end up in a place like this than under some invader's metal foot."

Off to one side, Bumblebee revved his engine. It was a sound that had become as familiar to Sam as his own heartbeat, one that had served to inspire and energize him on more than one previous occasion. It did so again now. The rumble, and the words that had been spoken over the car's radio.

"Okay—*okay.* Let's think this through. When I killed Megatron by jamming the Cube into his chest, it must have affected me as well. I think some stuff must have gotten transferred into me. Stuff from the Cube. Knowledge of some kind." He looked over at

Leo. "All those symbols and equations I was writing on the walls of our room, stuff like that. I don't know what it all means, but I knew how to write it out. How to transfer it." Reaching up, he rubbed his forehead. "All that knowledge went into my head, right?"

"Not just alien symbology, either, I expect." Mikaela was eyeing him with a mixture of sympathy and wonderment. "No wonder you aced your SATs and got a scholarship to an Ivy League school."

Ideas were flowing through him now, coalescing, starting to make sense. He had never taken the time to really think about them before. Or maybe his perception of himself had been blocked. Such blockage could be removed by all kinds of things, he realized. Drugs, diet, environment. An emotional crisis . . .

"So when I touched the splinter, got proximate to it, got shocked, that stored knowledge got *activated*. I started seeing symbols, which is what they're after—no," he corrected himself as fresh comprehension struck home. "Not the symbols—it's what they *represent*." His gaze grew distant, his voice faint.

"He's drifting," Leo remarked warningly.

Reaching out, Mikaela took Sam by the shoulders and shook him. "Sam! Stay here! Stay with us—focus!"

"What?" He blinked, turning away from the distant mysteries he had been viewing and back toward her. "I just—understood. Focus, yeah. Concentration. I know, I realize—the symbols? They're a message. A message—or a map. Or maybe both, I dunno." Reaching up, he grabbed his head. "This is *hard*. It *hurts*."

"That's thinking for you," Leo told him. "Gets you

every time. Okay—say you're a map. We don't know what you lead to or where you're starting from, but first things first: how do we *read* you?"

"Read, yeah. Translate what's in my head. A map can show, but it can't interpret. For that we need . . ." He shifted his attention to the attentive Bumblebee and the silent Twins. "You guys, any of this make any sense?"

Turning and using a forefinger, he started writing in the dust that caked the nearest wall, tracing arcane symbols in the grit and grime. The method and the medium were far from perfect, but the results were legible.

Mudflap spoke up almost immediately. "Oooh— ith the wangwadge of the Pwyimes! We don't know how to wead that!"

Mikaela made a face. "The—'language of the Primes'?"

Skids explained. "*Old* school, like *way* far back. Long before the time of li'l punks like us."

Bumblebee, as always, had something to add, his radio warbling from yet another old film. "*You say to-mayto, I say to-mahto. . . .*"

Sam was thinking hard. "Well, if none of you can read it, we need to find someone who can." He took in their surroundings. "But first we gotta find a safe place to hide out. We can't stay here. There's no power, so we've got no way to stay warm, and no way to know what's going on. And we're gonna need food and water, and . . ."

Leo interrupted him. "I think I might know some- one who can help: Robo-Warrior."

Mikaela responded with a disapproving look. "That a *friend* of yours?"

He returned her gaze, shaking his head sadly. "Y'know, someone looks like you shouldn't be so touchy."

For the first time in a while, Sam smiled. "Better watch what you say, man, or she'll reach out and touch you—with a torsion wrench."

☸ XI ☸

No one bothered to look twice at the green and orange cars traveling in line, though the lustrous black-and-yellow Camaro in front of them drew the occasional envious stare from several passing commuters. Their ogling didn't last long. Drivers approaching the bridge exit to Manhattan had to pay attention lest they take the wrong off-ramp and find themselves heading in the wrong direction—or worse, crosstown.

Such important last-minute decisions did not appear to weigh heavily on the Camaro's driver, perhaps because the hands he was resting on the wheel were positioned there only for show. For all the actual control he was exercising over the car he could just as easily have been riding with his feet up on the dash and his hands behind his head, except that that might well have attracted more than a little unwelcome attention from the other drivers. Allowing the vehicle to drive itself did, however, permit him to concentrate on the ongoing conversation with his fellow passengers.

"You're *sure* about this guy?" Sustaining the necessary fiction that the car had a human driver, Sam continued to face forward even as he addressed himself to the occupant of the passenger seat. Relaxing sideways in back, Mikaela listened intently to the continuing discussion.

Leo's reply was confident, but mixed with bitter acknowledgment that he was recommending his rival. "The 'Robo-Warrior'? Well, he's not a friend, he's a frickin' archrival. But he claims he's the Holy Grail on this stuff."

"He runs that 'Giant-Effing-Robots' site?"

"The dude swears he works outta some bot-proof bomb shelter in the middle of New York City—posted specs on how to fight 'em and everything. We tried to revenge-hack his firewall one time and I saw some junk on his site that looked like those symbols."

Suspicious from the start of every move Sam's roommate had made and everything he had said, Mikaela wasn't about to let his assurances pass unquestioned.

"So in other words, you're saying that you've never met him."

"So? I never met Jesus and he obviously looms large in our society. That's the beauty of the online world; you can be anything and do anything without exposing yourself. I mean, think about it: if the Sermon on the Mount had gone viral throughout the Roman world, wouldn't things have maybe gone differently? This dude we're going to see is the Holy Grail of alien mythology. The Matthew and John, if you prefer. Or Mohammed, or Buddha. Pick your Messiah. He feeds me and the rest of us in our worldwide group ultra-top-secret files, he's posted specs on how to fight 'em and everything, and he's got some kind of bot-proof bomb shelter in the middle of New York City—so if he can't help us, *no* one can."

"Maybe," Sam conceded, "but what're the odds 'Robo-Warrior's' just a ten-year-old girl with an X-box and a talent for improvisation? Or maybe somebody who wants to be a game designer and is trying out plots on unsuspecting viewers, pretending that their scenarios are based in reality?"

"Save us, Obi-nobody, you're our only hope," an unconvinced Mikaela muttered.

Sam's roommate shook his head condescendingly. "Ponce-de-Léon is on the case. Trust me."

Bumblebee kept driving throughout this exchange. The signpost up ahead read "Brooklyn," but Leo couldn't help but feel that he had crossed into a different dimension.

Trailed by the Twins, the Camaro slowed as it passed the restaurant. After confirming that they had indeed arrived at the indicated address, all three vehicles made a block to check that their destination was not under surveillance. Satisfied, they began to look for a place to park on the busy street. Enshrouded in their terrestrial guises, the Twins had no trouble. Finding a place for Bumblebee to settle in proved more problematic, but eventually that was done with a little creative rearranging of parked cars during a lull in pedestrian traffic.

As Leo led the way toward the busy restaurant entrance, they passed a newsstand whose owner was watching a small TV. The headline on one paper shouted, "5,000 DEAD AT SEA—CAUSE STILL UNDETERMINED."

The announcer on the compact set looked none too composed. "Though many people continue to doubt that what they saw in the now-infamous television broadcast was in fact real and denials continue to be issued by numerous governments, we are starting to see cases of stockpiling, looting, and panic, as the manhunt continues for this boy."

Sam's face promptly appeared on the screen. The same lousy photo, he noted as he pulled his hoodie farther down over his head and lowered his gaze. At least they didn't have far to walk. Halting outside the restaurant door, Leo double-checked the street number.

"Deli—good front. Low-tech, lots of customers. I'm starving." As they entered, he whispered to Sam and Mikaela, "You guys wait here. I'll check it out, give you the go/no-go. Shouldn't take long." Pushing his way through the milling, anxious crowd, he began working his way toward the counter.

Huddled close to Sam, Mikaela tried to keep from being knocked over by the continuous back-and-forth surge of customers. "Everyone sure is in a hurry."

Sam turned philosophical. "That's Armageddon for you. Gives everyone an appetite."

Rising above the requests for food and the demand for service, a booming voice floated across the crowd. "*Number Forty-two!* We got your kishka-knish-kasha-varnishk-and-kreplach combo right here! End-of-the-world specials, cash only, who's next?"

That voice . . . Rising pitch, naturally accusatory tone—where had he heard that before? Straining to see over the crowd, Sam finally located the source—

only to be shaken by something considerably stronger than hunger. Swathed in a butcher's apron and grease, the lean and sharp-eyed figure behind the counter was carving a corned beef as if it had committed some personal offense against him.

Simmons. Formerly *Agent* Simmons. Formerly Agent Simmons of former Sector Seven. Sam turned to Mikaela, as he did so gesturing in the direction of the source of his astonishment.

"You gotta be *kidding* . . ." She joined him in confirming the identity of the busy operator behind the counter.

Coming up behind the subject of their study, a short, stout, elderly woman unloaded a smack on the back of his head. Sam was reminded of all the black-and-white movies he had ever seen that involved old-style dynamite detonators.

"Moron! I told you to cure the lox in the brine, *then* smoke it! You ruined a beautiful piece a fish!"

Staggered, Simmons looked back and down. "Ma! You want me to cut my own hand off or what? I'm like a Ninja with a blade—it's an art form!"

Signifying that such altercations were a daily if not hourly occurrence, Simmons immediately forgot the confrontation as he turned to serve his next customer.

"What'll it be, kid? Time's money, business has *never* been this good, and there are starving people waiting behind you."

Leo paused a moment to make certain no one was listening. No one was: everyone was trying to get the attention of another of the several counter operatives. He leaned forward and lowered his voice.

"Robo-Warrior. Know him?"

Simmons made a dismissive sound. "Figment of your imagination, my friend. Never heard of him."

Straightening, Leo continued unabashed, "My imagination has no figment, *friend*. Never heard of a survivalist psycho stealing paid subscribers from an *authentic* alt-news provider: The-Real-Effing-Deal-dot-com?"

Recognition dawned in Simmons's eyes. "Oh, you must be talkin' about that amateur-hour blog operation with Gameboy-level security? That sends out 'cease and desi-si-st' letters without bothering to spell-check?"

"Robo-Warrior," Leo confirmed.

A brief nod from Simmons acknowledged the fact, and he countered, "Leonardo Ponce-de-Léon Spitz."

"Only my mother calls me 'Leonardo.' "

"Well, come to mama," Simmons mocked. "You just give information, I take it . . ."

"Why don't you get me a cookie, bitch?"

"All out," sneered Simmons. "How 'bout some kugel, bitch?"

Leo and Simmons locked eyes, literally growling at each other.

Leo turned and signaled to Sam and Mikaela. "It's him! It's this dude!"

The instant he set eyes on them, Simmons took a step back.

"No . . . *what? You! Again?* No—*way.*"

"Excuse me." An elderly man struggled to reach the counter by pushing past Mikaela. "But I'm in a terrible hurry, and . . ."

"Meat store's closed." The ex-agent gestured sharply. "Murray—out!" As the bewildered customer moved off in the indicated direction, Simmons leaned forward across the counter. "C'mon with me—can't have anyone seeing you here. Dangerous for business."

"What business?" Leo inquired quickly.

"Shut up, kid." Gesturing for them to come around the corner of the counter, Simmons shucked off his apron and started toward a back hallway, beckoning them to follow. As the noise of the crowd out front began to recede behind them, an incredulous Leo stared at his roommate.

"You *know* this guy?"

"Yeah." Sam sounded tired as Mikaela checked behind them. "We're old friends."

" 'Old friends'?" Simmons looked back in disbelief. "*You're* the case that shut down Sector Seven! Got the ki-bosh, disbanded, no more security clearance, scattered to the four winds, powdered, no *nuthin'*." With a wave, he took in his immediate surroundings. "So I'm waitin' in the weeds. I'll get 'em back, all cuza you and your little crim girlfriend." His gaze settled on the tight-lipped Mikaela. "Look at her now—all *mature* and everything."

A powerful yet feminine voice blasted through the noise from the front of the deli. "Seymour! Where's the whitefish?"

Muttering under his breath, their host turned to shout toward a one-toothed helper working near the meat grinder. "Yakov! You don't get Christmas bonuses just standing around! You want those new teeth you saw in Skymall? *Help her out.*"

Mikaela was ready with a few choice words the instant their dyspeptic host turned his attention back to them.

"You live with your momma—*Seymour?*"

He glared at her. "*No.* My momma lives with *me,* okay? *Big* difference." His attention snapped back to Sam as he looked his visitor slowly up and down. "They got your face all over the news, Alien Boy. And NBE-1? Still kickin'? How the hell'd *that* happen?" He raised a hand to forestall the reply Sam was not prepared to give. "Don't answer—I don't know what you're hiding, but I don't want anything to do with it. So g'bye, you never saw me. I got bagels to schmear. *Vanish.*" He eyed the silent Leo with obvious distaste. "And take Mr. Juvie-obsessive here with you."

Sam took a deep breath. "Look. I'm not happy about having to come here, either. But—I need your help."

Whatever response Simmons might have been expecting, it was plain from his reaction that this wasn't it. A slow, knowing grin spread across his face.

"Reeeeeally? *You* need *my* help?" He chuckled softly and with evident satisfaction. "Oh, how the wheel of justice turns. The big boy with the pet car and a personal line to its buddies needs the help of poor ol' Seymour Simmons." Looking past Sam, he glared anew at Mikaela. "Whose mother lives with *him.*" When she didn't take the bait, he shrugged and turned back to Sam. "And why. On Earth. Would I. Help *you.* I mean, considering all that you've done to—pardon the irony—*for* me?"

Sam didn't hesitate. "Three reasons. One, you get to save the planet. That's big. Two, they'll give you your old job back. And three, *'cause I am sick of this*

shit. I got toasters nunchucking my knees, an animatronic coed tried to pierce my spleen with her tongue,
a crab-bot stuck a worm in my brain and used it to
project alien symbols like a frickin' home movie, and
now I'm a wanted fugitive. You think *your* life's
rough? Say the word. *I'll* go feed your mom whitefish
and you can run for *your* life."

It was dead quiet in the corridor. Leo held his
breath. Mikaela's gaze kept flicking anxiously between Sam and the ex-agent. Unlike Sam's roommate,
she knew what Simmons was capable of. Fugitive
youth and trained operative stood staring at each
other for a long, long moment—until Simmons finally
proffered a reply.

"Go back," he said quietly and calmly, "to the part
about the crab."

Sam blinked. "Huh?"

"The crab-bot." The change in Simmons's de-
meanor was as stunning as it was swift. "You said it
projected symbols offa your brain?" Speechless, Sam
could only nod affirmatively. Apparently, that was
enough for the ex-agent.

"You. Her. Him. Meat locker. *Now.*"

Sam found himself hesitating. From the time of
their first encounter, Agent Simmons of Sector Seven
had always struck him as a bit—unsettled. Yes, that
was the word. Unsettled. It was a polite, almost def-
erential description. Also, it sounded so much better
than maniacally deranged. Did he really want to take
Mikaela and Leo and go into a meat locker with this
man? Even one that was kosher?

He steeled himself. They had come a long way
under difficult conditions in the improbable hope that

his new roommate might actually know someone capable of helping them. That the identity of the individual to whom they had been led was not one who would have been Sam's first choice to lend them assistance did not obviate the fact that he might be the best qualified to do so.

Mikaela was watching him closely, waiting for a sign. With a nod, Sam made the decision to follow their host.

Once inside the walk-in deep-freeze, Simmons quickly shut the door behind them. Sam observed that not only did Mikaela keep her distance from their guide, she had already checked out a large meat cleaver hanging from a hook on the wall and positioned herself between it and their host. Simmons's interest, however, was not directed toward neighboring utensils.

Continuing on, he paused about halfway into the frigid locker before turning to face them, his gaze meeting each of theirs individually.

"What you're about to see is completely top-secret. Do not tell your friends. Do not tell government operatives. Do not inform the military. Most especially, do not tell my mother."

Reaching up between hanging slabs of beef, he fumbled with something unseen. A click was followed by a low grinding sound as a hatch opened in the ceiling and a telescoping stairway extended downward. There was nothing remarkable about this, Sam knew. It looked like the kind of retrofit attic stairway available from any home-improvement shopping site. What was unusual was its location.

Gesturing, Simmons led them upward. A motion

sensor activated lights in the room above. As soon as they were all upstairs, he used a rope to pull the hatch and stair arrangement up after them. This gave them a chance to take a quick survey of the converted, windowless storage room above the freezer.

A wide-eyed Leo was drawn immediately to the partial alien skull clamped to a table in the center of the room. As he reached out to touch it, Simmons intercepted him.

"Huh-uh. Still radioactive. Hands off."

As soon as he was confident the youth would comply, the ex-agent moved to a file cabinet and began yanking open drawers. Extracting an armful of file folders, he carried them over to an unoccupied table and dumped the pile. As they spread out and fell open their contents became visible: photos of ancient ruins, close-ups of hieroglyphs, cuneiform, and friezes. Many of them conveyed no decipherable information, while others were so obscure that Sam and his friends could not even recognize their origin. But some—not many, but some—boasted inscriptions that were by now immediately familiar.

Although the method of scribing and the materials employed differed, they were unquestionably the same symbols that Sam had drawn on the walls of his and Leo's dorm room.

Simmons didn't know that, of course. At least, not yet.

"Okay, Cube-brain. Any of these look like the symbols that've been coming out of your head?"

A bewildered Sam examined one folder after another. They were crammed with images and pictures drawn from a wide diversity of sites throughout the Middle East. "Where—where'd you get these?"

Sam's manifest confusion appeared to please the ex-agent. "Before I got fired, I did a little copying. Filled up some flash drives and helped myself to some 'scratch' paper. I poached Sector Seven's 'crown jewel'—over fifty years of research into alien 'scribbling.' A lot of it—most of it—is the kind of junk you'd expect to find in such files. Overhyped interpretations of well-known ideographs. Von Daniken-style leaping to conclusions unsupported by actual facts. Drawings that seemed to mean something that when examined by experts really mean nothing. But some of it, enough of it, when properly correlated with recent research and the latest findings and studied by someone with *actual knowledge of the facts . . .*" His voice trailed away.

Leo finished the observation for him. "Like you?"

"Modesty forbids me," Simmons responded.

"Since when?" Mikaela shot back.

He threw her a sour look, then returned his attention to Sam and Leo. "Analysis and distillation of the available evidence points to one inescapable fact. The Transformers? They didn't just show up a couple of years ago. They've been here a long, *long* time."

Now even the skeptical Mikaela was intrigued. "Like—how long?"

He could have taken the opportunity to reprove her. But this time the seriousness of the subject matter under discussion muted his natural inclination toward sarcasm, and he replied as if he was a teacher earnestly instructing a student newly enrolled in his course.

"*Way* B.C. Twice as long as you think, and then even longer than that. Leastwise, if my math is correct. I'm talkin' 'Quest for Fire' was the national pastime, the wheel was just coming into fashion, and we were all riding around on Snuffleupaguses." He saw the doubt in their faces.

"How do I know this? Archeologists found these unexplained markings in ancient ruins all over the world. Macedonia. Mohenjo Daro. China. Luxor. Each instance was explained away as being part of some alphabet or set of glyphs for which a Rosetta stone equivalent had yet to be found. So how'd they all end up looking the same, these drawing and symbols from completely different corners of the ancient world? From entirely unrelated civilizations? Well, the owners of that particular Rosetta stone showed up and started beating the crap out of each other, and we've been caught in the middle. They're *alien* symbols. Utilized by the originators and copied by those of our ancestors who saw them and were lucky enough not to get stomped for their trouble. And I think some of those alien originators *stayed*."

Leo was staring at the file photos and shaking his head. "No way, man. If even one of them had hung around, it would've been singled out and sketched by some primitive van der Rohe."

Simmons nodded slowly. "Sure it would—if it had remained in its original form. But these are Transformers, remember. They can take any mechanical shape. A cart first, then more complicated machinery." He indicated a wealth of drawings and photos. A cotton gin. A steam engine. One of the first Model Ts.

"Robots—in disguise," the ex-agent insisted triumphantly. "Hiding here all along."

Sam's mind was whirling. "Megatron said there's another Energon source on Earth. He thinks whatever's in my head'll lead him to it." Reaching up, he pushed hair back off his forehead. "His way of trying to obtain it was a little too straightforward."

Simmons considered. "Have you asked the Autobots what it is? Or where it might be located?"

Sam shook his head. "Tried to with a couple of them. They said the relevant language predates them."

The ex-agent let out a slow whistle. "And I thought the stuff *I* was working with went back a ways. Well then, we're porked. Too bad we can't ask a Decepticon."

"Excuse me." They both turned to Mikaela. "Actually," she informed them, "we can."

Simmons made a face at her. "Uh-huh, right. I suppose you carry around a spare Decepticon in your purse?"

Hands on hips, she met his gaze without blinking. "Close."

The bare table in Simmons's hideaway was more than sturdy enough to accommodate the metal box Mikaela brought from Bumblebee's trunk. Leo and the ex-agent eyed it with interest, Sam with apprehension.

"I see the latches," the ex-agent declared. "Want me to . . . ?"

"I'll do it. Just a sec." Picking up the tiny welding torch she had brought with her, Mikaela snapped it alight. A soft roar accompanied the intense blue flame as she approached the container and popped the catches. Holding the torch firmly in one hand, she used the other to lift the lid and peer inside.

"Come on out—but *behave* yourself."

Like a nightmare Jack-in-the-box, something small, shiny, and multi-limbed hopped out of the metal container. It trailed a chain that restricted its movements. Espying the torch, it scrambled as far away as the restraining links would allow.

"*Hothothot*—keep away, keep away!" Then it saw the partial skull of Frenzy clamped to another table nearby and the tiny Decepticon shrieked like a child—albeit one with a metal esophagus. Trying to calm it, Mikaela gave a sharp yank on the restraining chain.

An utterly flabbergasted Simmons observed this girl–Decepticon pas de deux in stunned silence before finally commenting in disbelief.

"Spent my whole adult life combing the planet for aliens. First as part of Sector Seven, then via libraries and the Net—and you're schlepping one around in your luggage like a little tinfoil chihuahua." He shook his head in amazement.

Wasting no time, Mikaela selected a couple of especially detailed photos from the ex-agent's vast collection and positioned them in front of the shackled Wheels.

"Speak English! What do these mean?"

The Decepticon examined the images closely, then drew back in surprise. "Ohh—language of Primes! Words before time. Me know not, know not me. Only Seekers can explain you."

Sam frowned. " 'Seekers'? Who are they?"

Metal limbs gestured excitedly at a number of the photos piled on the table. "*Seekers*. Old Transformers! Oldoldold. Stranded, stuck, searching for something." Despite his predicament and restraints, his tone turned scornful. "Seekers *seek*."

"Well, duh." Leo was delighted for a change to be entranced by a robot instead of terrified by one. "What we want to know is what they're seeking."

Wheels's response to that was more subdued. "Don't know what. Old language. Old seeking. Wheels not old."

Simmons's reaction was half triumph, half disdain. "See? *Told* you they were here. Nobody listens to Seymour Simmons. Years of experience means nothin' to pencil pushers and key kissers. All they're interested in is moving up a rating—not in results."

"*We're* interested." Mikaela spoke softly as she turned back to Wheels. "What are these Seekers? Decepticons? Autobots?"

"Both," the frazzled prisoner replied. "Battle-battle, race-race. They know ancient language. Only they can translate. I know where Seekers are!"

Simmons pulled a wall map out of some fixture in the ceiling. "Show us."

Wheels, barely able to contain his excitement, projected a laser at ten locations across the United States. "There! The Seekers!"

As a man whose obduracy had once again been justified, if only by a trio of teenagers, Simmons was clearly pleased. "Closest one's in Washington, D.C. You got exact coordinates?"

Simmons placed a GPS device in front of Wheels, who quickly jacked into it. The GPS beeped, and Simmons grabbed it back. With a satisfied smile, he looked at the others and said, "I got news for you, gang. We're gonna need *tickets* . . ."

✪ XII ✪

The drive to D.C. produced only one bad moment: when a convoy of three police cruisers came up behind them with lights flashing and sirens off. When Leo tried to look out Bumblebee's rear window, Simmons quickly grabbed him and shoved him back down in his seat. Though the younger man tried to resist, the ex-agent's grip was surprisingly strong.

"Take a tip from someone whose business this was, kid. Never show your face when you don't have to. It's good to see who's after you, yeah—but it's better if they never see *you*."

Up in front, Mikaela and Sam had already hunkered down as far as they could in an attempt to hinder identification. They need not have worried. The police convoy wasn't trailing them. All three cars sped on past in the fast lane, their mission and destination unknown.

They swung past the city and headed for the Dulles Airport zone without further incident, Sam having to occasionally remind the impatient Bumblebee to remain not just at but below the speed limit and Bumblebee having to remind the Twins not to go wandering off sightseeing. Getting to their destination slowly was better than not getting there at all. When eventually they pulled into a museum parking lot, Sam heaved a sigh of relief.

Simmons proceeded to scan the building through a pair of small binoculars. "Looks clear. Usual security measures in place but I don't see anything exceptional. Steven F. Udvar-Hazy Center—part of the Smithsonian Air and Space Museum. Land of dreams in there. All I ever wanted was to be an astronaut. Even took the test. Failed." The regret in his voice was palpable.

Mikaela was unrelenting. "Yeah, I don't really see you being one of the best and the brightest."

Lowering the binoculars, he growled softly. "*Hey*— I had a cold that week, sue me."

Seated beside the ex-agent, Leo studied the huge, rambling structure. "Okay, I'll kick it out here, man— I'm not dealing with no Deathbots."

Sam was resigned. "What's your website again? 'I'm One-Hundred-Percent-Useless-dot-com'?"

Bumblebee parked alongside an empty motor home while the Twins closed in behind. The tight grouping provided cover while Simmons passed out the gear he had brought with him. Like a demented Santa, the ex-agent handed out tasers, maps, and copies of file photos.

When he had finished and everyone had stowed their equipment, Simmons eyed them appraisingly. "Okay. Watches synchronized, sharp mind, and empty bladder. You get caught, demand an attorney and don't *ever* say my name." He held up what looked like an aspirin. "And keep this little white pill under your tongue. It's the high-concentrate patented sucrose polymer they put in Oreo cookies. Tricks the polygraph *every* time."

One hand resting on the pocket concealing his taser, Leo let out a groan. "Whaddya think I am—some alien bounty hunter? I look like Boba Fett to you? I'm *management,* not labor. I can't risk my life. The future needs me."

Grabbing him by the collar, Simmons pulled Sam's roommate close. Leo's eyes widened as those of the ex-agent peered into his own. Suddenly, Simmons seemed far less like an overage geek living with his mother and working in the family delicatessen than the former chief agent of a secret government organization.

"Kid? What do you think we're doing here? Getting ready to trade snide blog comments? This is *real*. This is *serious*. If you compromise this operation for the rest of us, you are *dead* to me. And I will make you dead to everyone else." He loosened his grip on the younger man's shirt. "Now—tighten your sphincter. You were *born* for this mission."

Swallowing as he adjusted his collar, Leo stammered, "I was?"

"All right, maybe not born for it, but you're part of it now. This isn't a video game. There are lives at stake. Lots of lives. Maybe a planet."

Spitz nodded. Slowly at first, then with increasing enthusiasm. He might not be confident, but he was ready.

Hours passed. Visitors from near and far wandered toward the exits of the enormous building, crowd the gift shop until the last possible moment before drifting out to their cars or public transportation or waiting tour buses. The vast hall of the Boeing Aviation hangar echoed to the repeated clarion call of a recorded message.

"*The museum is now closed. The museum is now closed.*"

The entry hallway was silent. Having taken over from the day shift, the recently arrived night security guards began to settle in for the evening. They had checked out their respective stations and were just beginning to peruse the first of a hamper full of stockpiled magazines when they were confronted by the bizarre sight of an apparently semi-stoned teenager staggering out the restroom exit, bare-assed and with his pants trolling his ankles.

"Yo, you guys got any toilet paper out there?"

Rising from his chair, the first guard's challenge was rich with the ripeness of outraged authority. "Sir, what are you *doing*?"

"Two words," Leo replied amiably. "Thumper dumper. It's a slow process." He gestured phlegmatically in the direction of the hall entrance. "Guess I kinda missed the closing bell, huh?"

"Please pull up your pants, sir," demanded the second guard, "and exit the building, *now*." As he spoke, his colleague was already striding rapidly across the floor to force Leo back into the bathroom.

Leo stood his ground. "My butt-cheeks are having ___ m with your totalitarian regime, buddy!"

___," declared the first guard impatiently as he ___ the overstayer, "janitorial doesn't come on

duty until eleven, and I personally don't want
to clean up . . ."

Leo waddled back into the bathroom with the
guard, reached into his pants, pulled out the taser,
and jammed it against the guard's side. Shocked in
every sense of the word, the burly watchman collapsed against the teen. The guard was quivering and
twitching—but still mobile. And now reaching with
shaking fingers for his own weapon. Starting to
panic, Leo zapped him a second time, promptly
tripped over the pants still down around his ankles,
and fell over on top of the activated taser. Entirely
egalitarian when it came to targets, the still-charged
device proceeded to shock *him*.

As teen and guard convulsed side by side, neither at
present preoccupied with the other, the alarmed second sentry came running toward them. In doing so he
passed a tableaux consisting of several famous test pilots arrayed in noble, welcoming poses. As soon as
the watchman had passed, one of the figures stepped
out from behind him and jammed a fresh taser into
his back.

"Textbook," Simmons declared calmly as the
guard fell forward onto his face. Pulling a roll of duct
tape from a pocket, the ex-agent proceeded to tape
the man's hands and ankles, slapping a thick wad of
tape over his mouth while leaving his nose uncovered
so he could breathe.

"Sorry," he said to the guard, "national security."

Concluding the task with efficiency born of long
practice, Simmons then walked over to where the
other occupants of the outer hall still lay on the floor.

Having taken two shocks, the first guard had passed out. Simmons taped him up, then turned his attention to Leo.

Gazing up at the ex-agent out of wide eyes, the teen was still twitching helplessly. "How many times can you . . . get tasered in the . . . jewels 'fore you can't have kids, huh? Anybody know?"

A disgusted Simmons grabbed him and began dragging him toward the information desk. "You're pullin' your own pants up."

Outside, a brightly painted Camaro abruptly hurled itself onto the entry terrace. It was followed by a pair of garish cars doing doughnuts. When angry shouts and warning cries from the parking lot guards failed to send the three vehicles packing, the irate sentinels piled into their own official vehicles and took off in pursuit.

Back in the Aviation Wing, Sam and Mikaela emerged from the MIG engine exhibit in which they had been hiding. A quick look around showed that their immediate vicinity, at least, was now completely deserted. Withdrawing a small container from a pocket, Mikaela returned it to its owner. Sam did not have to ask what was inside; he remembered all too well. The cylindrical canister held the splinter of the Allspark. Maybe, he thought as he turned and started walking toward the main exhibits, the *only* surviving splinter of the Allspark.

"C'mon," he muttered as he and Mikaela strode silently among the well-preserved relics of humankind's first steps into the sky and the great void of space beyond, "show me something." Reaching into his own pocket, he withdrew a pair of tweezers. Carefully extracted from its container, the splinter did not look like much. Its passive appearance notwithstanding, Sam knew it might well be the single most important object on the planet.

They continued on, past the *Enola Gay,* past numerous other aircraft suspended from the high ceiling, with Sam holding the tweezered splinter out in front of him like a minuscule divining rod. Having rejoined his young companions Simmons trailed behind, his attention fixed on the small radiation tracker he was holding.

Back at the info desk, Leo grabbed the microphone, his voice booming through the open space, "Museum's closed, bitches!"

Sam came to an abrupt stop. Held firmly in the grip of the steel tweezers, the splinter had begun to glow faintly. It jerked once, twice, then started to vibrate steadily, forcing him to hold the tweezers tightly with both hands. His effort ultimately proved useless.

Before Simmons or anyone else could intervene, the splinter flew out of the tweezer's grasp and shot upward. As the ex-agent let out a cry of frustration, the fragment smacked into one of the metal struts that comprised the landing gear of a suspended SR-71 Blackbird. While the humans clustered below looked on in rising astonishment, the landing gear began to glow. Leo tried to turn and run, but his legs were still in no condition to obey him.

The light intensified and, with a single burst, rushed through the entire body of the sleek, twin-engined spy plane. Gazing up at it even as he was taking a couple of precautionary steps backward, Simmons was muttering knowingly to himself.

"SR-71 Blackbird spy plane. Still the fastest in the world. *Figures.*"

Starting to retreat, Sam and Mikaela saw the symbol that had begun to pulsate on the underbelly of the streamlined aircraft. By now it was as familiar to both of them as it was unwelcome.

It was the Decepticon symbol.

"Oh, shit," Sam mumbled as he sought cover for himself and Mikaela.

Above them the still-striking aircraft began to shift shape, to change in outline and in body. Having witnessed the process numerous times before, Sam and Mikaela exchanged a glance. What was taking place in front of their eyes in the great hall of the museum was unfolding according to those same previously observed transformations—but more slowly, and with the added component of a great deal of inorganic grinding and metallic wheezing.

When after what seemed like an interminable period of time the fully altered life-form finally completed its conversion, it straightened slowly—and promptly banged its head on the *Apollo 12* capsule that was also hanging from the ceiling. Regardless of whether the impact was what caused it to drop heavily to the floor and roll, there was no mistaking the symbol it flashed as it turned.

"*Decepticon!*" Backing up fast now, Simmons pointed to the display that dominated one far wall. "Everybody behind the MIG, *now!*"

No one needed to be told twice. As they raced for cover, the newly formed Decepticon let out a terrifying howl—half dominating robotic life-form voice and half twin jet engines.

The howl proceeded to drop to a scream and th^e to a whine before finally petering out in the unmistakable mechanical equivalent of a deep-seated cough.

"Aww, fragbottom—too low on juice—why bother . . ."

Their caution mixed with new uncertainty, the four humans peered out from behind the cover of the MIG display. As they stared at the ancient Decepticon, a set of lenses materialized from his head to flip down over his eyes. Scrutinizing them from a distance, Sam decided that more than anything else they resembled a pair of oversize if high-tech spectacles.

Turning slowly and squinting through the newly formed transparencies, the Decepticon struggled to make sense of his surroundings.

"Who's there? *Show yourself!* I'll annihilate each and every one of you!" The massive, angular head seemed to squeak slightly as it rotated, the eyes studying their immediate surroundings until they located the humans who were cowering off to one side.

"Fleshlings? Speak and identify yourselves, or suffer my wrath!" One huge arm came up and they could clearly see the missiles slotted in the rotating barrel.

Singled out and with nowhere to run, Sam felt it incumbent on himself to take the lead—wherever it led. Stepping out from behind the inadequate cover of the MIG exhibit, he took a couple of hesitant steps toward the towering alien. Familiarity with Decepticon and Autobot weapons caused him to keep his eyes fixed on the missile-laden barrel arm. If it started to rotate, or to whine, the best he could do was sprint

and hope the resultant fire was concen-
on him. At least it might give Mikaela and the
others a chance to escape.

"Yessir," he began politely as he continued his
watchful advance. "Sorry about the abrupt wake-up.
Accident. You can go back to sleep-shape now. We
won't bother you any mo . . ."

The activated armament arm with its load of missiles inclined downward in his direction and he
halted. As the arm declined, the missiles within unexpectedly slid out. One by one, they fell to the floor.
Wincing each time one hit, Sam turned away, but not
one of the unsecured explosives went off. After the
last had been dumped and as his tentative companions rejoined him, he tried to come up with an appropriate explanation for what had just happened. Two
words he had never anticipated using in the same sentence came quickly to mind—"ordnance" and "in-
continence." He did not voice them aloud. The
defective Decepticon could still step on him.

"Ah, crap," the giant bipedal shape muttered to itself as he bent to recover the unwillingly discarded
missiles. Before metal fingers could close around the
first one, his owner let out a metallic groan and his
arm began to tremble. Unbending with an obvious effort, he turned to go.

"Name is . . ." The Decepticon paused for a moment, seeking an appropriate descriptive based on the
brief bit of conversation he had absorbed from Sam
and those who had been whispering behind him.
"Name's Jetfire. I'm on a mission; no time for chit-
chat."

Lumbering forward and appearing to drag one leg

slightly, the giant headed for the main hangar door. Confronted by the barrier, he paused to examine the massive portal for a moment. Then one hand reached out, again shakily, and a finger touched a point where the door made contact with the wall. A couple of sparks flared and the door, its alarm system bypassed, began to trundle aside. As soon as the gap was wide enough, the Decepticon stepped through and out into the high-walled storage yard beyond.

Frowning, Simmons gestured to his youthful co-horts and followed. "Uh, something's a little off here. This one seems kinda dingy."

Sam moved up alongside the ex-agent. "He sure doesn't act very Decepticon-like. I don't think he's gonna hurt us."

Leo was looking back at the missile-laden floor. "I'm not sure he *can* hurt us. Reminds me of my Aunt Ethel. She was always trying to swing her cane at us kids but she could never get it more than halfway off the ground."

"Why didn't she hit you in the knee, then?" Mikaela asked tartly.

Leo shrugged. "She probably would've fallen over." He increased his pace to catch up to Simmons and Sam. The faint migratory moan of police sirens could now be heard in the distance.

As they passed the exhibit that featured the *Apollo 12* capsule, Simmons came to an unexpected halt. Sam eyed him questioningly.

"Just—just—just lemme do this," the ex-agent murmured. There was a catch in his voice Sam had never heard there before.

Carefully stepping over the low barrier and supplementary explanatory displays, Simmons climbed into the open capsule and settled himself snugly into the first seat. The smile that subsequently spread across his face seemed as unlikely as the restored Decepticon that was currently tottering into the museum's main outdoor storage area.

"Houston?" he murmured softly. "Captain Seymour Simmons, ready for my ticker-tape parade. Over and out."

He lingered in the capsule a moment longer. Then, beset by the fears, concerns, and paranoia that had come to dominate his life for the past several years, he climbed back out and ran to catch up to the trio of teens.

Moving even more slowly now than he had within the display hangar, the giant appeared bewildered by his new surroundings. Bits and pieces of hundreds of old aircraft and related machinery filled the storage yard to near capacity. None of it looked familiar to the old alien: not the technology, not the materials, not even the high fences that enclosed it all.

Trying to get in front of the suddenly indecisive entity, Sam was waving his arms and shouting for attention. "Hey, Mr. Jetfire! Stop. We just wanna talk to you, please!"

Something in Sam's attitude, or perhaps in his tone, persuaded the giant to halt. More likely it was due to the thought that had just occurred to him.

"Wait. Where am I going? What planet am I on?" As he scrutinized his immediate surroundings, his bewilderment only increased. "This doesn't look—

right. Doesn't look right, doesn't sound right, doesn't *feel* right."

"Uh," Sam ventured, "this is Earth."

Gazing up at the stricken, disorientated giant, Mikaela found herself experiencing something she never thought she would feel in the presence of a Decepticon—sympathy.

"You—you don't remember where you are?"

The great head squealed as it swiveled to look down at her. "Reach a certain mileage, Milady, the old circuitry begins to fail you. Tell me—is that point-less war still going on? Decepticons: such heathens and cowards! That's why I defected to the Autobots. Can't we all just get along?"

A small, gleaming shape scurried past the staring humans. Trailing a piece of the chain that had been used to restrain him and moving too fast for either Sam or Mikaela to grab, Wheels raced toward the towering robot. The smaller Decepticon had finally managed to break free of the metal box in which he had been imprisoned. All four humans watched help-lessly as the giant who called himself Jetfire scooped up his far tinier relation and brought him close to his face. While Sam and his companions looked on, the two machines began to converse energetically in their own language.

"They're talking much too fast for me to catch any-thing." Mikaela found herself fascinated by the ver-bal electronic byplay even as she wondered if it might be prudent to start running at full speed in the oppo-site direction. "Wonder what they're saying to each other."

all humans." Leo smiled wanly.

was shaking his head. "It doesn't sound hostile." He eyed the ex-agent. "What do you think?"

Simmons grinned contentedly. "What? You want *my* opinion again?" His attention swung back to the two briskly chattering robots. "I don't get it. The big one acts like he's escaped from someplace more medically oriented than a museum and the small one is yapping and dancing around like a puppy. I *will* agree with you that neither activity seems to presage the imminent deployment of lethal force. Of course, I'm templating human motivations onto alien mentalities. There's no telling what they might decide to do."

Whatever Sam and Simmons believed the Decepticons' next move would be, it was safe to say that neither man was anywhere near the actual mark.

Doing a backflip off Jetfire, Wheels landed next to Mikaela and reached out to grab one leg. Letting out a yelp, Leo jumped to one side. An equally alarmed Sam started toward Mikaela, only to have Simmons hold him back. The metal limbs gripping her leg were not twisting, not cutting, not piercing. They were . . .

Hugging?

Wheels was babbling anew in English. "Jetfire says can change sides! Change sides! Wheels on Warrior Goddess side. I worship Warrior Goddess! Need discipline!"

Her expression that of someone who had just stepped in something unappetizing, Mikaela struggled to shake off the clinging Decepticon. Refusing to be dislodged, Wheels clung to her tightly. Sam fought unsuccessfully to repress a smirk.

"Hey look, your new sadomasochist boyfriend needs discipline."

"Oh, that's cute," she growled at him. "Bet he's a better kisser than your dead girlfriend."

"Probably not as shocking," Sam snapped back.

They were interrupted by a flatulent *ploof!* as a large trapezoidal parachute unfurled from the general vicinity of Jetfire's dorsal zone. Catching the breeze that was gusting through the storage yard, the 'chute ballooned to its fullest diameter. Limited though it was, the resultant tug was enough to cause the ancient Decepticon to totter backward. Tripping over part of the fuselage of a yet-to-be-restored Antonov prop job, the alien landed backside first before collapsing all the way onto his back. Having reflexively self-conditioned himself to speak in the current dominant language, his words were probably more intelligible than he would have preferred.

"Seeping selenium sealants! Can't even *walk* properly. Updating says I've been stuck on this miserable little world for thousands of orbits around its insignificant little sun and that I've got a mission, but I keep forgetting what it *was*. Wait! Of course! We must destroy the dinosaurs!"

"Uh . . . I think that kinda happened already," offered Mikaela helpfully.

Still tentative but less afraid now, Sam approached the recumbent robot as closely as he dared. A dark shard on the ground nearby caught his eye. Bending, he quickly scooped up the scorched splinter of the Allspark from where it had fallen, having been jolted loose from the Decepticon by his fall.

"Uh, Sir? Mr. Jetfire? If you can help me, maybe I can help you."

Enormous inorganic eyes shifted to focus on him. "You? Help *me*? You are only a small fleshling of limited physical strength and low-energy neurological output whose cognitive abilities are additionally restricted by limited cerebral development that is confined within a fixed calcium-based envelope."

Mikaela nodded knowingly. "That's what *I* keep telling him."

Sam drew himself up to his full height. "Yeah, but I'm a small fleshling of limited physical strength and low-energy neurological output whose cognitive abilities are additionally restricted by limited cerebral development that is confined within a fixed calcium-based envelope *who knows something you don't know.*"

He manfully resisted the urge to stick his tongue out at both of them.

Symbol after precise symbol appeared as Sam traced line after line of ancient knowledge in the dirt of the storage yard with the tip of his fleshling finger. He looked as if he would keep at it until he fell over when an empathetic Mikaela finally reached out and gently placed her hand over his.

"Give it a rest, Sam. And remember to breathe once in a while." She eyed him with concern. "You were starting to turn blue."

Blinking and breathing deeply, he sat back and gazed in wonderment at everything he had just etched into the ground. What did it all mean?

It had better mean something, he thought. The police sirens they had been hearing for a while were noticeably louder now. Also, the hand he had been drawing with had gone to sleep. He tried to shake some feeling back into his numbed fingers.

"It just keeps coming. I get the feeling I could write this stuff forever."

Squinting through his lenses, Jetfire reacted in astonishment to the human's handiwork. "The Fallen? As in *The* Fallen?" Genuine excitement leached through the aged metal. "Young fleshling, you may have saved us all. *Now* I remember what I was seeking." His voice faded slightly as recollection filled him. "The Dagger—the Kings! And the key, of course, the key."

Sam and the others gaped at the babbling Decepticon. "*What* key? What dagger?"

"No time to explain." The alien seemed more alert than at any time since the splinter of the Allspark had revived him. "We have to get there before I forget where we're going!"

Raising his hands defensively, Simmons took a wary step backward. "Wait, *wait*—where? *Get where?*"

"To where we have to go, of course." Jetfire's tone implied that anyone who bothered to ask such foolish questions was more than a little intellectually challenged. "C'mon, you dimensionally challenged runts, have faith. Gather tight, stand still now, hurry! And let's just pray all my circuits are firing."

Mikaela's gaze had narrowed. "Why do *we* need to stand still?"

"So your parts get there in one piece," the former Decepticon explained amiably.

"*One* piece? As opposed to *what*?" Leo stammered.

Instead of replying, the Decepticon began to shudder. Violent groans and metallic grinding noises sounded from deep within his huge body. Behind their magnifying lenses the glowing eyes went dim as he appeared to be exerting himself toward some unknown end with every iota of his being. His voice, however, still resounded clear and intelligible, if plainly under great strain.

"Technology of—the Ancients. Discontinued in later models due to excessive rate of failure—reportedly prone to—catastrophic malfunction."

Leo swallowed hard, wondering if he should run like hell or if it was already too late and taking off running might result in his "parts" being scattered all over the storage yard. The police sirens were very loud now. He found himself hoping the cops would show—and fearing what would happen if they did. Something inside him, some instinct, was insisting loudly that this was not a good time to deal with such outside interference.

"Catastrophic," he muttered. "I hate that word . . ."

A tremendous convulsion shook the Decepticon. His armored breastplate began to open, the sections parting to expose his spark. Rising up from the ground (or maybe down from the sky—Sam couldn't be sure), a swirling blue vortex began to engulf them all. At that point the Witwicky gene for survival kicked in and he shouted at the top of his lungs.

"I think—we should run!"

He turned to do so. So did Mikaela, Leo, and Simmons. None of them made it more than a couple of steps from the now-violently vibrating, mechanically shrieking Jetfire before his spark expanded into a ball of blinding blue fire spitting forks of blue lightning in all directions. Expanding wildly, growing with unrestrained speed, it engulfed the stunned onlookers before spreading to parts of the museum itself—including the rear parking lot. Looking back as he tried to flee, Sam saw one such bolt firing in slow motion directly at him. His eyes widened and he opened his mouth to . . .

☷ XIII ☶

Normally at this time of day the fennec would be asleep in its den. Movement outside the opening had tickled it awake and drawn it forth into the blazing sun. Not that it was disappointed to have had its daytime rest disturbed. The fat lizard that had probed the opening was still close by and would make a fine meal.

It was just about to pounce when the earth exploded.

Two figures shot skyward out of the sand on either side of the startled fox. One was large, metallic, and troubled. The other was smaller, fleshy, and screaming. After rising twenty or so feet into the air from their respective points of ejection, both Bumblebee and Sam hit the ground hard. Adjusting his position in midair according to the precepts of his internal gyroscopic system, the yellow-and-black Autobot had no difficulty with the landing. His human counterpart was not so fortunate, ending up in a jumble of arms and legs. Thankfully, the soft sand helped cushion his fall.

Sand?

Struggling to a sitting position, a baffled Sam first checked to ensure that nothing was broken before beginning to study his surroundings. The desert expanse that stretched out before him in every direction was beautiful, the rust and ocher hues precise and sharply etched in a way no landscape of a mid-Atlantic state like New Jersey could ever match, the cute little big-eared fox gaping back at him lithe and limber and . . .

Hastily making tracks for the nearest hillside as it rushed to flee the location of inexplicable occurrences.

It was good that it did so, as three more figures who did not belong in its home territory burst out of the ground not far away from the first two. Training told Simmons he needed to roll over and take the measure of his surroundings the instant he hit the ground. The pain that was running through his body from teeth to toenails insisted otherwise. Pain won, and he lay where he had landed, groaning. Nearby, the Twins sat up and took stock of themselves, checking readouts, appendages, and assorted perceptive instrumentation.

The last two shapes to emerge geyserlike from the sand landed several hundred yards away from the others. Leo hit the ground first as Mikaela came down hard on top of him. The instant she tumbled off he rolled over, spitting out desert while clutching at himself.

"Whoa," he moaned sickly, "I was having this beautiful erotic dream about you." His face was screwed up in a rictus of pain. "Then I realized you had just landed on my testicles." Turning aw...
buried his face in the sand.

Regrouping, they walked up to the recumbent Jetfire. No one objected when Sam took the lead. The Decepticon was lying on his back on a rocky outcrop that protruded from the sand.

"What the—where are we?" Sam asked him.

"As still named according to your ancient tribal designations, Egypt. I told you."

Sam stared at the prone Transformer. "You didn't tell us *anything*! You—you blue-lighted us and something loud and painful and hallucinogenic happened and there was five seconds of Ted Nugent meets Thor and then . . . !" He forced himself to stop and catch his breath. "What d'you mean we're in *Egypt*?"

Jetfire ignored him. "Ohhh—my aching epidermal alloys! Haven't done transspatial porting for a long time."

Simmons frowned. " 'Porting'? As in going through a 'portal'?"

The Decepticon sounded pleased. "Oh, yeah. Fast, huh? Everyone check your appendages, make sure nobody is missing anything. Or got it switched." Sitting up, he began to take stock of their surroundings. "Hmm—I thought there'd be a particular body of water near here. It's gotta be close. My coordinates must be off by a little bit."

Sam was turning a slow circle, studying the environment while trying to make some sense of what had happened. "We're in Egypt? Halfway to halfway around the world? But *why*?"

Jetfire harrumphed softly. "Can't you fleshlings remember anything? I thought I explained that."

His hands balling into fists at his sides, Simmons glared at the Decepticon. "No, you didn't! You explained nothing!"

"Oh, right." Swinging his massive legs off the rock, Jetfire regarded the unlikely assembly of humans and Autobots. But while he took the measure of them all, the bulk of his attention remained focused on Sam.

"Your symbols, boy. They're a story. The greatest story ever told. The history of our race. How we began. And," his voice dropped slightly, "how we came to be divided." Raising a creaky arm, he gestured outward, taking in the vast sweep of empty desert.

"Long ago on these very lands a legendary battle was fought. A monumental slaughter that divided us all . . ."

Listening in rapt silence, the four humans and three Autobots waited for the old Decepticon to continue. Jetfire regarded them with paternal contentment.

Several minutes of extended paternal contentment led Leo to finally exclaim impatiently, "*And . . . ?*"

Jetfire peered down at the young human. "And what?" he inquired placidly.

"What about the *battle*?" an annoyed Sam inquired.

The old Decepticon was perfectly bemused by the question. "What battle?"

Sam rolled his eyes. "Aw, c'mon, pay attention, man! You saw what the wind did to my inscriptions. Don't make me draw those symbols all over again." For emphasis, he let his right hand flap loosely on its wrist.

The young human's conveyance of urgency seemed to jog something in Jetfire's memory. He was about to respond when a rising buzz in the air attracted his attention. It also drew curious stares from his audience.

The source of the buzz turned out to be a biplane of World War I vintage, only instead of a Maltese cross or French bull's-eye it flaunted Decepticon markings. Circling once, it then came in low and slow on a course that would send it directly at the placid figure of Jetfire. Humans and Autobots started to scatter, but before they could disperse the biplane's buzz choked, started up again, and then died as the unimposing aircraft nosedived into the ground at the Decepticon's feet. Covering Mikaela, Sam backed away as the biplane changed shape from terrestrial guise into bipedal form. Leo and Simmons retreated as well, but not the Autobots. Bumblebee regarded the interloper curiously, while the Twins set to arguing between themselves as to its true nature.

"Well, if it ain't Jetfire," the altered airplane declared boldly. "When you open up a transspatial portal, that kind of energy discharge is bound to draw attention—you no-good yellow-bellied traitor!"

At this Bumblebee took an angry step forward, only to have Sam move sideways to block the Autobot's path.

"Metaphor," Sam murmured. "That's all." He nodded in the direction of the looming confrontation. "They kinda seem to know each other. Let them settle it." Reluctantly, Bumblebee stood down.

"Been looking for you for a long time," the altered biplane muttered. "You think you can just mosey out on us?" He gestured contemptuously to his right. "Help *humans*? Today we *settle* things. Just you and me."

Drawing his arm-mounted weapons, he let loose with a volley consisting of—a single shot. It pinged harmlessly off the uncomplaining Jetfire. He eyed the spent shell thoughtfully, then raised a massive foot and brought it down hard. The silent desert air was treated to the atypical crunch of metal crumpling.

"Always disliked him," Jetfire commented. Lifting the foot he had brought down, he began scraping detritus from the underside. "But yes, now it all comes back. Ah, the timing of remembrances! We were Seekers, me and that angry little fellow there. Among others. What were we searching for?" Before Sam or Leo could say anything, he continued. "Glad I asked." He leaned forward. "Would you like to see?"

Leo spoke up uncertainly. "See? You mean, hear."

"No. I mean what I say—when I can remember to say what I mean. That's what I meant. I mean see."

And so see-saying, an image was projected from his chest. Three-dimensional, irregular in outline, it floated before an audience composed of three young humans, three much older Autobots, and one semi-paranoid obsessed curmudgeon who despite everything that had happened recently, including a substantial transspatial dislocation, still smelled faintly of pastrami and lox.

Everyone stared. It was, a part of Sam reflec

awe, the first time since he had made their acquaintance that the Twins had been motionless and silent for more than a couple of moments. In the center of the image was a pool. Surrounding it were thirteen massive but indistinct robotic forms. In the middle—in the middle was . . .

A reverential croak rose from deep within Bumblebee's still-impaired vocal apparatus.

"All—sparkkk. . . ."

"In the beginning," Jetfire intoned, his voice having regained some of the inherent dignity that attends great age, "we were ruled by the Dynasty of Primes—the first thirteen Transformers, created by the Allspark to bring life to Cybertron. And as Energon was scarce, the Allspark forged us a means to obtain more."

Motion infused the image. The pool in the center seemed to weep a tear of silver plasma. Within the daggerlike sliver a crystalline shape formed.

"The Matrix of Leadership," Jetfire explained solemnly. "Simultaneously a key and a driving force containing essence of the Allspark itself, it is used to both activate and power the Great Machine . . . a machine built to destroy suns and collect their raw energy."

"Wait a minute." Sam was gazing intently at the storytelling Decepticon. " 'Destroy suns'? Like blow 'em up?"

"Uh, we kinda need our sun," said Mikaela.

"Fortunate for you," replied Jetfire, "the Primes were bound by one rule. Life is precious . . ."

"That's what I've been telling everybody all day," agreed a self-satisfied Leo.

". . . thus any star system inhabited by living beings must be spared."

Mikaela spoke up, her tone subdued. "What happened to this 'Matrix of Leadership'?"

Jetfire was staring off into the distance, seeing something long ago and far away. "One of the Primes defied all the rules. 'The Fallen.' " At Jetfire's mention of the name, the otherwise cloudless sky seemed to darken slightly. "To claim the Matrix for himself, he murdered his brothers. All but one, who escaped with it. The Great Machine was left abandoned, too dangerous to be used.

"This last, noble Prime hid the Matrix . . . in a tomb built from the bodies of his brothers. And as a final sacrifice, he sealed it from within." He looked down at his spellbound listeners.

"This was done so that your sun would be spared, and your species would survive.

"The human race evolved, multiplied, and matured. Some of your first cities were built over scraps of our history, founded on rumors of an ancient greatness that had once dwelled, however temporarily, in such places." Once again an arm rose to encompass their pristine surroundings. It was silent for a long while. Somewhere, a desert crow called.

Sam was trying to make sense of it all. "This all started *here*—in the presence of our ancestors?"

"And The Fallen intends to finish it. If he claims the Matrix, he'll use it to activate the Machine. Once it begins to draw upon the fires of your sun to create Energon, there is a very real chance that all life on your planet will end."

"Then how do we stop him?" asked Mikaela.

"Only a Prime can defeat The Fallen. That is why he returned to Cybertron to wage war. All direct descendents of The Prime Dynasty were slaughtered. Except for one who was hidden away, an orphan, forever unaware of his destiny."

Sam looked up in recognition. "Optimus Prime."

"You've met one named 'Prime'? Alive? Here on this planet?" Jetfire inquired in surprise.

"He sacrificed himself . . . to save me."

"A Prime indeed, and a tragedy."

Reaching into a pocket, Sam withdrew the charred splinter of Allspark that had so forcefully and unexpectedly revived Jetfire and that he had recovered from the museum storage yard. An idea that had been growing in the back of his mind now moved to the forefront of his thoughts.

"You said the Matrix was made by the Allspark. It was *part* of the Allspark."

Jetfire nodded in confirmation. "Aye, they share the same energy." He looked thoughtful.

Sam voiced a thought that had been growing rapidly in his mind. "Just a touch of that energy brought Megatron back. So is there any chance contact with this Matrix might work for—Optimus?"

Mikaela stared at him. "Optimus?"

"To heal him and bring him out of stasis lock."

Jetfire considered carefully. "Hmm. Never been tried. But an interesting concept. Such is not the purpose of the Matrix. It is the key to activating the Great Machine. Then again, it holds a power beyond all understanding."

"Then how do we find the Matrix before the Decepticons find me?"

Tilting back his head, Jetfire let his lenses catch the sun. "All I can do is translate your symbols. I'm no longer any good to you. Were I to attempt to continue on with you, I fear I would only draw unwanted attention." His eyes began to dim.

"Wait!" Sam stepped forward anxiously. "You didn't tell us how to find it."

"Sadly, I don't know. Never managed to reach it myself. All I can do is translate relevant text as it was set down, utilizing the most recent terms and references I recall that might have some meaning to you. 'When dawn alights the Dagger's tip, Three Kings will lead the way.' "

" 'Dagger's tip'?" Mikaela's tone reflected her confusion. "What 'three kings'?"

There was no response. The rangy, metallic head fell forward, the sharp-edged chin came to rest on Jetfire's chest, and the aged Decepticon was silent.

Leo had reached his limit again. "No way. I'm not going on your little scavenger hunt. Life's precious, especially mine; he said so himself. Who's with me? *Vamanos! Viva la revolución!*"

Leo sat down in the sand next to the silent Jetfire. But rather than reply to his most recent outburst, Sam and Mikaela simply turned and hopped into Bumblebee, ready for the next stage.

Simmons turned to Leo. "Better if you stay; you're slowing down the mission. Give ya twenty minutes before the vultures start pickin' at ya like lunch meat. Try swallowing your tongue, end it quick, go out with dignity."

"Good luck, Leo," Mikaela called from Bumblebee.

"Yeah, enjoy the heat," added Sam.

"YOU GUYS SUCK!" was the best Leo could do.

Bumblebee roared off, followed closely by the Twins. Left alone, Leo panicked and started running after the departing cars. "Wait, don't leave me with this old-ass plane!"

Point made, Bumblebee slowed and allowed Leo to jump in the backseat.

The vehicles sat silently in their barred containers. To an outsider they looked like any shipment of cars and trucks being prepped for transport. One who knew them for what they actually were might have considered them chained prisoners. They made no noise, gave no evidence that they were anything other than what they appeared to be. Invisibly, imperceptibly, they conversed silently among themselves on frequencies undetectable to the covey of armed humans working around them.

This was what Optimus had wanted, the group decided, so this was how they would respond. They would not resist; they would not fight back. Despite the current situation, it was not humans who were their enemies. Those remained farther afield and out of reach. The Autobots would stay quiet and quiescent in their present terrestrial guises. Only time would resolve the existing deadlock in which they found themselves.

As Autobots, they knew all about time.

A couple of the humans looking on from nearby

had no such extended concept of time. Unlike their Autobot friends, they were angry and impatient. But there was nothing either Lennox or Epps could do except watch as their friends and allies were bundled up like so many Detroit rejects for transshipment under guard back to Diego Garcia. The authorities in Washington who currently held sway over such matters would not allow them to travel back to NEST's base of operations unfettered and without guards. Given all that the surviving Autobots had done for humankind, Lennox thought it insulting and Epps, downright harsh.

Worse, it was undignified.

It might have encouraged the two men if they had been present at the discussion that was even then taking place in the depths of the Pentagon. Having convened in the "tank," as it was called, the Joint Chiefs were no less upset than the two lesser-ranking members of NEST.

"How can the President accept the loss of five thousand sailors, marines, and observers and do nothing?" The army chief of staff did not quite pound on the table with his fist—such melodramatic reactions were the province of cinema, not real life. But he wanted to.

His air force counterpart voiced the frustration that was seething in all of them. "What can he do? We have no one to retaliate against. Not anyone that we can locate."

"Or any *thing*," added the navy's second-highest-ranking admiral.

Morshower was too tired to shout. In any case, those he wished to rage against were not among the men present.

"Even if we find *them*, with my team on ice we've lost our best ally against the enemy."

The army chief met the chairman's gaze. "What about our ongoing efforts to have the Autobots restored to active engagement?"

Morshower shook his head. "The administration needs a scapegoat for the loss of the *Lincoln*, and the French haven't let up alternating requests for explanation with demands for retribution." He smiled thinly. "You know how it is when you're running a country. If you can't eliminate the real enemy, invent one you can deal with. We have no influence over these Decepticons, but we do over the Autobots. So— the Autobots take the fall."

The chief of the navy summed up the situation succinctly: "It stinks."

Morshower nodded in agreement. "Like old motor oil. But we have to live with it, gentlemen. Unless something happens to alter the existing situation."

Leaning back in his chair, the army chief slumped against the thickly padded backrest. "Sometimes at times like this I wish I'd stayed in Payroll. That's one part of the military where everybody leaves you alone to do your job."

"When dawn alights the Dagger's tip, Three Kings will lead the way." Repeating Jetfire's mantra didn't make Leo feel any more confident of success. What he wanted more than anything else was to be back in his comfortable, utterly ordinary dorm room.

In short, he desperately wished to be normal again.

Instead of normality, he found himself riding in the backseat of a car that wasn't a car alongside a spectacularly alluring girl who wasn't his girl as they trundled down a desert road on the approach to greater Cairo in search of some potentially world-destroying ancient artifact that might or might not even exist. The rest of his company consisted of alien robots of varying size, capabilities, and in the case of the Twins, sanity; a perpetually paranoid ex–government agent; and his roommate, who might simultaneously be more important and crazier than any of them. Leo Spitz licked dry lips.

What he wouldn't give for a cheap, pseudo-beef hamburger and a Coke the size of a bed pillow!

Simmons had been working his cell phone ever since they had come in adequate pickup range of a relay tower. It had taken longer than expected to acquire the information he sought, because he had been forced to go through multiple channels and numbers in order to avoid being traced. But he had eventually been able to obtain answers to some of his questions.

"Old secret agents never die," he explained with a sly smile. "They just set up their own networks."

"So, what were you able to find out?" Seated behind the wheel of the Camaro, Sam kept his eyes on the pair of compact vehicles that were leading the way. Each boasted a rezzed simulation of a driver lifted from a car billboard. That these advertisements had featured supermodels had not yet attracted undue attention.

Simmons spoke without turning, likewise keeping his attention forward. "Okay, here's what my CIA contact in general history says. Because of its shape, the ancient Israelites used to call the Gulf of Aqaba 'the Dagger.' It's part of the Red Sea, divides Egypt and Jordan like the tip of a blade, with a bit of Israel occupying the topmost portion."

Leo spoke up from the backseat. "Jetfire referred to a body of water. Maybe he was talking about the Gulf of Aqaba."

Simmons nodded approvingly as he squinted at the image being displayed on his phone. "At the very tip the Israelis have a long-established holiday town called Elat, and the Egyptian side around Ras al Masri is lined with resort hotels and scuba safari enterprises. But the Jordanian side is pretty deserted except for the town of Aqaba itself. So we know what the 'dagger' is. What we don't know is how these 'Three Kings' relate to it."

"Uh-oh," Sam murmured.

They were approaching a police checkpoint, the first of its kind they had encountered since rumbling out of the western desert. Idling in wait, Sam watched nervously as first Skids and then Mudflap were waved through.

"How'd they do that? I can understand the sim drivers passing for human, but what'd they use for papers?"

Leo ventured a possible explanation. "Did you see the women the Twins reproduced to put in their drivers' seats? If you were an Egyptian cop stuck out here in the wind and the sand all day and someone who looked like a cross between Gisele Bündchen and Tyra Banks suddenly showed up at your gate, would you spend your time asking for papers—or staring at simulated boobies?"

In the seat next to him, Mikaela shook her head knowingly. *"Men."*

One of the guards was gesturing for them to come forward as his colleagues gazed, no doubt longingly, after the departing Twins. Sam lightly tapped the wheel.

"Okay, okay, we gotta go—we can do this."

"Yeah?" From behind him, Leo voiced skepticism. "What're *you* gonna flash 'em, Sam? Your winning smile?"

"Shut up, shut up, lemme think." His fingers gripped the steering wheel more tightly as Bumblebee edged toward the checkpoint.

Simmons tried to dispel the growing anxiety among his youthful companions. "Let me do the talking. Everybody be chill; these are my people."

Sam looked around sharply. "I thought 'your people' were Jewish."

"I'm one thirty-sixth Arab," the ex-agent informed him. "Hey, kosher, halal—it's all the same thing."

While Sam kept his window up Simmons rolled his down, greeting the approaching guard with a wide smile and a blast of air-conditioning. Bending forward the guard glanced inside, no doubt regretting that this unexpected and striking American car was not occupied by more of the recently departed supermodels.

"Rayih fayn?"

By way of reply, Simmons nodded emphatically.

His eyes fixed on the road ahead, Sam muttered without turning. "What's he saying?"

Continuing to nod and smile at the guard, the ex-agent replied cheerfully, "No idea."

The guard's dazed expression, a legacy of the Twins' rezzed supermodels, was beginning to wear off fast. *"Rayih fayn?"* he asked again, more forcefully this time. *"Ismak? Bit amal? Bititkallam Arabee?"*

As the man continued to pepper Simmons with increasingly agitated queries and the ex-agent responded only with shrugs and smiles, Sam's gaze drifted away from the road and out his window. His eyes widened at the sight of a CCTV camera. Mounted on a post, it was pointing directly at him.

"Shit, they got cameras! We gotta get outta here! *Bumblebee!*"

Spitting dust and gravel, the Camaro blasted away from the checkpoint. Whirling in their seats, Mikaela and Leo peered out the back window. Two of the guards were shaking their fists at the fleeing car while the third was trying to level an AK-47 in their direction. By the time he had it raised to his shoulder and was taking aim, the accelerating Camaro was already out of effective range.

"Not good," Leo muttered as he slumped back into his seat. "This is not good at all."

Leaning forward, Mikaela put a hand on Sam's shoulder. With no need to sustain the charade, Sam relaxed and let Bumblebee do the "driving."

"Do you think they got your picture, Sam?"

"I don't know. We got out of there pretty fast." He

looked over at Simmons. The ex-agent was calmly contemplating the road ahead.

"You don't look worried. Shouldn't you be worried? Shouldn't *we* be worried?"

"Kid, when you've spent your entire adult life either being worried or worrying about someone else or worrying whether or not someone was doing the appropriate worrying, you don't let little things like cameras get to you." He nodded in the direction they were going. "In a few minutes we'll hit the outskirts of greater Cairo. I understand the traffic there makes midtown Manhattan at rush hour look like a farm road in northern Nevada. Relax. I got a feeling you'll need the adrenaline later."

Simmons's reassurance, however misplaced, had a calming effect on his companions. "Maybe," Sam said, "we got out of there before the camera snapped me."

An excited crowd was gathering around a console in the Cairo office of Interpol. Of all the active monitors in the room, only this one was screaming an alarm from its integrated speakers. The somewhat vacuous expression on his face notwithstanding, there was no mistaking the identity of the American teenager whose image was being ⬚⬚⬚⬚⬚⬚⬚⬚⬚ video.

"Red flag at Marsa Alam!" ⬚⬚⬚⬚⬚⬚⬚ charge was shouting. "Send a te⬚⬚⬚ get it out on the wire *now*."

In a very large room in a very se⬚⬚⬚ other town half a world away, ar⬚⬚⬚

turned and yelped to his colleagues, "We got a hit on the kid. Cairo."

"Illinois?" wondered the woman next to him.

The first officer shook his head. "He's gone the other direction. *Egypt.*"

A flurry of movement filled the room, none of which boded well for a certain astrophysics student now long absent from class . . .

☙ XIV ☙

Simmons was right, Sam decided. The traffic in Cairo was by far the worst he had ever seen. The coating of dust they had accumulated out in the desert helped veil Bumblebee somewhat and deflect a little, if not all, of the attention the sporty American car attracted. Besides, none of the other drivers could stare for very long lest they end up crashing into the vehicles in front of or on either side of them—or worse, miss their turn.

Traveling on the highway they had passed a fair number of official vehicles representing one department or another before a police car finally spun around behind them, changed lanes and direction, and gave chase. Siren wailing and lights flashing, it closed in on them rapidly.

"Sam . . . ," Mikaela murmured.

"I *know.*" Wrenching hard on the wheel to give impetus as well as instruction to Bumblebee, he followed the Twins off the highway.

Exhibiting remarkable acceleration for so modest a police vehicle, the Egyptian patrol car slammed unapologetically into the Camaro's rear bumper.

"We've got to shake them!" Simmons was looking around anxiously. "Any minute now this chase will start drawing notice. Gotta lose one pursuer before a dozen show up."

"Yeah, but how?" Mikaela turned and shouted *"Hey!"* as something small, metallic, and active scrambled out of the trunk, utilizing the fold-down access between the rear seats.

Instantly sizing up the situation, Wheels clambered out the open window on Simmons's side of the car, scrambled over the roof, and leaped off the trunk cover to land on the windshield of the pursuing car. His screams as he began pounding on the safety glass were exceeded in volume only by those of the two cops inside who found themselves under attack by the biggest, ugliest, maddest bug either of them had ever seen. While the wide-eyed driver fought to keep the car on an even keel, his partner fumbled for his service revolver.

Leaping into the air with a matched perfection that would have drawn a "10" from any gymnastics judge, the Twins allowed Bumblebee to pass cleanly beneath them as they changed form. By the time they landed atop the weaving police cruiser they had fully reverted to their natural Transformer shapes. Assailed from the front by what looked like an insane giant metal spider and from both sides by glaring alien robots, the driver of the cruiser could have been excused for abruptly leaving the road. The car rolled a couple of times before it finally came to a stop upside down at the bottom of a dry ravine, its lights and siren silenced.

Staggering away from the upturned pursuer and clutching a dislodged windshield wiper as a symbol of his victory, Wheels let out a Cybertronian cry of triumph as he tottered over to the Camaro that had stopped not far ahead. A single leap brought him back inside the waiting car.

"See, see? Change sides, like Jetfire! Me protect! You safe with me!" Disdaining a return to the trunk, he settled down in Mikaela's lap and buried his face in her cleavage. Glancing around, she saw all three of her male companions looking on in silence.

"*What?*" she said. "He's *cute.*"

Settling back down in his seat, Simmons stared out the windshield and back up at the busy highway. "No one's stopping to see what happened. My understanding is that the public isn't real fond of the local cops. But we gotta get off this main road. We can't keep traveling in the daytime." Reaching out, he let his open palm brush across the Camaro's dash. "Your crazy car kinda stands out in a city full of Fiats and Renaults. We'll lay low till sunset. Find someplace where the authorities won't think to look for us. Then decide what to do next. Try to figure out what the old Decepticon meant by the three kings and how that relates to the dagger—to the Gulf."

Sam was shaking his head. "We're running out of time. We gotta send a rendezvous message to Lennox. Get Optimus to the 'Dagger's tip' of the Ancients."

The ex-agent shot the notion down immediately. "Negative, kid. You're number one on the worldwide wanted list. You get on a military frequency, they'll track us down again."

"Military frequency . . . ," Sam murmured. "Yeah, that makes sense. Yeah—military. . . ."

*   *   *

So far away in space, if not in time. So different in feeling, if not in empathy. So . . . busy.

The sun was shining on the patio at the back of Lennox's house. Sarah Lennox juggled her two-year-old on her lap while Ray Epps's wife, Monique, attempted the impossible task of keeping track of their five offspring. Their four daughters were chasing one another around the pool, occasionally pausing to hop madly up and down in the spray from a hose-fed plastic fountain. Above the happy hysteria the insistent ring of a cell phone was barely audible.

Still maintaining a firm grip on her terrible two, Sarah looked around in confusion. While she could hear the phone, from a practicable standpoint it might as well have been invisible.

"I think one of your kids has my . . ."

Though she was not in the military, Monique Epps had a fine drill sergeant's voice—a requirement for keeping a handle on five rug rats.

"Shareeka! Shaniqua! Sheleeka! Mozambiqua! Where's your brother? Where's Fred?" Spotting her isolated male progeny hard at work hollowing out the Lennoxes' sandbox, she rose and hiked over to him. He gazed up with the guilelessness of a precocious three-year-old, plastic sand shovel in one hand and lips wrapped around the other. "Fred, what'd you do with Mrs. Lennox's phone?"

Formulating a response required Fred to execute a cursory search of his infantile hard drive. This unleashed a moment's digging in the sand, where excavation soon exposed the still-yammering communications device. Maintaining his innocence, he picked it up and held it out to his mother. She glared down at him.

"You best wipe the sand off that phone or I'm gonna reach out and touch your *behind*."

Fred complied, motivated more by his mother's stern maternal tone than her only marginally comprehensible words. Half satisfied, she took it from his small fingers and walked back to return it to her host. Sarah put it to her ear as she acknowledged the call.

"Hello? Hello, who is this? We don't have a very good connection." She smiled speculatively. "Maryann, are you calling while riding your Mercedes through the car wash again?"

It was just as well that the Lennoxes did not subscribe to caller ID. Had the phone's screen come back with a number combined with its location, *City of the Dead, Egypt,* she might have hung up without a word.

Most people would have.

On the other end of the call, his back turned against a light breeze that whipped not-so-light sand around him, Sam squinted as he sought shelter from the blowing desert while cupping his hand over the mouthpiece of the battered pay phone. Nearby, a partially occupied yellow-and-black Camaro and a pair of only intermittently occupied compact cars stood watch.

"Hi—Mrs. Lennox? My name's Sam Witwicky. You don't know me but I know your husband, Major Lennox. Met him two years ago when it started—the thing we all know about but can't talk about."

Sarah's voice quickened over the receiver. " 'Sam'? You're the kid who . . ."

"*Yes*—I'm 'who.' And the fate of more or less the entire *world* depends upon me getting a message to him, but people are gonna be listening for certain key words. I need your help."

Silence reigned at the other end, and for a terrible moment he was afraid she had hung up on him. Then a terse but self-assured feminine voice finally responded. "What can I do?"

He proceeded to tell her.

He was nearly done when a tall, slim figure draped in local dress came running directly toward him. Preliminary panic gave way to amusement and then to admiration as Sam admitted to himself that Seymour Simmons didn't look half bad in local attire. His arms were full of wind-whipped clothing. While Sam had been setting up the call and talking, the ex-agent had gone shopping.

"Local police must've gotten word. They're searching the town. We gotta move *now*."

Nodding understandingly, Sam started to replace the handset in its holder. "I gotta go. You got the coordinates I gave you?"

"*Yes*. Sam, I . . ."

"Thank you."

Slamming the phone down, he nodded at Simmons and together they raced back toward the waiting Camaro. Now thickly coated with dust and sand, all three cars peeled out of the parking area. Moments later, several Egyptian police vehicles pulled in to form a heavily armed circle around the now-deserted and forlorn pay phone.

Close, Sam thought as they accelerated away. Too close.

*   *   *

The huge pallet and its irregularly shaped payload was clearly visible from the operations control room as it was being loaded onto the waiting C-17. Standing side by side, a disconsolate Lennox and Epps followed the procedure. *There ought to have been an honor guard,* Lennox told himself. And a band solemnly playing. And flags flying. Optimus Prime deserved all that and more. Instead, he was being crated and shipped like an oversize FedEx parcel. It wasn't right. Beside him, Epps was muttering his own opinion under his breath. The words he was using were considerably less polite than those coursing through the thoughts of his friend and superior officer.

Behind them, Galloway was reviewing an intelligence file when a communications officer appeared and bent to whisper something in his ear. Frowning, he raised his gaze to the far window where Lennox and Epps continued to stare, for some unfathomable reason, out at the runway.

"I don't care," the advisor informed the officer. "There are *no* private calls. Not even from wives to husbands—or vice versa." Slapping a button on a nearby phone box, he put the incoming call on speakerphone.

The voice of Monique Epps echoed through the operations room.

"Ray? Is Ray on the line?"

Startled to hear his wife's voice, Epps turned and started in the phone's direction. "Yeah, baby, I'm here. You're on speaker. What is it?" Looking around, he saw that the other operations personnel were studiously and politely doing their best to ignore the conversation taking place in their midst. "We're workin'."

Speakerphone. Monique Epps hesitated, looked at Sarah, who was standing next to her, glanced at the kids racing around the Lennox kitchen, and strove to figure out how best to proceed. A questioning look at her friend generated only a raising of hands and a helpless shrug. They would have to improvise as best they could.

"Don't you dare gimme 'we're working,' Raymond. This is an *emergency*. You gotta stop what you're doing and be *listenin'* to me." Beside her, Sarah Lennox nodded encouragement.

Trapped in the wide-open operations room and shooting the occasional murderous stare in the direction of now-smirking co-workers, Epps had no choice but to reply. A glance in Galloway's direction showed that the advisor had turned away and had apparently returned to his work.

"Okay, baby, okay," he murmured soothingly. "Calm down. Remember, I'm on speaker here. What's going on?"

"Well, for one thing I'm not getting any *younger,* is what's going on," she shot back. "I just took a good long look in the mirror this morning and it hit me all at once that I've popped five kids outta this factory and I'm feeling like a damn *truck*." A few chuckles sounded around the operations center, only to turn to silence when Epps glared in their direction. Embarrassed but helpless, he had no choice but to continue listening to his wife rant.

"Like a big ol' eighteen-wheeler," his wife was complaining, "that woulda been easier to *drop* than five smaller versions, you feel me?"

Epps looked over at Lennox but found no enlightenment there. Cupping a palm over the phone's handset, he lowered his voice affectionately. "Uh, I kinda feel you, I think."

"You better *believe* you feel me," his wife continued, " 'cause I got a big-ass booty to prove it. I've been thinking a lot about this, Raymond, and my mind's made up. I'm getting it *done*. Face-lift, tummy tuck, super-boobs, the whole chimichanga redo from Doc Samuels."

Epps's lower jaw dropped. "*What?* When did you—who's 'Doc Samuels'? You been seeing a plastic surgeon without telling me, Monique? You know I don't allow plastic in my house."

"Let me remind you it's not *your* house, it's *our* house, and you're 'bout to be sleepin' in the *dog* house, 'cause you are *not listening. Sam*uels, Doc *Sam*uels. He's young, you both met him a couple of years ago at the *car* show? He had that new custom job, probably paid for it with a couple of dozen front end lifts."

Epps looked at Lennox, who stared back. Dawning realization was beginning to penetrate the solid bone of both soldiers' skulls sufficiently to reach into the gray matter beneath. A nearby guard remained at attention, inadequately equipped to catch on to the real gist of the ongoing domestic conversation. Lennox decided to announce his presence.

"Oh, yeah, the car show, I remember now, Mo-

nique. That doctor, he had bought himself one *fast*
ride."

"Glad you both remember," Epps's wife was saying, " 'cause I truly feel that I'm just coming up on my
prime now—my *optimal* prime. So I told this doc that
I was feeling like a big ol' truck that was just falling
down and he thinks he can bring the whole kit and
kabooty back to life. You hear what I'm saying
now?"

The voice of Sarah Lennox broke in. "I keep telling
her it's not the end of the world if she doesn't get this
work done, Ray, and she keeps insisting that it *is*."

"Oh yes, *it is*!" Monique insisted vehemently.

The watching guard did his best to stifle a smirk.
Under ordinary circumstances Epps would have
punched him out, stockade or no stockade. Instead,
he just gazed back at Lennox. The real meaning
buried in the seemingly insouciant conversation had
hit them both hard.

Lennox nodded toward the mic pickup. "Ray—
your wife is waiting for a reply."

Epps nodded, bent, and spoke. "Sugar Muffin, I'm
sorry for getting angry. You need a tune-up? Who am
I to say no?"

"Doc *Sam*uels says it has to happen, like *now*,
baby. After all, the body we're talking about is important to *both* of us. It's a body that deserves to *live*
again."

"I couldn't agree more, Sugar Plum. Believe me, I
understand *completely*. I mean, what's truly important is truly important, right?" He glanced over at
Lennox, who did a quick scan of the operations center. Bored from listening to the marital byplay, the

others had returned to their work. No one was paying the two soldiers the least attention except their guard, and he continued to operate under a perfectly wrong set of assumptions. Which meant they could proceed.

Epps nodded and addressed the mic afresh. "So, uh, Sugar, what's this operation gonna cost me? Gimme some hard numbers. I need to know where we're *going* with this."

Having prepared for the conversation by pulling the family atlas from its place on the living room bookshelf, Sarah Lennox already had it open to the relevant section. A Post-it note on the page opposite the critical one was filled with her neat handwriting. Pulling it free, she handed it to her friend. Holding the note in one hand and the phone in the other, Monique resumed talking to her husband.

"Well, right now it's looking like around twenty-nine. With all the extras, it comes to exactly twenty-nine point three-one, maybe east of thirty-five—depending on whether we go with 'saline' or 'silicone,' but it's *definitely* in that neighborhood."

Epps nodded as he memorized the numbers. "I got it. Wow. Those are some far-out numbers. As near as I can see, they're way off base. You tell the doc that's half my salary. But I think we can swing it. I promise you I'm gonna do my damndest, and I'm sure Bill Lennox will help out in every way he can. Won't you, uh, Sir?"

Lennox nodded. "You can bet on it, Sergeant. We've been friends too long to let this one slide."

Epps smiled. "Thanks. Sugar, kiss the kids and tell 'em—tell 'em we're all comin' home soon." He broke the connection, paused, and stared. Turning, Lennox saw what had drawn his attention.

Galloway had risen from his chair to come up right behind them.

"In my long career," the advisor began gravely, "I bet I've heard ten thousand wiretapped conversations. And the one thing I've learned?" Both soldiers stiffened. Lennox saw that the guard was paying close attention and might be difficult to jump.

"What's that, Sir?" he inquired carefully.

Galloway never hesitated. "The wife is *always* right." Having delivered himself of that immutable truth, he walked past the two of them and out through the nearest doorway. Lennox and Epps watched him go, then exchanged a glance. Nothing was said, but their respective heart rates slowed proportionately.

The C-17 pilot was NEST, but Lennox and Epps still confronted him cautiously. Both men knew there would be only one opportunity to make this work. If the pilot refused to cooperate . . .

They made a show of looking busy, doing their best to give any onlookers the impression that they were discussing the plane and its forthcoming mission. Which indeed they were, but not according to the procedure that had already been laid out. They kept their backs to the operations center just in case a lip-reader or a monitor manning an audiosnoop might be peering at them through a scope.

"Coordinates," the pilot was repeating quietly, "twenty-nine degrees thirty-one minutes north, thirty-five degrees east." He frowned. "That's the northeast branch of the Red Sea. Gulf of Aqaba, up where the three countries meet. Eastern shore." His eyes met Lennox's. "Not a real peaceful part of the world, Major."

Epps's eyes had widened as he listened to the pilot. Up until now he'd only had the numbers and not a real location. "*Jordan?* You kidding? Even if we had a way to get Big Daddy there, how's the kid gonna bring him back to *life?*"

Lennox took a deep breath. "If the Decepticons want Sam Witwicky bad enough to try and snatch him straight out of school and reveal themselves the way they did, it must be because he either knows something they don't or has something they want—which for all we know could be one and the same. Which means that one way or another he *definitely* knows more than us about what's going on." He shrugged resignedly. "We gotta trust him."

"With something this big? With our careers, not to mention our families' future?"

Epps's doubt infected Lennox—but only briefly. He turned back to the attentive pilot. "Say you had engine trouble on the way to Diego base. Considering the sensitivity of your cargo, it's reasonable to assume that you'd have a tough time getting authorization to land somewhere and take on supplementary fuel. Wouldn't it be more expeditious to lighten your load first, for safety's sake, and then divert to Soccent? That would mean flying over someplace empty in order to make the dump while properly complying with security directives. Hard to imagine an emptier place on route."

The pilot grinned understandingly. "Standard operating procedure, per eleven dash four-oh-one. Safety of plane and crew paramount."

Pulling out a small steno pad Lennox wrote down the coordinates, just in case the pilot's memory should happen to fail him. After passing the slip of paper across, he scribbled a second note and folded it twice. On the way back to operations central they confronted the base's air boss.

"Sergeant," he told the attentive noncom, "once we're airborne and clear of U.S. airspace, Chairman Morshower of the Joint Chiefs has to get this information ASAP. I take full responsibility, but you're the only one whose security clearance here will let him do it. The chairman's personal secure cell number's right here on the back of this note." He leaned a little closer. "For your own sake and future, just pass the information along as indicated. No recreational reading."

The air boss hesitated, then nodded and took the folded note.

Loaded and fueled, the C-17 lifted off from McGuire not long thereafter. The air boss watched it go, looking on as the heavy cargo jet banked slowly to finally vanish eastward over the Atlantic. Around him the base was quieting down as it returned to more familiar operational procedures. In his pocket lay a small piece of folded notepaper.

In due time he would open it, and make a phone call.

Morshower was bent over his desk. Hard work was about all these days that kept him from saying undiplomatic things to important members of Congress. He barely looked up when the J3 entered, saluted, and passed him yet another in the endless stream of sheets of paper. He started to wave the courier off.

"I think you should take a look at this one, Sir."

"What? Oh, why not." Picking up the printout, the chairman read. And as he read, he sat up straighter in his chair. The note itself was brief.

FROM LENNOX—29° N, 35° E—GET READY TO BRING THE RAIN

Morshower stared at the piece of paper, his mind churning at the implications of what it did not include. "We check these coordinates?"

"Yes, sir." Moving to a wall, the J3 hit a series of controls. The wall lit up with a Robinson projection and zoomed in on one small area: a narrowing body of water where three countries met.

"Gulf of Aqaba, Sir."

Morshower rose to get a better look. "Lennox knows something. If he didn't, he wouldn't take the risk of contacting me directly with this. We have to be ready to back him up if this goes hot. Have NSA task our keyhole satellites to target the indicated coordinates on a thirty-minute rotation. And get me . . ." He broke off and sat back down in his chair. "On second thought, don't get me anyone. Not just yet." He smiled.

"We could all do with a little nap."

Known to the ancient world as the northern of the two Pillars of Hercules, the rock of Gibraltar rose green and populated on its western slopes while the eastern side dropped almost sheer into the Mediterranean Sea. While tourists and soldiers took roads or the cable car up the vegetated side, only the most avid rock climbers attempted to reach the summit from the opposite direction.

The fighter jet that braked impossibly fast changed shape as it reached an isolated point of the gleaming white limestone. No British fortifications clung to this unreachable spot. Shrouded in fog on this particular morning, none on the many vessels anchored below could see the powerful bipedal shape that stood on the small ledge, peering out to sea. Passing ships called mournfully to one another as they entered the straits on their way to Mediterranean ports or prepared for the rigors of the open Atlantic.

Too much organic growth, Megatron thought to himself as he stood there in solitary malevolent majesty. Insects, fungi—it was enough to make even him shudder. One day he would bring a cleansing to this benighted world. One day, if events proceeded as hoped, that was not too far in the future.

Touching a small portion of his wrist sent a signal twisting outward, warping its way through the space–time continuum. A shape appeared before him, a face—the visage of The Fallen.

"I sense that you've found the boy."

"Yes, Master. Not far now, across this sea and another, smaller one, in the land of the original riverbank."

"Of course," the unfathomable voice replied. "How quite natural. Where the battle began, and ~~here~~ it is destined to end. It is only fitting. Once we ~~get~~ the Matrix, we will activate the Machine and then . . ." The voice paused; contemplative, perhaps enjoying. "You have regained my trust, prodigal. I will tell you where the Machine is hidden."

"I will find it, Master. Is there anything else?"

"Only one thing more," the voice declaimed. *"Prepare my arrival."*

⬡ XV ⬡

The old tourist center had been built in the 1930s on a now unused flat area well west of the famous monuments. An attempt to be all things to all visitors, it had ended up being none of them. Located well away from the official entrances to the Giza pyramids, back when it was constructed the complex must have been a lonely outpost of tourism indeed.

Simmons led the way through the broken fence of some long-forgotten entrepreneur's abandoned hopes and dreams. Some of the whitewashed buildings were still intact. It was unlikely that the police would look for them here, right near the center of the country's most famous tourist attractions. Whatever else the authorities thought of Sam, it was doubtful they would expect him to be playing sightseer.

At the moment none of this mattered to Sam and Mikaela. As Simmons and Leo slept inside one of the structures and the three palm frond–covered Autobots rested behind old walls, boy and girl stood next to each other beneath the stars and gazed out over moon and pyramids as thousands had done before them.

"One week without me," she murmured, "and

look what happens to your life. Don't say I didn't warn you."

"Okay, I won't," he quipped back. In a more serious tone he added softly, "I shoulda let you break up with me. You'd have been better off if you had. Being my girlfriend's turned out to be pretty hazardous to your health."

She snuggled a little closer. "Yeah, well, you know how it is. Girls like dangerous guys."

He turned toward her. "That's been my nickname since kindergarten—Mr. Dangerous."

Their lips were very close. She hesitated, he hesitated, and then she spoke—clearly disappointed.

"Still can't say it, can you?"

"Sure I can." He mustered a minimal touch of male bravado. "After you."

She drew back slightly. "Why do I have to say it first?"

" 'Cause 'ladies first,' it's a rule."

"Oh, suddenly you're a gentleman? That one of your kindergarten nicknames, too? You held the door open for four-year-olds?"

"You're still pissed I kissed a Decepticon."

Her expression narrowed. "I thought you said *she* kissed *you*. And you didn't *know* she was a Decepticon."

"That's what I meant—I mean . . ." Male bravado, as it usually does, found itself crushed by feminine accusation.

"Actually," she continued, "I *wasn't* thinking about that, but obviously *you* were."

Having lost the high ground, he fought for air. "Do

girls have a special class where they learn how to turn things around on guys?"

She sat up straight, more beautiful than ever in the moonlight. "No, Sam, it's genetic. And for your information, I just flew three thousand miles to stop you from getting *killed*! And another four thousand or whatever through some kind of transspatial dislocation, and now we're standing in front of the three most romantic pyramids on Earth under a full moon and stars in actual real desert, and you can't even admit you love me! So don't tell me how you're doing my life such a favor because . . ." She broke off, noting that he had turned away from her. "Are you listening to me, Sam Witwicky, 'cause . . ."

"What'd you say?" All the upset and uncertainty and confusion had gone out of his voice. " 'Pyramids and stars' . . ."

Looking away from her, he found his eyes drawn to an old fountain. The thin film of water lying within, the product of some recent storm or aged leak, was lined with scum and unfit for drinking or bathing. But it was more than adequate to reflect the night sky and the gaggle of stars within. Three in particular drew his attention. Lifting his gaze, he sought and found them immediately. Two connections were made: between the three stars and their reflection and between three stars and a small bit of knowledge. Suddenly he was off and running toward the nearest semi-intact building.

"*Wake up! Simmons, Leo, wake up!* I know where the Three Kings are!"

Inside, the ex-agent was instantly awake—old training leads to permanent habits. He stared as Sam struggled to shake some consciousness back into his considerably more bleary-eyed roommate.

"Wha—what are you blabbering about, dude?"

"Our astronomy class." Sam struggled to keep a lid on his excitement. "The textbook, page forty-seven, remember?"

Leo squinted up at him. "No, I don't remember. I was only in college two days."

Mikaela had come in behind him. Now she watched as he rambled on.

"The pyramids of Giza: when they were built they were lined up with Orion's Belt. 'Cause those three stars were known as 'the Three Kings.' It's like an arrow staring us right in the face! At dawn over the top of the Gulf, they gotta point to a spot on the horizon." He looked at his watch. "Dawn will be a little later here, but not much. We can work out the timing."

"Three kings will lead the way," Mikaela reiterated.

He led the rush to the rooftop of the old building. Despite the glow of Cairo's lights, the three main stars that comprised the belt of Orion stood out plainly. In fact, the city lights helped highlight and isolate the constellation from the surrounding stars.

Simmons was working silently with his GPS. When he had done all he could, he raised an arm and pointed.

"There—that way. Using the belt and drawing a line from it to where it would be pointing when dawn breaks over the tip of the dagger—the Gulf of Aqaba—we get a location in Jordan."

"Jordan!" Leo rolled his eyes. "Oh, man, do we need passports!"

"We're gonna need everything the Autobots can give us if we're gonna get there before dawn." Simmons tapped the GPS screen. "The coordinates I get are for the area right around Petra. That's two hundred and fifty-six miles and a different country from here, give or take a tomb or two."

Sam nodded his understanding, then gestured down toward the shielded parking area where Bumblebee and the Twins waited. "We'll make it." He grinned at the ex-agent. "Remember—I've got a fast car."

The national park had not yet opened when the travelers reached the central part of Petra. With the help of the three Autobots they had not entered via the usual route, coming up the main canyon, but had instead worked their way down the surrounding steep slopes, in the process succeeding in avoiding the few sleepy night watchmen.

Now they entered the tomb that, according to Simmons's best guess, represented the nearest approximation of where the row of Orion's belt would line up with dawn at the tip of the Gulf. The barred gate at the entrance had yielded easily to Bumblebee's delicate ministrations.

Light provided by the three Autobots revealed the murals that had been left on the high walls by the conquering Romans. Studying them, Simmons was uncharacteristically subdued.

"That's the Romans for you. They painted over a lot of stuff when they conquered the Mediterranean world, including what the founding Nabateans left here."

"Thanks for the history lesson," Leo mumbled. He was sleep-deprived and exhausted. "There's no alien tomb?"

Sam was searching the walls, the floor, even the distant ceiling. "If this is where the Three Kings—the three stars—point when dawn breaks over the tip of the Gulf, then it's gotta be here somewhere."

"Why?" Leo snapped. " 'Cause we're trusting Grandpa Blackbird, who can't even remember what friggin' planet he's on? Okay, lemme do a quick search—nope, nothing. Did it ever cross your mind, guys, that archeologists *have been here before*?"

This was enough for Mikaela. "Do you even *have* balls?" she asked.

"Hey, what're you pissed off at me for? Robo-Warrior's the one who led us into this dead end!"

Simmons was seething. Getting up into Leo's face, he began, "News flash, kid: Real life isn't a cushy college campus where they fix you three meals a day. Real life is heartbreak. Despair. Sometimes you get to the end of the rainbow and the leprechauns went and booby-trapped it!"

Undeterred, Leo countered, "How did you ever work for the government? Seriously, who'd ever hire you? I want to see some kind of documentation that proves you were once entrusted with an actual job!"

"Okay, everybody needs to chill," interjected Mikaela.

"It's not over," said Sam, "listen up . . ."

"We ain't listenin' to you sucka," challenged Twin 2, "what he ever done for us?"

Mudflap immediately spoke up for the human. "Killed Megatron. How about *that*?"

Instantly, Skids was in Mudflap's metal face. "Well, he didn't get the job done, 'cause Megatron's *back*."

Alarmed, Simmons took a step forward. "Hey, don't make me have to separate you two."

"Awww, whutha matter?" Mudflap stared at the approaching human. "You thcared?"

"Sure he is. Scared o' yo ugly *face,* mutha," declared Skids.

Mudflap regarded his brother with (naturally) equal intensity. "We're *twinths,* you shtupid geniuth!"

Simmons just shook his head. "Anybody ever get the feeling we teamed up with the *losing* side of the Transformers?"

Skids shoved Mudflap. Mudflap pushed back, whereupon his doppelganger promptly punched him hard, sending his counterpart crashing into the near wall. The sound of metal striking rock reverberated down the long passageway. More intriguingly, the impact cracked the wall on which the nearest Roman fresco had been painted. Beneath the plaster something was etched in the stone that was decidedly not Roman, Nabatean, Egyptian, Assyrian, or anything else that had been conceived and inscribed by representatives of the dozens of empires that had left their mark on the hard sandstone.

Sam recognized it immediately. He should have. It was one of the symbols he had written on a wall of his dorm room and later in the dirt of the main outside storage yard of a branch of the Smithsonian Air and Space Museum.

Bumblebee recognized it, too. Within seconds, the Autobot was using his fingers like chisels to chip away the rest of the Roman mural. The Jordanian antiquities department would not be pleased, Sam thought as he watched the Autobot at work, but far more was at stake in this old tunnel than a wall of Roman graffiti.

Their momentary spat now completely forgotten, Leo, too, was staring entranced at what the Autobot's busy hands were rapidly exposing to the light.

"Cool," he murmured as the Roman artwork was progressively whittled away. "Gives new meaning to the term 'caesarean section.'"

When the last of the plaster backing had been pulled off, three symbols stood revealed, engraved in the wall. Or rather, embossed, Sam saw. Behind the plaster and the stone, metal ribbing was now visible. The Romans had known the working of bronze, and lead, and gold and silver and copper, but he doubted that in their wildest metallurgical dreams they had ever conceived of a material like the one he and his companions were presently confronting. It gleamed brightly in the light provided by the Autobots.

"This is it," Sam heard himself mumbling. It had to be. It had better be. They were running out of time.

After instructing the humans to move clear, Bumblebee leveled an arm and let loose with one of his lesser weapons. This was no time to worry about whether or not their activities would be overheard by any patrolling guards. The detonation blew an Autobot-size hole in the wall.

Beyond lay darkness.

Without waiting for the dust to settle, Sam wa

stepping through, followed closely by his companions. They did not find Transformers.

They found themselves *inside* them.

No larger than a good-sized room in a human dwelling, the walls, floor, and ceiling of the metal grotto had been fashioned from the fused bodies of twelve Transformer endoskeletons. Tremendous heat had been applied to meld them together, while time had applied its own special patina. Empty eyes gazed out beyond twisted limbs. Mouths gaped open as if in the act of voicing incomprehensible warnings. Sections of torso and hip flowed together as if rendered for a surrealist sculpture.

It *was* a surrealist sculpture, Sam mused as he turned a slow circle to examine their implausible surroundings. And they were standing inside it. But they were not here to marvel, and there was no time for sightseeing. Lowering his gaze, he began searching.

It did not take him long to find what he was looking for.

Whereas every other limb had been fused to form part of the gleaming cavern, one arm protruded sharply from a rippling wall. Hand open, palm upward, it was clearly offering something to any who might enter the tomb of the ancients. Sam rushed to it, peered down between the slightly upward-curling fingers, and discovered in the open metal palm . . .

Sand. A small mound of black sand.

Having found even less, his companions gathered around him.

"No . . . ," Sam mumbled. Coming up behind him, Simmons eyed the handful of grains matter-of-factly.

"Thousands of years—we don't know how many

thousands. Must've turned to dust. Rapid dec
that energy would consume itself, leave nothing behind but—this."

Sam looked away, shaking his head in disbelief.
"No—*no*. This is *not* how this ends."

The ex-agent smiled sanguinely. "Give you the
bright side, kid. Means there's nothing here for the
Decepticons either. Consider that . . ." He broke off,
frowning. "You hear something?" When no one answered, he ran for the entrance. No one followed
him, but they could hear him shouting from the far
end of the main corridor.

"C-17s! They're air force, they're ours!"

Simmons's declaration did not move Sam. He was
too numb, too disappointed to care. Staring down at
the little pile of black sand, he contemplated the end
of his hopes, of all that he had aspired to accomplish
in this far-off place. Mikaela moved close, wishing
there was something she could offer other than a re-
statement of reality.

"Sam—there's nothing left. We tried. We revived
an ancient Decepticon and we came partway around
the world via a transspatial portal and we dodged police, and now we're here and—there's nothing left.
Nothing left to try. You can't bring him back."

"Don't tell me there's nothing," he muttered un-
happily.

Leo was pacing impatiently back and forth, kicking
at the grainy floor underfoot. "It's sand, are you kidding me? We came all this way for worthless sand!
Are we done now? Can we go?"

Looking up, Sam let his gaze travel around the
room, taking in the contorted, flowing faces of the

Ancients whose very bodies had been utilized to construct the chamber. It made no sense. Something rendered out of the Allspark itself wouldn't just disappear, wouldn't simply decay into grit. Bending, he pulled off a shoe, peeled off the sock, and began shoveling the black sand into the only suitable container at hand.

"They hid it, you hear me? They *hid* it! They sacrificed their lives for this. Everyone's after me 'cause of what I know? Well, I *know* this is gonna work."

Mikaela just looked at him. "How?"

"Because I believe it," he told her as he started tying a knot in the neck of the sock.

The loud buzzing and flashing lights that suddenly filled the passenger section of the C-17 caused Galloway to look up sharply from the report he had been reading. All around him the soldiers who constituted the bulk of the group being returned to Diego Garcia were rising from their seats, moving with confidence born of extensive training. The big jet began to shake and rattle, then banked sharply to starboard. Before the alarmed advisor could ask what was going on, the voice of the pilot sounded over the intercom.

"We've got an emergency engine situation up here. Indicator lights just came on for both port engines. We're losing altitude fast. We're going to try to divert to Soccent, but there's a real chance we may not be able to make a safe landing. Procedure in this instance calls for lightening all noncritical materials and emergency evac of personnel. Move, people, move!"

Galloway looked over at Lennox. " 'Emergency evac,' what's that mean?"

Lennox was addressing his troops. "Okay, boys, grab your chutes. Soon as we're down to fifteen thousand, open bay doors."

Preparations proceeded smoothly and with little conversation—too smoothly and with too little conversation for Galloway, who was immediately suspicious. Extensive training or no, a call for an emergency evacuation ought to have prompted at least *some* obvious anxiety among the affected soldiers. Instead, they were going about the necessary planning as if it had been—planned.

Lennox was in his face before the advisor could voice his reservations. The major was polite and proper, all business now.

"Familiar with a standard-issue air force chute, Sir?"

"Of course not!" Galloway sputtered. "I've never had to jump out of an airplane in my life! *What the hell did you do?*" Peering past the major, he saw technical sergeant Epps conversing with several other soldiers. Epps was smiling and joking, which seemed somehow out of place onboard a plane whose pilot had just declared that it was at risk of going down.

"You heard the pilot, Sir," Lennox explained. "Engine trouble. Both port-side engines. Right now the guys up front are doing a terrific job just keeping us in the air, but there's no telling how long they'll be able to manage that. This is a serious situation, Sir. I'm sure you realize the diplomatic ramifications if an air force plane was to go down in this politically sensitive area. The pilots'll have a much better chance of making it to Soccent if they don't have to worry about passengers and cargo and the plane is made as light as possible." Picking up a tightly packed chute, he advanced on the advisor.

"There's nothing to it, really, Sir. These things are pretty much idiot-proof these days. Here, let me assist you . . ."

Raising his hands defensively, Galloway stepped back from the helpful officer. "There *is* no trouble; *you're* behind this . . ."

At that moment at least two and possibly three of the big plane's engines shut down. The result was an eerie lack of noise inside the fuselage.

Lennox persisted. "No idea what you're talking about. This is regulation procedure, pilots are doing what they're supposed to do—and now it's our turn to comply. I just follow orders. 'To the letter.' Isn't that what you said?"

With nowhere to go, Galloway halted. His tone matched his expression. "You just signed the death warrant on your career, Major."

"Always wondered what it would be like to be a warrant officer." Lennox was urging the chute on the other man. "Better put this on quickly, Sir. We'll only get one chance at a clean drop."

The howling wind near the open cargo doors compensated for the lack of engine noise as everyone gathered near the rear of the cargo plane. Wearing his chute, a terrified Galloway stood at the back and clung tenaciously to the nearest drop line. Only then did he notice that while Lennox had quickly and efficiently helped the civilian into a chute, the major had yet to don one of his own.

"Why aren't you putting on your chute?!" He had to yell at the top of his lungs to make himself heard over the noise.

"Gotta secure VIPs first, Sir!" Lennox spoke loudly and very fast. "Listen carefully and memorize what I say. Each chute has an integrated GPS tracker so the wearer can be located by Search and Rescue. Right next to that's a fabric webbing called a bridle. The bridle holds the pin that keeps your main chute container closed—you with me?"

The wind was making Galloway's eyes tear up and hurting his ears. "Yes—*no*—stop, slow down!"

Lennox did neither. "When the pilot chute inflates in the airstream, it pulls the pin and opens the main container. Red cord's your backup, blue cord's your main. I want you to pull the blue cord, and you need to pull it *hard*."

Confused and frightened, with the plane jumping and bouncing around him, Galloway hurriedly complied and yanked hard on the indicated cord. His main chute promptly began to unfurl.

Taking a step back into the plane, Lennox finally allowed himself to grin. "No, no, Sir—I didn't say *now*. You pull the cord when you *jump*."

"YOU SONOFAB . . . !"

The rest of the advisor's mostly unprintable comments sailed away along with him as the rapidly ballooning chute grabbed air and yanked him out the open back of the plane. His shrieking, along with his body, faded rapidly with distance.

Coming up alongside his friend, Epps watched as the advisor's parachute swiftly disappeared behind and below the C-17, which continued to lose altitude.

"Sounds like the engines are working okay again even though we're going down fast."

Lennox nodded solemnly. "How 'bout that? Gotta hand it to the guys up front."

Epps squinted as the descending chute slipped completely from view. "So rude, he didn't say good-bye." Looking back into the fuselage, he nodded meaningfully. "Left in such a big hurry that he forgot his briefcase. I guess without his laptop and cell phone he'll just have to wait awhile for pickup." He sighed. "Where we supposed to meet up with our 'contact'?"

"Rendezvous point'll be an abandoned town by the sea. Jordanian authorities have been informed that we'll be conducting an 'exercise' there so they should've closed the north–south highway south of Aqaba and north of Tala Bay. That should give us enough room to operate without having to worry about busybodies." Making sure his headset was on, he spoke into the pickup.

"Arcee, spread the news—let's go go go!"

Turning back into the cargo bay, Lennox, Epps, and their fellow NEST soldiers began to release the straps and bonds that secured the body of Optimus Prime. At a word from the major to the cockpit, the C-17 abruptly angled upward. Freed from its restraints and grabbed by gravity, the massive shape began to slide out the open rear cargo doors. As it did so it was accompanied by a small squad of armed, grim-faced, exceedingly determined men. Free-falling beside the descending bipedal mass, they looked like sparrows attending a broken branch.

Having followed the lead cargo on its downward path, the pilots of the C-17 reduced their altitude. In the big plane's cargo bay the engines of the tightly packed Autobots suddenly flamed to life in unison as their terrestrial motors started up. Exhaust belching from multiple tailpipes quickly filled the huge storage area with fumes. Coughing and gasping for oxygen, unable to get his breath, one of the guards hit the emergency release on the cargo bay doors. As they continued to descend and fresh air began to replace the smoke that had filled the interior, all three MPs suddenly found themselves confronted by the multiplicity that was Arcee. Gun muzzles came up—and hesitated as their wielders found themselves facing weapons of considerably greater potency.

"Just stand there and watch, boys," advised the tripartite Autobot. Wisely, the soldiers complied.

Throughout the cargo bay heavy-duty straps and metal bands began to snap and break, ricocheting against walls and ceiling as the Autobots freed themselves. One by one they began to roll out the open cargo bay doors. When the last had finally dropped clear, Arcee turned to the watching guards.

"Have a nice trip, fellas. This now concludes our in-flight service." And with that, she turned and leaped out into the open sky.

It was just as well that there were no beachgoers in the vicinity and that the Jordanian government had cleared the strip of land along the Gulf coast. When Optimus's body slammed into the ground, the concussion would have been sufficient to deafen anyone situated close by. As it was, only a few startled seabirds fled the scene in panic.

Landing around the fallen giant, Lennox and his

team snapped off their chutes and hurriedly regrouped. Around them, aged and worn structures
spoke of an earlier time. The old fishing village was
long abandoned, its sons and daughters having surrendered family traditions in favor of far better-paying
jobs in the hotels and tourist venues that spotted the
coast and air-conditioned condos and houses in the
city of Aqaba itself.

Weapon at the ready, one of the United Kingdom
team members hustled up alongside Epps. "It's a little
bit like—now what?"

"Now we wait and find out," the American noncom informed him as he studied the surrounding
empty buildings. "We just dropped a thousand tons
of alien robot in a ghost town. Sure as hell hope
there's a reason."

Lennox came up behind them. "Cordon and
search, find the kid. Ray's little phone chat with his
missus suggested he'll show up here somewhere. Autobots, stay out of sight—low-visibility recon. This
area's supposed to be clear of civilians, but never bet
against a family that's prepaid for a beach vacation."
He gestured toward the old town minaret. "Graham,
get up high."

The UK soldier nodded and ran toward the indicated tower.

Epps moved closer. "What next?"

Lennox was pondering the motionless form of
Prime. "Might be a chopper come down this way, private plane—or worse. Don't want any rubberneckers
posting stuff on YouTube. Let's get him under cover
best we can."

Epps nodded, backed up, and began yelling orders

at the waiting, wary troops. Working togethe
managed to scavenge enough corrugated scrap from
collapsed roofs and walls to cover nearly all of Optimus's body.

That task accomplished, they settled down to wait.

They didn't have to wait long.

From his position in the minaret, it was Graham
who spotted the rising dust through his binoculars.
Whatever was in front of it was moving at law-
breaking speed southward along the main road. But
that road was supposed to be closed to traffic, he reminded himself.

Unless . . .

He waited a moment longer for the image to more
clearly resolve itself before shouting down to the soldiers hugging the shade below.

"*Got a visual!* Yellow team! Two kilometers out!"

Almost simultaneously a distant whine became audible off to the west, out over the Gulf, and grew
steadily louder. Raising his own binocs, Epps checked
it out. The sound was too high-pitched to come from
a C-17, and in any case the silhouette he identified
was far smaller, sharper, and sleeker than that of a
cargo jet.

He recognized it immediately.

"F-22 Raptor," he murmured to no one in particular. "Just one. Way out here." He shook his head
slowly. "Got a bad feelin' festering, tellin' me we got
the leading edge of an alien war on our hands."

The sound from high above changed abruptly. As it
shot painfully through Epps's headset he wrenched it
off, then spoke into the pickup.

"EMP burst! Anyone copy? *Copy?*"

Lennox came running over to him. "Just lost all electronic communication."

Working in unison they rechecked their headset units, then Lennox pulled his cell phone. The device was deader than the famous inland sea that lay far to their north. He tried their last remaining comm unit.

"Anybody on radio? Hello?"

Epps gave voice to his disgust. "Ah, man, I hate it when they cut the damn phones. These aliens got their shit *down.*"

"Y'know," Lennox told him as they started off toward the old village center, "I do not need the negativity right now."

"You *know* it means we're about to die," the sergeant replied cheerfully. "Ain't no credit card's gonna save us this time . . ."

XVI

The vivid blue of the Gulf of Aqaba contrasted brilliantly with the paler sky and the golden-brown of the mountains and desert off to their left as Bumblebee and the Twins roared down the deserted coastal road. Each lost in his or her own thoughts, the Camaro's passengers rode in silence. Leo was half asleep, Simmons was planning, and Mikaela was sneaking worried glances at Sam, who just stared at the sand-filled sock he held in one hand.

All such meditating vanished instantly as the roadway erupted in front of them.

Bumblebee and the Twins swerved to avoid the resultant crater as two huge winged shapes shot past overhead and then swooped around sharply to come straight back at them.

Megatron. And Starscream.

"Get out of the way!" Sam screamed, the sock and its intimations of failure momentarily forgotten. Behind him Leo was waving his arms frantically in front of him, as if by some magical means that could ward off the developing attack.

"They're coming right at us!"

Accelerating in front of the Camaro, the Twins ecuted a series of unpredictable crisscrossing m vers on either side of the road that threw up a dust cloud thick and wide enough to obscure not only themselves but the larger vehicle in their midst. Within the cloud they projected multiple rezzed images of themselves, further confusing the two attacking craft and leading their probing pulse-blasts astray.

The newly erupting clash on the highway served to punctuate Graham's warning. Soldiers who had been resting in the shade rushed to recover their weapons and take up their assigned positions. As they did so, Lennox happened to glance skyward.

Thirteen shapes were descending straight toward the abandoned town, and every one of them was a Decepticon.

"Oh, my God," he mumbled, "we're dead."

"You call *me* negative?" Eyes also on the sky, Epps pressed against the wall behind them. "Now *that's* negative."

Both men waited apprehensively, as did the rest of the troops, as one by one the alien intruders touched down on the opposite side of the town from where the human soldiers had taken cover. Thirteen Decepticons began taking up strike positions on one side of the abandoned village, while deeper within waited a ten-man human strike force team and half a dozen Autobots.

High overhead, at a distance from which the town under attack was less than a dust mote against the sandy yellow-brown of the Jordanian coast, a military surveillance satellite aimed its high-resolution cameras at a selected sliver of Gulf shoreline. Silently, it beamed images back to Washington, D.C. and to the Pentagon, where Chairman Morshower and his subordinates gazed anxiously at the relayed feed.

"Satellite's approaching coordinates over the Gulf. Image in twenty seconds." The console technician made the announcement as he adjusted his instrumentation.

Without fail, the pixilating image on the main monitor began to resolve, to clear, and to graduate from black and white to color. It showed the scene on the ground closely enough for those in the Joint Ops Center to plainly pick out the waiting Autobots. The Decepticons . . .

The Decepticons were not there. Their malicious presence had been eliminated from the satellite image.

"All quiet on the western front," one of the many military aides present observed with satisfaction as he studied the screen. "We'll have the imagery for about ten minutes, sir. Then we lose 'em."

"Understood." *Odd,* Morshower thought. Nothing of much consequence seemed to be taking place. Well, no doubt clarification would be forthcoming. "Let's establish comms."

On the backside of the hacked surveillance satellite, Soundwave chuckled to himself as he continued to monitor and doctor the communication. The next step would be to lock and subtly manipulate the transmitting images so that it would appear that the Autobots were simply changing their position from time to time. *A pity,* he thought to himself, that the humans on the ground would not be able to see what was actually taking place.

As for the orbiting Decepticon, his vision of what

was happening far below was considerably different from the one he was passing along to the human authorities, and he was enjoying both versions immensely.

A human driver in a car of any kind would have long since been chewed up and spit out by the repeated attacks of Megatron and Starscream. Able to anticipate, predict, and avoid the tactics and weaponry of the two alien aircraft, Bumblebee and the Twins somehow managed to avoid being blown to bits and their human occupants turned to organic sludge. Being able to go off-road on the flat, hard desert surface that flanked the two-lane pavement aided their evasive efforts considerably. But they could not avoid the relentless assault forever. One did not have to be an experienced military strategist to realize as much.

"We gotta split up." Sam seemed to be speaking to empty air, when in fact the individual he was addressing was all around him. "Bumblebee, you lead 'em away."

"Sir, yes Sir!" the Camaro's speakers barked, quoting from yet another unknown radio recording.

A tense Simmons looked across at the young driver who was not driving. "I'll go with the Twins and help draw their fire. You kids get to those soldiers and get *outta* here!"

Their eyes met. For the first time, something besides animosity and suspicion passed between the two men: one young, afraid, and determined, the other experienced, world-weary, and knowing. Admiration, perhaps, seasoned with a touch of gratitude.

Sam nodded. He might have gone with agent, but there was Mikaela to worry about, and the still-extant faint hope that he might, just might, be able to do something for someone who had once saved *his* life.

"Thanks." Reaching forward, he lovingly stroked the dusty dash. "And Bumblebee—give 'em the ride of your life."

They waited until both Decepticons were approaching the distant terminus of their most recent dive. Then the three cars pulled close together and screeched to a stop. Sam and Mikaela scrambled out of Bumblebee while Simmons headed for Mudflap.

"It's up to me, one man alone. Betrayed by the country he loves and the planet that doesn't even know him. Now he is their last hope in the final hour of need!" Half singing to himself, half monologuing, he turned and looked back at those he had once thought to imprison.

He was smiling.

"Plus you guys, of course. Mission's a go! Move-move-move!"

Sam nodded gratefully. Considerably less appreciative, Mikaela eyed the ex-agent a moment longer. Then she relented, blew him a kiss, smiled, and joined with Sam as together they raced for the nearest buildings.

Simmons was just settling behind the wheel of Mudflap when the passenger-side door of the tiny car swung open and a second figure slid into the empty seat. Face flushed with the kind of excitement that replaces fear, adrenaline pumping wildly, Leo looked over at the startled ex-agent.

"*Drive*. I'm coming with you!"

Simmons shook his head. "You'll never make it, kid! Bravery'll only get you so far."

Sam's roommate didn't back down. "Wanna talk about bravery? You live with your *mother*!"

"Okay, that was a test," Simmons replied more sociably. "You passed. And hey, when all this is over—just make sure there's a plaque for me in Washington. Be great to get the Navy Cross—'cept I was never in the navy."

Leo grinned back. "Bet I can get your picture up in the post office."

Simmons started to snap back, paused, and broke out in a wide grin. "Whatever. Good luck." Turning his attention forward, he slapped both hands down on the waiting wheel. "Okay, small-but-tough—let's see what you can do!"

As the Twins and Bumblebee roared off in opposite directions, Sam and Mikaela safely reached the outskirts of the abandoned town. Rusting construction equipment provided temporary cover as they worked their way toward the nearest intact structures and the camouflaged, heavily armed men waiting among them. More than once they had to duck under shelter as the frustrated Decepticon leader and his main minion came thundering past overhead.

Doing everything but popping spinning wheelies and flashing their trunk lids at the airborne enemy, the Twins taunted the two Decepticons with sounds as well as gestures. Within the complaisant Mudflap, Simmons worked the wheel like a Nascar driver on a rainy track in Mississippi.

"My little alien friend, prepare to be driven like

never before. You got the *maestro* behind the wheel."
Weaving crazy curves in the desert and wild turns on
the road, he sang out as he directed the diversionary
effort. "One man alone, oh it's one man *alooonnne*!"

In the passenger seat beside him Leo was screaming, but with ire rather than enthusiasm.

"Stop *saying* that. *I'm in the car too!*"

Alive and unscarred, Sam and Mikaela reached the
first of a series of empty whitewashed buildings and
ducked inside. There was a back door, but it had been
bricked up. A front window had been hand-made
from pieces of bottle glass. As they debated whether
to expose themselves and break for the center of
town, something weighty shook dust from the ceiling:
heavy footsteps, just outside. Covering Mikaela, Sam
crouched low.

"I don't think they saw us come in here. Get
down—*not a peep!* Once it's clear we run as fast as
we can for Optimus." One hand gripped the sock full
of glistening black sand as if it were a truncheon.

She indicated the sock. "What if this doesn't
work?"

"It's gonna work," he growled hoarsely.

"But what if it doesn't?"

"Look, I don't *know* what's gonna happen. I just
know that we have to try—because Optimus would
do it for *me*."

His response steadied her. This was the Sam
Witwicky she knew, the Sam she had fallen in love
with. Right or wrong, success or failure, she was with
him. Whatever might come.

His other hand tightened on her arm as he st

window. "Okay, on three we run. Outside
e left. Ready? One—two—*shit . . .*"

Massive and slow-moving, more footsteps sounded just outside their refuge. Shadows obscured the light that had been pouring through the window.

As they drew farther back into the building, they were careful not to disturb any of the debris that was piled in places on the floor. A length of rusty rebar caught Sam's eye, and he used it to delicately punch a hole through the crumbling wall. It was enough to allow him to see outside but not enough to draw attention.

What he saw was not encouraging.

Though the hole did not allow enough of an angle for him to make out individuals, the metal figures outside were clearly speaking Decepticon. While he could not see faces, all too many previous encounters did permit him to recognize one set of massive feet.

Starscream.

Conversing among themselves, the Decepticons sounded none too pleased. Starscream in particular was ripping off rapid-fire streaks of angry dialogue as if he was ready to start tearing into the ground itself. As Sam looked on, his eye glued to the peephole he had made, something suddenly blocked part of his view. Attracted to the hole, the bug came crawling toward him.

Well, fine. He'd let it in and it could pick out its new home while he resumed his watch. But instead of flying toward safety, once inside it came straight toward him, landed on his leg, and let out a single sharp chirp. A decidedly electronic chirp.

It was a very small Decepticon.

The satisfaction Sam felt in smashing it w
gated by the sudden silence that descended
their hiding place. It lasted just long enough for him
to realize that he much preferred the sounds of Decepticons arguing among themselves to the ominous
hush when the roof was ripped aside.

Executed with a decided lack of surgical precision,
the removal caused the rear doorway to crumble. As
intent alien lenses searched the interior of the old
structure, its two inhabitants bolted toward the town.

With no time to choose another hideaway, they
rushed into the nearest open doorway—and fortunately kept moving toward a rear stairwell as the
room behind them was torn apart. The stairwell led
to a traditional flat roof. Now within the town itself,
they were able to jump from rooftop to congruent
rooftop. Behind them the enraged figure of Starscream pursued, tearing apart every intervening wall
and structure in his path.

Leaping from roof to roof with no more plan in
mind than to stay ahead of the rampaging Decepticon, they landed on the next in line—and promptly
crashed through the rotten ceiling boards to land
hard on the floor beneath.

Chairman Morshower found himself growing increasingly discomfited as he studied the main monitor
in the Joint Ops room. It continued to display high-
resolution images of the Jordanian gulf-side village
and the men of the NEST team moving in and around
the abandoned buildings. Moving, searching, and apparently finding nothing.

What was starting to really bother him, howeve

was that they were *saying* nothing. He turned to the row of tech specialists.

"Something's not right here. Lennox's team's got the latest quantum crypto gear; we should have heard something from them by now." His eyes swept over the group of aides and technicians. "Somebody tell me why we can't establish radio or cell phone contact."

"We're hailing them on every frequency and mode in the book," the nearest aide responded. "We'll keep trying, Sir."

Cupping his phone, the admiral standing nearby looked up to relay a message. "Sir, White House Chief of Staff wants confirmation for our intel for deploying the *Roosevelt* battle group into the northern part of the Red Sea."

Morshower pursed his lips. "Understandable. Tell him—it was a hunch."

Like anyone who had achieved such exalted rank, the admiral had been in the service a long time. Long enough to take the chairman's response at face value. "Don't think the President's gonna like that answer, Sir."

"Nope."

Admiral and chairman regarded each other for a moment. Then the admiral nodded, turned, and resumed speaking softly into his phone. Meanwhile, Morshower returned his attention to the main monitor. His gaze took in first one readout and then one subsidiary set of monitor images after another before __ __ le yet another critical call. Having gone as far __ __ ad, there was nothing to be gained by exercis- __ __ tion now.

"This doesn't add up," he declared to any and all within hearing range. "We should've heard from Lennox long before now. We need to contact the Jordanians, see what air assets they've got in the area. They've cooperated by blocking off the zone. Tell them we're experiencing difficulty getting a clear view of what's happening on the ground and that we need better imagery *now*." He turned his attention to the officer in charge of communications.

"Get General Fassad. I'm gonna ask him to clear some UAV overflights. We need some way of confirming the satellite visuals we've been receiving. Another channel, different eyes—something."

The aide was hesitant. "If they say no and we launch a Global Hawk into their no-fly zone, it's an international incident."

Morshower was adamant. "We've *got* to verify what's going on down there. Launch it. Rather beg their forgiveness than be too late with something. I'll take the heat." A grin spread slowly over his face. "Tell them we're checking up on clandestine Israeli naval maneuvers and that we'll pass along anything we learn. That ought to satisfy them in Amman *and* Cairo."

The minister did not like to run. He had bought his shoes in Milan, and running tended to scuff their otherwise mirrorlike surfaces. But he had no choice. Not today.

He was out of breath by the time he reached the king's office, and his honorific bow was perfunctory at best, but the king took no umbrage.

"What is it, Marouf?"

"Majesty: the Americans are requesting our assistance as well as fly-over clearance."

The king frowned and put down the pen he had been using. "It's not a drill?"

"No, Majesty. It has to do with this peculiar business on the coast south of Aqaba. The one we were told involved some sort of covert training exercise. They believe there may be a problem with some of the technology."

The king considered this, then nodded slowly. "Give them what they need. Keep an eye on them, but give them what they need."

The Twins were forced to skid to a halt as the side road they had taken dead-ended in an open quarry. At the far end, looming above the open pit, stood an ancient pyramid, its massive size accentuated by the deep excavation. As both Autobots paused in their uncertainty, Leo looked out the back window.

"They're not following us anymore. Neither of 'em. I don't think this worked. Or if it did, they've caught on to us."

Simmons nodded and climbed out while the younger man exited on the other side. Together they stood examining the road behind them as well as their present surroundings. It was evident that the quarry, unlike the town, was the scene of ongoing activity. A giant green-painted hauler stood next to a big dump truck. Not far from these two vehicles, a front loader idled next to a giant construction crane. As the two visitors stood and stared, shading their eyes from the glare of the sun, three more construction vehicles came rumbling into view from another part of the quarry.

"So, uh," Simmons commented as he studied the oncoming machines, "what exactly do you think these people are working on here? This equipment is too big and clumsy for archeology." He gestured at their surroundings. "It looks like they're digging for something, but I don't see any cut stone, slag heaps, mine tailings—nothin'." He was tensing up all over again. "And I don't see any people workin', either."

"Maybe they're all on lunch break?" Leo sounded more hopeful than certain. "Assuming they have lunch breaks around here. Maybe they're mining sand."

Simmons eyed him as if he had just flunked the third grade. "Why would you have to 'mine' sand around here? It's *all* sand."

Leo was ready to argue that there were many different kinds and grades of sand when the three newly arrived construction vehicles joined up with the four that were already present. They did not park parallel to one another, or trundle off in a line to commence some excavation work; instead, seven shadows began to merge against the sun-baked floor of the quarry as the seven metal shapes fused together, piling one atop another to form a single Decepticon whose massive bulk blocked out the sun.

"Did you know they could do that?" asked a stunned Leo.

The ex-agent had to tilt his head back to take it all in. His reaction was characteristically Simmons.

"This ain't gonna go our way . . ."

*   *   *

the far side of the abandoned town, Lennox's team had taken up the best defensive positions available. Men were loading sabot-tipped Sideswipe missiles and preparing equally devastating yet compact munitions, while the altered Autobots stood ready to give free rein to their own weapons.

Such a sight would surely have been encouraging to Sam and Mikaela—had they been able to pause long enough to admire it. Explosions had begun to erupt all around them as the perturbed Decepticons stopped ripping buildings apart in favor of blowing them up. The subsurface passageway into which they had fallen provided some cover as they ran down its length. Raising an arm, Sam pointed unnecessarily. The corridor ended at a set of stairs that were fortunately still intact. Without waiting to see where these led, they scrambled upward and found themselves running down an empty alleyway.

It didn't stay empty for long.

The concussion as the huge Decepticon landed behind them nearly jolted them off their feet. Fighting to maintain his balance, Sam reached out to help steady Mikaela. In so doing he found himself looking straight back down the alley at the Decepticon that had come up behind them. As he stared, its chest opened to reveal a sizable internal compartment. Instead of firing at the two fleeing humans the Decepticon leaned forward, dumping the contents of this compartment into the dirt. To Sam's shock, they were immediately recognizable.

Ron and Judy Witwicky.

Mikaela grabbed his arm, urging him to keep running, but he could not. How could he when ents were sprawled on the ground behind him, grow ing as they tried to pick themselves up? As they fought to rise, one of the Decepticon's arm cannons inclined downward until it was pointed directly at them, its muzzle held only feet away from his mother's back.

"Give me the Matrix," the Decepticon growled, "or your parents die."

No debate, no equivocation. That was the Decepticon way. Comply without delay or face the consequences. Still, Sam hesitated. The sock and its gritty black contents dangled from his right hand as he stood in the alley, swaying slightly.

Having picked himself up, a bruised and filthy Ron Witwicky blinked at his son. "Please, Sam, please— listen to me, son. I want you to . . ."—he looked back up at the metal giant towering above him and his wife—"I want you to *run*. Whatever it is these things want, don't give it to them! Go, get outta here!"

Sam didn't move; he could hardly react. The choice he was being given was no choice at all. Whatever he did would end badly. But he had to do *something*. The unknown Decepticon wouldn't wait forever. Standing out in the open, staring, the sunlight was blinding Sam, making his eyes water. He rubbed at them, trying to clear his vision, turning away from the glare and to his left. From which direction yet another figure was now approaching.

Bumblebee.

Advancing in the shade of multistory ruins, the Autobot could not perceive the details of the scene that was being played out farther down the intersecting alley. He couldn't see the impatient Decepticon. But he *could* see Sam, analyze his posture, match the expression on his face with others in his data banks, note the terror in Mikaela's eyes, and come to a realistic conclusion. Halting, keeping low as he started to back up, his gesturing to Sam was unmistakable.

Distract it.

Wiping at his eyes again Sam slowly started forward, his attention focused on his battered parents. Behind him, a frightened Mikaela was retreating one step at a time, her gaze flicking from him to the monster blocking the alley.

"Don't hurt them," Sam implored in his best pleading voice, "just don't hurt them, okay? Look . . ." He held up the sand-filled sock. "This is everything I've got. I'm giving it to you . . ."

Flying off a nearby roof, a black and yellow shape slammed into the Decepticon from above, knocking it backward. Though caught off-guard the Decepticon reacted with preternatural reflexes, flipping backward even as he unleashed a killing spike that Bumblebee hastily dodged. It slammed into the ground near the Witwickys as they raced toward their son.

The Decepticon was bigger and stronger, but Bumblebee was moving like his terrestrial namesake. For every glancing blow the enemy struck, the lightning-fast Autobot landed several. Metal clanged on metal as shells and short-range missiles tore the surrounding structures to pieces. But bit by bit, the Decepticon was succumbing to the relentless punishment that was being meted out by the furious Autobot.

As his parents stood nearby looking on in amazement and Mikaela moved to join them, Sam stepped forward with fists clenched. "*Kill* him, Bumblebee, kill him!"

The Autobot needed no urging. Not with his human family at risk and the memory of Optimus's fall still fresh in his memory. As the Decepticon unloaded a murderous swing, the faster, smaller Autobot ducked beneath it, grabbed hold, and swung around behind his enemy. The force of his forward movement combined with his weight was sufficient to produce a grinding noise as metal joints gave way and the arm snapped. The Decepticon roared, trying to break free and flailing with his remaining good arm. Bumblebee promptly grabbed this one as well and pulled it back behind his foe. Rising into the air, he kicked out straight with both legs as hard as his servos would permit. The Decepticon's body went flying, but his arms remained locked in Bumblebee's grasp. As the armless body went rolling into the dirt, a protective shield slid down into place over the Autobot's face.

Serving primarily as a translator and then as an interlocutor, it had been a long time since he had either been in condition or in the mood to don his battle mask.

Sam's parents embraced their son so forcefully that in their enthusiasm and relief they threatened to knock him down.

"Sam, oh, Sammy," his mother was wailing, "thank God!"

Ron eyed his son proudly but briefly. His attention was still diverted by the battling robots. "I don't know what the hell's happening here—I don't even know where we are—but I do know that we gotta move. *Follow me*." He started to turn down one of the narrower side alleys.

Sam reached out to stop him. "No, Dad—they're after *me*. You and Mom get in Bumblebee. He'll get you out of here." Turning, he whistled and waved. *"Bumblebee, take 'em!"*

Scored and dented but unbowed and still very much in fighting mode, the yellow-and-black Autobot came close—speaking, for the first time in quite a while, in a voice that was raspy but intelligible and decidedly lifted from a song or old radio show.

"Stayyyy withhhh yyyyooouuuu."

Ron looked evenly at his son. "He's right, Sam, this isn't a discussion!"

"No, it's *not*," Sam agreed, drawing himself up. " 'Cause this is *my* scene. Both of you do what I say. You don't hide, you don't stop. You get to safety and I *will* find you. You understand? *I've got things I have to do*."

Ron Witwicky stared at his son. Who was the young man standing before him and speaking so resolutely? The same tentative, almost timid youth he had so recently seen off to college? Shifting his gaze, he eyed the black-and-yellow metallic life-form standing silently behind Sam. No—his son had become something else. Something more.

It seemed that not only alien robots were capable of striking transformations.

The same epiphany had affected Judy Witwicky. Reaching out, she put a hand on her husband's arm, her face glowing with pride and understanding as she smiled at her progeny.

"Ron, it's okay—let him go."

Throughout the fleeting conversation, explosions had continued to detonate all around them. Some were coming closer. Changing shape, Bumblebee roared forward and skidded to a halt beside the waiting humans. Doors flung themselves wide. Ron glanced in the Camaro's direction, then turned back to his offspring and nodded in understanding.

"We're with you, son—whatever happens."

They embraced—father and son, then mother and son. As his friend carried his mother and father away from the scene of battle, Sam stood gazing after them. Only a touch from Mikaela broke the emotion-laden reverie into which he had fallen. She glanced down at his right hand.

"I know you're not going to give up that sock, but if you don't relax your fingers you're liable to break your own bones."

⟁ XVII ⟐

Towering above Simmons and Leo, the colossal Decepticon took stock of his surroundings. Significant if not prominent among them were two humans and a pair of comparatively diminutive Autobots. That was sufficient motivation for Devastator to open a great, whirling cavern of a mouth. A wind rose immediately—not from the south, nor from the mountains to the north, but from within the Decepticon himself as he leaned forward and directed it toward his targets. Sand, then rocks, and finally boulders rose to vanish into that widening maw.

Simmons had already started backing away. Now he turned and yelled.

"RUN!!"

Not all of the construction equipment at the quarry site was capable of animation. Some was exactly what it appeared to be: little-used or abandoned machinery. The ex-agent took cover behind the biggest dozer he could find while Leo dove into a car that had spent too much time out in the desert sun. Behind them, the Twins ran for their lives. Bravado and boldness were indefensible attitudes when faced with a Decepticon the size of Devastator.

It did not matter what was sucked into that bipedal tornado—rocks, chunks of wood, small bits of machinery—Devastator drew them in, ground them up, and spit out a steady stream of gravel, chips, and metal fragments. When Leo felt the shell of the car in which he had taken shelter begin to shudder, he scrambled madly out the opposite door and rushed to lock both arms around the railing of an iron stairwell.

Not that his efforts would do him much good if the Decepticon chose to consume the stairwell as well.

Mudflap likewise managed to secure a grip on a solid structure, but his counterpart was not so fortunate. Struggling to hold on to a steel beam, Skids found himself lifted off the ground and sucked toward Devastator's vast mouth. As it slammed shut with the smaller robot inside, Mudflap let out an electronic howl as piteous as anything Leo had ever heard emerge from the mouth of an Autobot.

Devastator started toward the remaining two humans and the twin of the Autobot he had consumed—and then started to wobble. Standing up straighter, the giant halted in his tracks. His head shook to the left, then to the right, then left again. A peculiar grinding noise came from deep within the massive head.

Skids exploded out of the Decepticon's right eye, not only unharmed and very much alive but firing directly into the colossus's face while clinging to its jaw. Hurt and enraged, Devastator stumbled wildly as he sought to get a grip on the fast-moving Autobot. He couldn't fire at Skids without shooting himself in the face. When one gigantic foot slammed down too close to Simmons's own hiding place, the ex-agent burst from cover and started running again—this time straight at the Decepticon.

"Only safe place is right under it!" Simmons shouted back. "Run *at* it! Run for its feet—it's big, but it's slow."

Having learned to listen to the ex-agent's advice, Leo released his grip on the dubious stairwell and rushed to join the older man. *Run at it*—yeah, sure, he thought. That makes sense. Jump on your enemy's foot. But as he joined Simmons in a potentially lethal dance beneath the immense, slow-moving feet, he had to admit that hiding in plain sight had one virtue: the Decepticon couldn't bring any of his weapons to bear between his own legs.

Meanwhile, Mudflap scrambled up the nearest tottering leg to fire a cable toward his brother. Grabbing hold, Skids swung safely to the ground, firing continuously at point-blank range as he did so. Both Twins landed cleanly right in front of the two scrambling humans.

In town, Sam and Mikaela did their best to stay out of sight by keeping to the smaller alleyways as they ran. A succession of intensifying concussions caused Sam to look back the way they had come.

Yet another Decepticon had appeared in their wake. Leaping rather than running, pogo-sticking its way across town, it pulverized every structure it encountered. Alerting Mikaela with a tug and a nod, Sam led her sideways just as the building behind them was flattened.

At this rate, he thought as he rolled over and spat out plaster and mud, pretty soon there wouldn't be anyplace in town beneath which to take cover because there wouldn't be any town left.

The fully armed jets sat on the deck of the *Roosevelt* locked to their catapults and ready to go. All they needed was the launch command.

They had been sitting thus, in carrier-launch terms, for quite a while now.

In the Pentagon, Chairman Morshower was listening to the quiet but firm complaints of the officer in command of the *Roosevelt* battle group.

"We can't remain at this level of readiness indefinitely, Admiral. No matter how good the acrobat, sooner or later he'll start to lose his balance."

"I know." Aware that the eyes of numerous senior officers were on him, Morshower held his ground as he responded. "Hold as long as you can. Nobody leaves until I have *confirmation*."

Devastator started after the Twins—and then suddenly and unexpectedly stopped, turned, and started off in the opposite direction. Unable to flee without revealing themselves, Simmons and Leo stayed beneath the striding Decepticon as he headed back toward the quarry wall.

"Keep directly underneath, kid." Simmons was whispering as he tried to match his pace to the stride of the colossus towering above them. "When he looks distracted, we'll make a break for it." Keeping pace alongside him, Leo nodded nervously.

The massive Decepticon began climbing the steeply pitched side of the excavation site. It was all the two humans could do to scramble up the side while ke-

the hulking beast. At the top, standing im-
~~mutably~~ as it had for thousands of years, was the
great pyramid.

Simmons barely had time to regret his choice. The
sky above cracked open like a blue eggshell. There
was a brief vision of—something. Another world, another place, another incredibly far distant corner of
the space–time continuum. It did not last long, because the view was largely blocked by a shape that
was coming through the gap. Simmons did not have
to look at the apparition to know that it represented
something—or someone—of great importance.

He knew because the gargantuan Devastator bent
low in supplication and abasement. And because alongside the swirling, metallic shape, Megatron looked
only—ordinary.

"Master. Your Machine remains in place, where it
was hidden."

The Fallen surveyed his surroundings. They were
not to his liking, but that did not matter. Very soon
now he would simply change them to suit his wishes.

"Where is the Matrix?"

"With the boy," Megatron informed him.

The Fallen was mightily pleased. "Then we are
very near. Bring it to me, and our destiny will be complete."

"Near to what, my lord?" Megatron inquired uncertainly.

, to our apotheosis, my prodigal. And to the
this foolish and Energon-wasting war on
u and yours have been forced to expend so

much time and energy." An immense arm rose and gestured. "Go now. Exultation is at hand."

Unlike Devastator, Megatron did not bow, but he did turn obediently to bullet off in the direction of a nearby and presently human-occupied desert town.

The battle there was not going well for the defenders. As explosions erupted all around them, a pair of Blackhawks arrived and began to unload special forces troops. As they rappelled down to a pair of adjoining rooftops, one was blown to fragments by a rampaging Decepticon. Debris, shrapnel, and body parts rained down over a wide area as the second chopper broke off. Trying to provide covering fire, both Ironhide and Sideswipe took repeated hits. The Autobots were outnumbered and the presence of a few human allies, no matter how experienced and well trained, was hardly enough to make up the difference on the battlefield.

Seeking a clear route away from the increasingly desperate combat, the second copter's flight path took it straight toward the open quarry. The Fallen watched it approach with as much detachment as an entomologist studying a particularly uninteresting species of ant. Unlike the lesser Decepticons, the Master did not unlimber a weapon, did not fire a single shell or missile. Instead, he merely waved a hand in the aircraft's direction.

The chopper turned upside down as neatly and swiftly as if gravity itself had suddenly reversed. The Fallen looked on with interest as the out-of-control craft zoomed past him to slam into the floor of the quarry and burst into flame.

*   *   *

Are those helmets I'm seeing ahead of us? Sam wondered as he continued to stumble forward. He and Mikaela had been running, diving, and dodging for so long now that he could not be sure of anything. But the closer they drew, the more the rounded shapes seemed to be sitting on top of people instead of posts.

Another explosion sent earth and gravel vomiting skyward behind them and they were forced to take cover behind a row of pillars. The detonation also drew Lennox's attention. Spotting the two teens, he yelled at the men on both sides of him to direct some covering fire their way. If the kids could just make it across the last remaining stretch of open ground . . .

Then they might be little better off than they were right now, he told himself realistically. But at least in among his troops they would not be surrendered without a fight.

As Devastator began to climb the side of the great pyramid, Simmons and Leo used the opening his departure presented to make a dash for the smoking ruins of the downed Jordanian chopper. Once they reached the still-smoking wreckage, they worked to help the wounded get away from the rubble and under the cover of nearby boulders. At the same time, they tried their best to keep track of what the Decepticons were doing.

At present, a bemused Leo decided as he squinted toward the crest of the pyramid, the alien activity was not making any sense.

Having reached the summit, Devastator had started banging away with both massive metal fists at the point of rocks that capped the ancient structure.

As more and more stone was smashed aside, something tapering and shiny was gradually becoming exposed. Shading his eyes, Leo continued to stare upward.

"What the hell's it doing up there? Is it trying to get inside? There's some kind of metal spire or something."

Rising from the injured soldier he had been ministering to, Simmons came up beside the younger man and joined him in gazing toward the line of rocks. His eyes widened.

"Oh God—the machine—*the machine that plane, Jetfire, was taking about.* The pyramid was built around it! We're sittin' at the *endgame*!"

He hesitated a moment longer, contemplating, planning, and weighing options. Then he turned, snatched a radio comm from one of the bewildered, shell-shocked soldiers, and took off toward the base of the pyramid.

On the bridge of the *Roosevelt*, the captain wished for more room in which to pace. It was something the ship's designers had not taken into consideration, he knew, none of them ever having found themselves in a position akin to that of a commanding officer.

As he was running over the available options in his mind for the fortieth, or maybe the fiftieth, time, a communications officer looked up sharply from his console.

"Captain, we have secure radio traffic coming from Jordan using outdated encryption. He wants to talk to you. He's . . . ," the officer hesitated, "he doesn't sound Jordanian."

The captain's brows arched. "What *does* he 'sound,' like, Lieutenant?"

The junior officer half smiled. "He sounds like 'Brooklyn.' Or at least, New York."

"Put it through." Stepping forward, the captain spoke into the nearest pickup. "This is Captain L. W. Wilder, commander U.S.S. *Roosevelt*. Please identify . . ."

Static distorted the voice on the other end, but it could not mute the outrage that underlay the angry response.

"Where the hell are all our people! Our tanks, our planes? We got three hundred friggin' satellites up there banging off each other! What are they all doing—providing feeds to the Weather Channel?!"

Captain and communications officer exchanged a glance. On the bridge, everyone had turned to look up from their own stations. Wilder growled a tense reply.

"I am Captain L. W. Wilder, commanding the U.S.S. *Roosevelt*. I repeat—*identify yourself. Who* is this, *what* are you talking about, and *how* did you get on this frequency?"

"You telling me no one knows what's goin' on here but me? That I'm the *only* guy on the ground talking to you?" A brief pause, then, "Okay, *listen up*. This is Agent Seymour Simmons, Sector Seven! Never heard of it? There's a reason! Now you wanna have a verbal throw-down about my lack of clearance, or you wanna help me save about a gazillion lives!"

Wilder struggled to digest what he was hearing. Quite possibly nothing but the ravings of some lunatic who had somehow hacked the command frequency and was having his little joke at the captain's expense. Or . . . A number of "lunatic" occurrences lately had resulted in thousands of deaths. Like every officer and enlisted man in the navy, the loss of the *Lincoln* remained uppermost in his mind. Furthermore, they were presently operating under a Red Alert. In the past, lunacy and Red Alerts had often turned out to be connected.

He decided to take a chance. If he was wrong, he would only come off looking like a fool.

If he was right . . .

"All right, 'Agent' Simmons," he said into the pickup, "I'm listening."

The static seemed to clear slightly, as if the radio was steadying—or the hand holding it was.

"We got ourselves an alien remodeling a pyramid. What you need to know is that if he finishes the job, a whole lotta everybody is gonna wish more attention had been paid to—well, no time for that now. I've studied these things, okay? Our best hope at this point is a prototype weapon, a rail gun. Shoots a steel projectile at Mach Seven. Bombs and missiles these guys'll be looking for, but a rail gun slug might come in under their radar. You carry some on your destroyers now."

Wilder stood straighter, glanced sideways at his executive officer, and moved his lips closer to the pickup so he could lower his voice. "That information is—classified, mister."

"You can call me 'mister,'" the highly excitable voice shot back, "but don't talk to me about 'classified.' My father, Felix Simmons, *invented* the word. If you got a suitably equipped ship in the Gulf, which I suspect you do, tell 'em to *ready that weapon*. I'll radio exact targeting coordinates in T-minus five!"

Nothing but static followed the mysterious transmitter's last words. Wilder looked over at the nearest comm officer.

"Channel's still open. He's just not talking. What—what are your orders, Sir?"

Wilder considered. He had listened. Now he had to decide whether or not to commit. The whole battle group would be waiting on his decision.

"Get me Captain Jackson, on the *Zumwalt*."

Coming in low and fast over the Jordanian coast, the Reaper was shooting video even before it crossed the shoreline. Moments later it was sending pictures to a low-flying satellite that was linked directly to Soccent headquarters in Dubai. That station in turn further encrypted the images and relayed them back to Washington via a routing that was not being monitored or controlled by the orbiting Soundwave.

Cries and exclamations arose unbidden in the Joint Ops room as the peaceful view of the tranquil village in Jordan was replaced by black-and-white images of carnage and chaos. A few men and women rose from their seats to yell at the monitors or at those seated next to them. Morshower's reaction was no less heated.

"Shit, it's a *trick*! Send everyone! Get the marines from the battle group in the air and on that ground as fast as possible. Tell General Fassad to move his armor south—and somebody let the Israelis and the Saudis know what's going on so they won't get the wrong idea! Whatever ground assets they can give us—bring them!"

From the Persian Gulf to the Red Sea, from Amman to Cairo, forces were set in motion. The Decepticon threat knew no borders, and as soon as the requests that were coming were verified, the armed forces of multiple governments began to respond proportionately.

But it took time to get armor and aircraft in motion.

Meanwhile, Sam and Mikaela were dealing with fire and destruction all out of proportion to anything they had encountered before, including at Mission City. At times it seemed as if the ground itself had vanished, to be replaced by gouts of flame and geysers of earth and pulverized stone. The American and British NEST troops were literally a stone's throw away, but the barrage beneath which they were presently hunkered down made any notion of rising and running toward them suicidal.

They remained pinned down for some time, until a new sound made itself heard above the ongoing struggle. Lifting his head, Sam strained to wipe grit from his eyes. Something was coming up behind the remaining soldiers. At first he thought it was another Decepticon. As the shape drew nearer, he wasn't so sure. Looking to his left he muttered to Mikaela, choking slightly as he did so on the swirl of acrid fumes that now permeated the town.

"Is that—is that a *tank*?"

The clanking interloper did not change shape, either to Decepticon or Autobot. Instead, it parked itself behind the uneven line of NEST soldiers. As it so, a single figure detached itself from cover to race over to the massive war machine.

"Let the world know we're here!" Lennox shouted up to the gunner crouched low within the top hatch. "We got a dozen Black Dragons laying siege to this place!" Turning, he gestured with the muzzle of his own weapon. "Gonna need cover to reach civilians down by those pillars!"

The gunner above nodded to him. "Marines got you covered, Major!"

Rattling up behind the first tank, others spread out in line abreast. While internal communications shuttled back and forth, turrets swiveled and cannon were brought to bear. As a pair of Decepticons closed in on the two trapped teens, sabot fire erupted from the muzzles of the half dozen parked and ready Abramses. The heavy barrage did not destroy the enemy— but it certainly gave the two robots pause, slowed them down, and distracted them.

That was enough for Lennox and Epps. Together, they charged out from behind their cover and zigzagged at top speed toward the line of pillars. Though both men dove for the ground as soon as they reached their objective, Lennox still had wind enough to grin up at Sam.

"Hey, kid. Long time. *Tell* me you got what you came for."

Sam's expression was as explicatory as his words. "Where's Optimus?"

g to a sitting position, Lennox gestured back
he had come. "First we've got to get you out
Couple of hundred yards across that court-

yard, then we make a break for the beach on my signal. Optimus—we'll deal with him later."

Reaching into a pocket, Sam silently pulled out the sock full of black sand. Lennox glanced at the sock, saw nothing worthy of comment, then raised his eyes back to the teen's face. Mikaela was watching both of them expectantly.

"Look, there's an air support attack coming." Lennox put a hand on the younger man's shoulder. "We can't sit here and wait for it. You need to stick right behind me—*understand*?"

Sam blinked and looked up. This was not what he had come all this way for, but—there was Mikaela, staring at him, waiting for him to make a decision. Turning back to the officer, he nodded, his lips tightening. At a gesture from Epps, they all rose and started to run southward.

They made it only a few strides before a big Decepticon stepped out right in front of them.

Howling defiance, Lennox and Epps opened up on the monster that was blocking their way. Their small-arms fire did not even slow it. One hand thrust forward, reaching for Sam.

It never touched him.

Landing atop the startled Decepticon with both arm weapons aimed straight downward, Jetfire proceeded to blow the foe to pieces before it knew what had happened. Touching down, the old Decepticon silently regarded the quartet of staring humans. He could not smile, but a creaky hand lifted slowly in greeting was evocation enough.

Seconds later an entirely different kind of Decepticon erupted from the ground beneath him to plunge a restored and regenerated tail straight through Jetfire's chest.

Skorponok had not shown himself in a very long time, a stunned Lennox knew.

Roaring in pain, Jetfire reached down and with strength born of desperation and memory, ripped the impaling Decepticon's arachnoid head clean off its body and flung it aside. Both hands then dropped to wrench free the skewering tail and body. Heaving these in the opposite direction was all the aged Decepticon could manage. Falling to one knee, he stared down at himself. Through the gaping hole in his chest could be seen a blinking, sputtering spark.

Green smoke rose skyward from the far side of the courtyard: the signal. Radio clasped to his ear, Epps yelled confirmation back toward his companions.

"Coming in hot in forty seconds!"

Jetfire looked up, his voice subdued, his posture downcast. "So many memories. So many wasted lives. Run, my friends! *Get to safety.*"

Distant from the ongoing action in miles but not in perception, the crew of the AWACS plane went about their business with the somber efficiency for which they were noted.

"Slayer One-Six, this is Top Hat. F-18s inbound, B-1s fifteen seconds behind you—you are cleared hot."

Four B-1 bombers sped up the length of the Gulf no more than a hundred feet above the calm blue water. From another direction, ten F-18s off the *Roosevelt* approached. Their target was the same.

On the edge of the abandoned village, the marine tanks were already pulling back. Not retreating, but accelerating toward cover. Across the battered and blasted empty space between them and the line of standing pillars, Lennox looked over at his young charges.

"When I give the word, do not stop running—we've got *seconds* to clear! Everybody with me?"

Sam and Mikaela nodded. Now was not the time for questioning.

Epps yelled as loudly as he could. *"Incoming! Go!"*

Lennox was already on his feet. *"Go go go!"*

As they raced after the retreating tank battalion, the two soldiers let loose with their magazines while the backward rumbling Abramses barraged the milling Decepticons to try and occupy their attention. A few explosions erupted around the quartet of fleeing humans, but the bulk of Decepticon fire was directed at the more distant and far more threatening human war machines.

The break in the heavy fire around him allowed Sam to get a glimpse of a shape off to his right. Something large and massive and motionless. Without breaking stride, knowing what he had to do, he veered off sharply in the direction of what he had espied.

"Sam!" Mikaela didn't slow. As she tried to join him she ran into Epps, who half pushed, half carried her onward.

"Kid, no!" Lennox yelled.

Missiles launched from the oncoming F-18s began to arrive and slam into the Decepticons who now towered over the rubble that had been the town. Sam did as Lennox had advised him: he did not stop running. It was just that he was not running in the direction the major had specified.

From on high came a whistling sound: a one-ton bomb dropped by one of the B-1s. The blast wave from the cratering explosion knocked Sam off his feet. His face bloodied, he was back up and running as soon as he recovered from the initial shock. Behind him there was now only black smoke and debris still falling out of the sky. That, and something that was emerging from the wall of smoke. A tank shape—but not Abrams, not marine.

Megatron.

Halfway to the recumbent body of Optimus, a shell tore up the ground near Sam's feet and sent him flying. Megatron adjusted his weapon, taking aim at the lone figure sprawled facedown in the dirt. But his appearance had drawn the attention not only of the troops on the ground but also of the recently arrived aircraft circling overhead in search of new targets. Pounded by the humans from all directions, the Decepticon leader was forced to change shape and take to the air in order to save himself.

Breaking free from Lennox, Mikaela ran toward where Sam had fallen. As she dropped to her knees beside him she called his name. It had always brought a smile, a twitch, usually accompanied by some wise-ass remark no matter how badly he was hurt or how exhausted.

Not this time. He didn't move.

"Sam—*Sam!* Wake up! *Please* wake up!"

She could see his face. His eyes were half open, but this time they did not focus on her. She passed her hand over them, close. He did not blink.

Moments later, Lennox was at her side again. Reaching down, he ripped open Sam's shirt and pressed an ear to the teen's dirt-smeared chest. Straightening, he yelled back the way he had come.

"I need medevac here now! No pulse!"

The chopper with the red cross on its side set down beside them with commendable speed. Medics surrounded the body as Lennox pulled Mikaela aside. Paddles were slapped against Sam's chest and his body convulsed as current from the defibrillator shot through him. Another medic jabbed a liquid-filled needle into an arm and rejuvenating fluid was forced into his bloodstream.

Shoving the defibrillator paddles aside, the medic in charge began pounding on Sam's chest. One-two-three—he counted and repeated the action several times. Each time the result was the same. Wiping sweat from his face, he looked up at Lennox, then over at Mikaela. It was time for the most difficult motion of all.

He shook his head, slowly.

Tears streaming down her face, Mikaela fell forward onto the unmoving body. "Please come back to me, Sam. I—I love you. I love you so much. Come back to me."

Others were gathering as the Decepticons were slowly forced back from the town. NEST soldiers, marines, and fighters who were not human. Ironhide and Ratchet, the badly wounded Jetfire, and most prominently a distinctive black-and-yellow figure that had dropped down on all fours.

Reaching out with one hand, forefinger extended, Bumblebee traced the air above the face of his friend.

Then the gleaming metal digit shifted sideways, to where one hand lay sprawled palm upward toward the desert sun. The clenched fingers were clutching a sock. A steady trickle of black sand fell from it, mimicking the line of blood that was seeping from a corner of the young man's mouth. The rest of the sand had already spilled from the torn fabric to lie dark and meaningless against the paler grains beneath.

White light, so bright it was almost blinding. Sam blinked against it but was unable to shut it out entirely. Around him lightning flashed, somehow more intense than the white glare from which it emerged. Images from his life frozen in time sparked briefly into existence around him only to vanish as swiftly as they had appeared. His vision cleared slightly.

Just enough to allow him to make out the singular exoskeletal entities that drifted in a circle around him.

A voice was speaking within the eddy of light: his own. He hardly recognized it.

"Where am I? Am I dead?"

"We are The Dynasty of Primes," one of the shapes murmured. "We have been watching you. For a long time—by your measure."

Sam shook his head. At least he thought he did. He had no sense of movement, no feeling in his extremities. "Watching—*me?*"

"You do not yet know the full truth of your past," declared another of the spectral figures sympathetically. "Or your future."

"I don't understand," he murmured.

"You will." There was the impression of smiling, but not of humor.

"The Matrix of Leadership is a force capable of great good," explained still a fourth shape. "Or great destruction. You have proven worthy of it. First, by sacrifice. Now, through courage."

"Most notably, you did not seek this power," added a fifth. "You wish for it only to help others. These are the virtues of a true leader. The Matrix of Leadership is yours."

His thoughts were as cloudy as the ether in which he found himself floating. What were they saying? Could they possibly be talking about *him*? Samuel Witwicky?

"But I don't understand. It's dust, that's all. Sand. There's nothing left."

"Determination brought you this far," said a sixth of the twelve. "Don't lose it now."

Another flash of lightning, directly in front of him, drew his attention. His lips parted, but no sound came from his mouth. The flash silhouetted a vision of Mikaela. She was holding him, crying atop his own body. His dead body.

"Sam, I love you . . . come back to me . . ."

He took the deepest breath he had ever taken in his life.

His pupils dilated so rapidly that the one medic still lingering over him fell backward. Blinking, Sam stared up at Mikaela. Shocked, but ultimately relieved, she embraced him while still crying. He struggled to make his mouth and larynx and lungs all work in harmony. It required a tremendous effort to render the three words audibly. The effort was worth-while.

"I love you." This time he was able to hear himself.

So focused on the unexpected, impossible resurrection were those around him that no one noticed the slight gust of wind that had sprung up. Whipping across the ground, hugging close to the surface, it began to swirl the sand. But only the sand lying close beside Sam's right hand, and only the grains that were a deep, deep black.

Something was welding them together. A shape was taking place. Metallic, with a crystal somehow embedded intact in its heart.

Rolling over, Sam gripped the dagger shape that had appeared beside his torn sock. Gripping the alien metal tightly, he rose from where he had been lying dead and began to walk, then to run. Not knowing what was happening, Lennox and the others followed. Not caring what was happening, so did a joyful Mikaela.

Up on the motionless metal hand Sam climbed, then the arm, until finally he was standing in the center of Optimus's broad chest. Searching the gleaming surface beneath his feet he found no slot, no opening of the right size and shape. Behind him the battle raged on, surging back and forth as first the humans and their Autobot allies, then the Decepticons gained the upper hand. There was no time to wait for advice, no way to ask another what he should do. Then he realized that he already knew. He had done this before, with an opposite goal in mind. He had taken a spark.

Now, if dream and memory served, he would give one.

Gripping it tightly with both hands, he plunged the metal dagger directly into the center of Optimus's chest. The point ought to have shattered against the alloyed armor. It ought to have been turned to one side or the other. It did neither of those things. Metal met metal—and the glowing dagger sank into the smooth surface like hot steel into butter.

The tremor that raced through the gigantic form dropped Sam to his knees. Light and energy gushed through the prone form. Forward of where he was kneeling, twin blue lights suddenly flared to life. Pulling out the Matrix, Sam climbed down, retreating as he rejoined his friends.

In front of them, Optimus Prime rolled over. Slowly, as strength returned, he rose to his hands and knees. His head came up and his eyes found the torn and bloodied figure of a single human. One who stared back at him confused, injured, but *determined*.

"I knew there was greatness in you, Sam."

"I—I'm sorry I didn't listen."

"Ah," Optimus murmured, "but you did."

The concussion that shook the earth knocked nearly all the humans and several of the Autobots off their feet as well as sending Optimus back to ground. Supremely confident, an enormous figure now towered above them all.

The Fallen had arrived.

As soon as they had recovered their balance, Ironhide and Sideswipe charged, firing all weapons. Raising a hand, hardly appearing to exert an effort, The Fallen swept them backward. When Optimus tried to rise, a second wave of the enormous hand knocked him down. It was as if The Fallen was fighting an infant. Then he turned.

And bent toward Sam.

The voice of The Fallen was even, perfectly controlled—and utterly, utterly malevolent.

"Now, at last, I claim the energy of your sun."

A finger reached out and the dagger shape was torn from Sam's grasp. He could no more have held on to it than he could have restrained a fleeing elephant.

In a swirl of energy, The Fallen vanished. Squinting into the distance, the stunned and dazed onlookers saw him reappear kilometers away on the summit of the nearby pyramid. Sam's tone was agonized, and not from the pain that wracked his battered and bruised body.

"Somebody—somebody stop him! He's gonna turn on the Machine!"

Raising a hand, Optimus implored his companions. "Autobots—stop him."

A shape drew near. "Optimus . . . you are the last of the Primes. You possess powers beyond your own imagining. Take my components . . . fulfill your destiny," Jetfire told him. "You don't need wheels, or feet—you need *wings*." He glanced skyward. "Never done a damn thing worth doing with my life—till now."

And with that, his head bent forward onto his chest as he willfully snuffed out his own spark.

Not only the Autobots but also the humans stood staring. Then Optimus was moving, rising from where The Fallen had crushed him—momentarily.

"Sacrifice should not be wasted. We have no time to mourn or to praise." He nodded at Ratchet.

Coming over, the medical Autobot quickly set to work. Charges and energy flew, stirring up whirlwinds of dust and dirt. When they settled, a familiar figure stood once more before those who knew him. Familiar, but altered.

Ratchet stepped back and contemplated his handiwork. As he did so, Ironhide leaned forward to point.

"I think you missed a seam there, just below . . ." Before he could finish, aged but still powerful engines roared, and Optimus Prime rose swiftly into the desert sky.

Another figure was also rising into the sky, ascending far more slowly and painfully but with a resolve and purpose of his own. Clinging to the bare rock, keeping out of sight of the still stone-bashing Devastator, ex-agent Simmons continued to work his sweating, gasping way up the far side of the pyramid. As he did so he occasionally paused to catch his breath—and to murmur into the radio he was carrying.

"Hang on, boys—gonna have a heart attack here."

Far below and behind the downed helicopter, Leo followed the older man's progress. His eyes were shining and his voice was alive with admiration.

"Whoa—*he* is the Robo-Warrior . . ."

Having outflanked the remaining Decepticons, a separate column of Jordanian and American armor had begun to close on the pyramid and was now firing at the two figures on top. Annoyed, The Fallen turned from Devastator's work and extended his arms. Lifted off the ground, tanks and mobile cannon found themselves suddenly helpless and suspended in midair. Bringing his arms inward, The Fallen examined the primitive war machines curiously. With a contemptuous flick of both hands, he then sent them tumbling like so many toys down the sides of the pyramid.

Near the pinnacle, Simmons ducked behind a massive quarried stone as a collapsing tank bounced over his head and on past him, heading downward. Choosing an opening, he rose and rushed up behind Devastator. Gulping air, he whispered sharply into his radio.

"Prepare—to target—your weapon! I am *directly* below—the enemy's scrotum." Softly and carefully he spoke a string of coordinates into the radio's pickup. "And gentlemen, if you miss by so much as one meter—you tell my biographer I was proud to serve!"

Too busy to look for insects, flanked now by Megatron and Starscream, The Fallen bent to precisely insert the Matrix of Leadership into a slot at the base of the spire of alien metal. Within the ancient device the embedded crystal began to glow more brightly. Standing nearby, Devastator looked on proudly—until his attention was drawn to a strange object flying in his direction. He raised his fists and readied himself to deal with the oncoming Optimus Prime.

Out in the Gulf, a weapon that had previously been fired only in secretive trials emitted a steadily rising scream as hundreds of electromagnets propelled a solid metal projectile along its length, each one accelerating it incrementally until it had reached a velocity nothing short of astounding. Fired from the still-distant destroyer, it struck its target squarely in the chest before Optimus could reach the pyramid. Devastator's body was shattered by the impact and literally flew apart. Below him, a fleeing Simmons sought cover from the sudden rain of metal fragments and splintered components. Part of an arm landed nearby and went rolling down the steep slope. As the ex-agent recognized it, a slow grin began to spread across his weary face.

His attack unimpeded, Optimus ever so slightly altered his angle of approach.

The Matrix crystal began to glow a white so intense not even The Fallen could look directly at it. A rising whine emerged from the depths of the metal spire as the ancient machine returned to life. An intense beam of white light thrust skyward from the apex of the spire. Even traveling at light-speed it would take eight minutes and thirty seconds to cross the gap between Energon-generating device and energy source, between unknowing planet and endangered star.

More than enough time for Optimus, arms fully extended side by side to form a finger-tipped ram, to smash right through the upper portion of the spire.

Collapsing in upon itself, the beam flickered briefly. Each fading flicker was powerful enough to burn holes in the bodies of the Decepticons flanking the spire. Wounded, melting in spots, Megatron and Starscream wailed in agony. Himself injured, the startled Fallen attempted to bring his mystical weapon to bear upon Optimus.

The Fallen was in a rage. "You dare challenge me? I am a Prime!"

With seeming ease, Optimus Prime blocked the

blast. "You abandoned that name when you slaughtered your brothers. There's only one Prime now, and my ancestry will be avenged."

Now the battle was truly joined. Optimus waded into the fray, wielding broken girders like clubs in a blur of motion that none could withstand.

Megatron, recognizing that the tide had turned, looked at The Fallen with incredulity bordering on contempt. "You promised, Master. You promised me the power of a Prime!"

Optimus answered for The Fallen, "Primes are born, not made, Megatron. You were betrayed."

Sensing defeat, The Fallen opened a wormhole portal. He needed to escape, to flee the onslaught of his enemy. Anything to get away from the searing light of the Matrix. But escape would not be so easy on this day.

Coming back around, Optimus ripped off the top of the spire, shot skyward, and then dove earthward. Intent on escape, The Fallen did not see him until the last instant.

"Megatron, help me!" cried The Fallen. But Megatron was unmoved. His former master had lost what power he once held over the Decepticon leader. There would be other days to fight, other means to destroy the Autobots. Commander once again, he led Starscream into the portal.

Left behind, The Fallen faced the vengeance of the Last Prime alone. Powered by Jetfire's engines and driven forward with all the strength in his rejuvenated body, Optimus powered the tip of the spire directly into the skull of The Fallen.

A metallic mouth opened wide, emphasizing an expression that was as much one of surprise as of shock and pain. Poised at the very entrance to the opening in the continuum, The Fallen collapsed. A few sparks fizzled from his skull and from his chest before he crashed forward. As he tumbled over the edge of the pyramid and rolled to the ground, it was with no more energy than any metal object of similar size and mass. When the ancient alien body finally came to rest against the rocks at the bottom, it sounded—ordinary.

With a sizzle and a sonic boom, the opening in the continuum closed, and the sky behind it was once again blue and unaltered.

Landing near the base of the spire, Optimus examined the still-pulsing Matrix carefully. Satisfied with his assessment, he reached out and slowly, cautiously, removed it from the lower half of the machine. The dagger shape was warm in his hand. Warm—but not threatening.

With the ruined town in front of them and the sea behind, soldiers and Autobots waited anxiously, their attention concentrated on the distant rocks. When a single shape rose from the summit and came toward them, respiration paused—until the figure grew large enough to recognize. Then men and women embraced one other and, according to their disposition, began to sob or cheer. Some, unabashedly, did both.

Wavering slightly but standing on his own two feet, Sam allowed himself to close his eyes. They opened when warm words filled his right ear.

"Took all this," Mikaela whispered tenderly, "to tell me you love me."

Still weak and unsteady, he turned to face her.

"You . . ." Exhausted, he had to catch himself before he could finish the thought. "You—said it first."

Grinning, she wrapped him in her arms. He immediately reciprocated; out of love, out of desire—but mostly so he wouldn't fall down.

When they finally separated, it was in time to see other familiar figures coming toward them. An utterly drained but triumphant Seymour Simmons, being carried in the arms of Mudflap. Beside him, being pulled along on a piece of Devastator like a kid on a sled, a beaming Leo Spitz. And running toward them, their faces shining, his mother and father, whose second honeymoon had not turned out exactly as planned . . .

Returning planes crowded the deck of the U.S.S. *Roosevelt*. Mechanics ministered to them while medical personnel moved among the marines who had been brought aboard for treatment. Under Ratchet's supervision, human technicians worked to repair the damage that had been done to a number of the Autobots.

Two individuals stood alone on the bow, gazing out across the desert sea as the battle group steamed south toward more open water and, eventually, home. One figure was small, slight, and all too human. The other was huge, powerful, and as different from human as different could be.

Or maybe not quite so much.

"The symbols in my head." Sam sucked in a deep lungful of the bracing sea air. "They're gone."

"Not gone." Looming beside him, Optimus shooed away a gull that sought to perch on his shoulder. "Absorbed within the substance of the Matrix." Dropping his gaze, he regarded that precious—and dangerous—relic of a distant past that was now attached to his hip.

"Peaceful." Sam nodded at the water sliding past beneath the great ship's keel. "Hope it lasts." He grinned to himself. "I've got a lot of classwork to make up."

"Hope, as you have proven, Sam, is all that's required." The leader of the Autobots paused for just an instant. "Thank you for saving my life."

Tilting back his head, Sam peered up at his massive friend. "Thanks for believing in me."

They stood quietly like that for some time before he spoke again. "The Primes—if they weren't a dream, or a hallucination—said I didn't know the truth about my future. Do you?"

Optimus considered. "I know one thing. Whatever it may hold, it is a future we'll meet together. Our planets, our races, united by a history long forgotten, yet to be discovered." Tilting back his head, he peered up at the sky and through it, to the stars beyond.

EPILOGUE

It was cold, and impossibly dark. In this place, *where* and *when* held no meaning.

But something moved in the darkness. A rough beast, slouching forward in his injured state, pitiless in his desire for revenge and domination, Megatron made his slow and painful way through the decks of the *Nemesis*.

It was a place perfectly suited for his needs. The *Nemesis* would provide sanctuary while he restored himself to his former might. It would take time, but this second defeat produced not despair but silent determination in Megatron. Here he would heal; here he would gather to him the surviving soldiers of his evil cause.

And there was something else. The *Nemesis* held a treasure trove that Megatron would tap. A resource that would ensure his victory over the Autobots, and the destruction of their pathetic human allies.

Dim lights flickered on, and Megatron surveyed the expanse of the cargo bay. Row upon row, level upon level of sarcophagi rested in the immense hold. Each contained a slumbering protoform, each

a mighty warrior that would swear undying alle-
giance to him.

With a vision of the devastation to come, Megatron uttered his first command to his legions.

"Arise!"